John Baptist Mary David, M. J. (Martin John) Spalding, John Baptist
Mary David

A spiritual retreat of eight days

John Baptist Mary David, M. J. (Martin John) Spalding, John Baptist Mary David

A spiritual retreat of eight days

ISBN/EAN: 9783742895301

Manufactured in Europe, USA, Canada, Australia, Japa

Cover: Foto ©Andreas Hilbeck / pixelio.de

Manufactured and distributed by brebook publishing software
(www.brebook.com)

John Baptist Mary David, M. J. (Martin John) Spalding, John Baptist
Mary David

A spiritual retreat of eight days

A

SPIRITUAL RETREAT

OF

EIGHT DAYS.

By the Right Rev. JOHN M. DAVID, D. D.
FIRST COADJUTOR OF BISHOP FLAGET.

EDITED, WITH ADDITIONS, AND AN INTRODUCTION,

BY M. J. SPALDING, D. D.,

BISHOP OF LOUISVILLE.

LOUISVILLE:
WEBB AND LEVERING.
MDCCCLXIV.

Stereotyped by Hills, O'Driscoll & Co.
No. 141 Main St., Cincinnati.

PREFACE.

Twenty one years have elapsed since the
pious death of the saintly Bishop David, the
founder of the ecclesiastical Seminary, and of
the Sisterhood of Nazareth, in the Diocese of
Louisville. Besides these living monuments
of his devotion and successful zeal, he left
behind him a considerable amount of writings,
chiefly on spiritual and ascetic subjects. The
most important of these, besides his Prayer
Book, entitled True Piety, and his Catechism, which have been already published, are
his Eight Days' Retreat, and his Manual
for the Sisters of Nazareth. The latter was
never completed, death having, it would appear,
surprised him in the midst of this, his last

labor of love. Of the Four Parts of which
it was to be composed, only the First and
a small portion of the Second were written.
As the First Part, however, is complete in
itself, and contains much useful instruction
on the religious life, which may be profitable to other religious communities, whether
of males or females, besides that of Nazareth, I here publish it in an Appendix.

Of the twenty four Meditations which were
to be embraced in the Eight Days' Retreat,
three are wanting, all belonging to the last
Week. These I have supplied from "Manresa, or the Spiritual Exercises of St. Ignatius
for general use," a valuable London publication. From the same source I have freely
borrowed whatever seemed to be necessary
for rendering the present little work a more
complete and practical Manual for the performance of the Spiritual Exercises; such as
the practical advices, or Additions, of St. Ignatius to those who wish to make a Retreat

with fruit, his methods of Prayer, and of
Examination of Conscience, both general and
particular, and Considerations for each day
of the Retreat. I have also thought it well
to prefix to the publication a brief biographi-
cal sketch of the saintly BISHOP DAVID, together with his short but admirable Method
of Mental Prayer.

I could have wished that some one more
skilled in the science of the spiritual life had
undertaken to edit this work. But having
failed in my efforts to induce some member
of the Society of Jesus to perform the task,
I decided to do the best I could myself under
the circumstances; and for this purpose I drew
on my notes of Retreats which were preached
to the Students of the Propaganda College
in Rome, about thirty years ago, by some of
the most eminent disciples of St. Ignatius,
including the late General of the Order. This
I have attempted to do in the Introduction,
in the preliminary remarks at the beginning

of each Week, and in the general ordering of the Exercises.

Many pious persons, both in Kentucky and elsewhere, have already used the Meditations of the good BISHOP DAVID with much relish and fruit. In publishing them for general use, I have merely endeavored to furnish a not wholly unsuitable frame for a picture of great and solid merit. All that I ask of those who will use this little work is, that they will strive to profit by its contents, and will have the charity to breathe forth occasionally a short prayer for the unworthy Editor.

CONTENTS.

(vii)

EIGHT DAYS' RETREAT.

FIRST WEEK.

FIRST DAY.

SECOND DAY.

THIRD DAY.

SECOND WEEK.

x   CONTENTS.

FOURTH WEEK.

BIOGRAPHICAL NOTICE

OF THE

RIGHT REV JOHN B. DAVID,

BISHOP OF MAURICASTRUM.

———

JOHN BAPTIST M. DAVID was born in 1761, in a little town on the river Loire, in France, between the cities of Nantes and Angers. His parents were pious, exemplary, and ardently attached to the faith of their fathers. Though not wealthy, they were yet blessed with a competence for their own support, and for the instruction of their offspring. Sensible of the weighty responsibility which rests on Christian parents, they determined to spare no pains or expense, that might be necessary for the Christian education of their children.

Young John Baptist gave early evidences of deep piety, of solid talents, and of an ardent thirst for learning. At the age of seven, he was placed under the care of an uncle, a pious priest, who willingly took charge of his early education. By this good priest he was taught the elements of the French and Latin languages, and also those of music, for which he manifested great taste. He was enrolled in the

(9)

number of *enfants de chœur*, or of the boys who served at
the altar and sang in the choir.

At the age of fourteen, he was sent by his parents to a
neighboring college, conducted by the Oratorian priests.
Here he distinguished himself for regularity, close application to his studies, solid talents, and, above all, for a sincere
piety, which soon won him the esteem and love of both
professors and fellow-students. But what all admired in
him most, was that sincerity and candor of soul, which
formed, throughout his long life, the distinctive trait in his
character.

From his earliest childhood, the young John Baptist had
manifested an ardent desire to embrace the ecclesiastical
state, that he might thus devote his whole life to the service
of God and of his neighbor, in the exercise of the holy
ministry. His parents were delighted with these dispositions
of their son; and to second his purposes, they sent him to
the diocesan seminary of Nantes. Here he entered with
ardor on his sacred studies, in which he made solid proficiency. In the year 1778, the eighteenth of his age, he
received the tonsure, and, two years later, the minor orders,
from the hands of the Bishop of Angers.

In the Theological Seminary he remained for about four
years, during which he completed his course of studies, and
took with honor the degrees of Bachelor and Master of Arts.
In the twenty-second year of his age he bound himself
irrevocably to the sacred ministry, by receiving the holy
order of sub-deaconship.

M. David was ordained deacon in the year 1783; and,
having shortly afterwards determined to join the pious
congregation of Sulpicians, he went to Paris, and remained
for two years in the solitude of Issy, to complete his
theological studies, and to prepare himself, by retirement

and prayer, for the awful dignity of the priesthood, to which he was raised on the 24th of September, 1785.

Early in the year following, his superiors sent him to the Theological Seminary of Angers, then under the direction of the Sulpicians. Here he remained for about four years, discharging, with industry and ability, the duties of Professor of Philosophy, Theology, and the Holy Scriptures—always enforcing his lessons by his good example. At length the storm of the French Revolution broke over Angers; and, late in the year 1790, the seminary was seized on by the revolutionary troops, and converted into an arsenal. The professors and students were compelled to fly for their lives: and M. David took shelter in a private family. In this retreat he spent his time in study, and in constant prayer to God, for light to guide him in this emergency, and for his powerful aid and protection, to abridge the horrors of a revolution which was every where sacrificing the lives of the ministers of God, and threatening the very existence of the Catholic Church in France.

After nearly two years of retirement, he determined, with the advice of his superiors, to sail for America, and to devote the remainder of his life to its infant and struggling missions. He embarked for America in 1792, in the company of MM. Flaget, Chicoisneau, and Badin. On the voyage, he applied himself with such assiduity to the study of the English language, as to have already mastered its principal difficulties ere he set foot on American soil.

Very soon after his arrival in the United States, Bishop Carroll ascertained that he knew enough of English to be of service on the missions; and he accordingly sent him to attend to some Catholic congregations in the lower part of Maryland. M. David had been but four months in America, when he preached his first sermon in English; and he had the consolation to find that he was not only well understood, but that his discourse made a deep impression on his hearers. For twelve years he labored with indefatigable zeal on this mission, in which he attended to the spiritual wants of three numerous congregations. He was cheered by the abundant fruits with which God everywhere blessed his labors.

Feeling that mere transient preaching is generally of but little permanent utility, he resolved to commence regular courses of instruction in the form of Retreats; * and so great was his zeal and industry, that he gave four Retreats every year to each of his congregations. The first was for the benefit of the married men; the second, for that of the married women; the third and fourth, for that of the boys and girls. To each of these classes he gave separate sets of instructions, adapted to their respective capacities and wants.

His discourses were plain in their manner, and solid and thorough in their matter. He seldom began to treat, without exhausting a subject. At first, but few attended his Retreats; but gradually the number increased, so as to embrace almost all the members of his congregations. But he appeared to preach with as much zeal and earnestness to the few, as to the many. He was often heard to say, that the conversion or spiritual profit of even *one* soul, was sufficient to enlist all the zeal, and to call forth all the energies of the preacher.

Great were the effects and most abundant the fruits, of M. David's labors, in the missions of Maryland. On his

---

* As far as our information extends, he seems to have been the first clergyman in the United States who adopted a practice which has since proved so beneficial to religion.

arrival among them, he found his congregations cold and neglectful of their Christian duties; he left them fervent and exemplary. Piety everywhere revived; the children and servants made their first communion; the older members of the congregations became regular communicants. Few that were instructed by him could ever forget their duty, so great was the impression he left, and so thorough was the course of instructions he gave. To the portion of Maryland in which he thus signalized his zeal, he bequeathed a rich and abundant legacy of spiritual blessings, which was destined to descend from generation to generation : and the good people of those parts still exhibit traces of his zeal, and still pronounce his name with reverence and gratitude. In the year 1804, Bishop Carroll found it necessary to recall M. David from the missions, in order to send him to Georgetown College, which was then greatly in need of his services. The good missionary promptly obeyed the call, and for two years discharged in that institution the duties of professor, with his accustomed fidelity and ability.

In 1806, the Sulpicians of Baltimore expressed a wish to enlist his services in the Theological Seminary and the College of St. Mary's, under their direction in that city. M. David belonged to that body, and he promptly repaired to the assistance of his brethren. He remained in Baltimore for nearly five years, discharging various offices in .the institutions just named, and devoted all his leisure time to the duties of the sacred ministry. He labored with so great zeal and constancy, that his constitution, naturally robust, became much impaired. Still he was not discouraged, nor did he give himself any rest or relaxation. A pure intention of promoting the honor and glory of God, and a constant spirit of prayer, sustained him, and hallowed his every action.

In the year 1808, the new Diocese of Bardstown was formed, embracing within its limits the States of Kentucky and Tennessee, although the delegated jurisdiction of the Bishop was to extend over the whole Northwest, as far as the Mississippi river. Rumor had fixed the appointment to the burdensome office of bishop for the "Far West," on Father David; but the choice of the Holy See fell on his intimate friend, M. Flaget. Surprised at the news of this unexpected elevation, M. Flaget hastened to Baltimore, to hear the sad intelligence either contradicted, or, if it proved to be true, to use every possible effort to shake off a responsibility which he believed to be entirely above his strength. The first person he met on the steps of the Seminary, was M. David, who, embracing him, confirmed the news, and, with tears in his eyes, added : " They told me that I was to be the Bishop of Bardstown ; I did not believe it. But I determined, that, should this happen, I would invite you to accompany me. But the case being happily reversed, I tender you my services without reserve."

Owing to the long persevering unwillingness of M. Flaget to assume the heavy burden of the episcopal office, he was not consecrated till the 4th of November, 1810, and it was only in the month of May following, that he was enabled to set out from Baltimore for the new field of his apostolical labors. On the 22d of May they embarked from Pittsburg in a flat-boat, chartered especially for the purpose. It contained, beside the Bishop and Father David, Mr. Fenwick, M. Savine, a Canadian priest, a sub-deacon—M. Chabrat, and a student. Father David had previously been appointed Superior of the Seminary ; and though "his health was in as bad a condition as the Bishop's purse," yet he presided over all the spiritual exercises which were carried on as in a regularly organized seminary. "The boat on which we descended the Ohio"—he subsequently wrote to a friend—"became the cradle of our seminary and of the Church in Kentucky. Our cabin was, at the same time, chapel, dormitory, study-room, and refectory. An altar was erected on the boxes, so far as circumstances would allow. The bishop prescribed a regulation, which fixed all the exercises, and in which each had its proper time. On Sunday, after prayer, every one went to confession; then the priests said Mass, and the others went to communion. After an agreeable navigation of thirteen days, we arrived at Louisville, next at Bardstown, and finally at the residence of the vicar-general."

This residence was an old log house, now converted into the "Episcopal Palace;" whilst another cabin harbored the seminarians, and Father David occupied a small addition to the principal building. There the seminary was conducted by him for five months, when in November, 1811, it was removed to the present farm of St. Thomas, which a pious Catholic, Thomas Howard, had bequeathed to the Church. Five years later the present neat church of St. Thomas was erected, and a brick building, intended for a Seminary, put up. The life of a Seminarian, in those days, was rather fuller of hardships and privations, than it is at present. It is well described in a letter of Father Badin.

"The seminarians made bricks, prepared the mortar, cut wood, etc., to build the church of St. Thomas, the seminary, and the convent of Nazareth. The poverty of our infant establishments compelled them to spend their recreations in labor. Every day they devoted three hours to labor in the garden, in the fields, or in the woods. Nothing could be more frugal than their table, which is also that of the two bishops, and in which water is their ordinary drink; nothing, at the same time, could be more simple than their dress."

2

The young seminarians, indeed, corresponded well with the parental solicitude of their good superior. They caught his spirit, and entered heartily into all his plans for their spiritual welfare. They united manual labor with study. They cheerfully submitted to lead a painful and laborious life, in order to fit themselves for the ministry, and to prepare themselves for the privations they were destined to endure on the missions.

As superior of the seminary, Father David was a rigid disciplinarian. Both by word and by example he enforced exact regularity in all the exercises of the house. He was himself always amongst the first at every duty. Particularly was he indefatigable in discharging the duty of instructing the young candidates for the ministry in the sublime maxims of Christian perfection. He seemed never to grow weary of this occupation. A thorough master of the interior life himself, it was his greatest delight to conduct others into the same path of holiness. He was not satisfied with laying down general principles; he entered into the most minute details, with a zeal equaled only by his patience.

He sought to inspire the young seminarians with an ardent desire of aspiring to perfection, and of doing all their actions for the honor and glory of God. To arouse and stimulate their zeal, he often dwelt on the sublime grandeur of the ministry, which he delighted to paint as a coöperation with Christ for the salvation of souls. A favorite passage of the Holy Scripture with him, was that containing the words of our blessed Lord to his apostles: "I have placed you, that you may go and bring forth fruit, and that your fruit may remain;"* as also this other decla-

* St. John xv. 16.

ration of the Saviour : "I have come to cast fire upon the earth, and what will I but that it be kindled ?"*

The first fruits of his seminary he reaped on the 10th of May, 1818, when two of his pupils, natives of Kentucky, who had gone through the whole course of their studies under his direction, were raised to the dignity of the priesthood ; although others, who came from Europe, had previously been ordained at St. Thomas's—among them several Lazarists, belonging to the Diocese of New Orleans, who stayed nearly two years in the seminary of M. David, whom, on that account, we may justly style the *Father of the Clergy of the West.*

Though he sometimes rebuked faults with some severity, yet he had a tender and parental heart, which showed itself on all occasions. For all the seminarians he cherished feelings of paternal affection. It was his greatest happiness to see them advance in learning and improve in virtue. He rejoiced with those who rejoiced, and wept with those who wept. No one ever went to him for advice and consolation in vain. As a confessor, few could surpass him in zeal, in patience, in tenderness. But what most won him the esteem, confidence and love of all under his charge, was his great sincerity and candor in every thing. All who were acquainted with him not only believed, but *felt*, that he was wholly incapable of deceiving them in the least thing.

He was always even better than his word : he was sparing of promises, and lavish in his efforts to redeem them when made. If he rebuked the faults of others, he was free to avow his own; and more than once have we heard him publicly acknowledging his imperfections, and with tears

* St. Luke xii. 49.

imploring pardon of those under his control for whatever pain he might unnecessarily have caused them. He was in the constant habit of speaking whatever he thought, without human respect or fear of censure from others. This frankness harmonized well with the open character of the Kentuckians, and secured for him, in their bosoms, an unbounded confidence and esteem.

Those under his direction could not fail to profit by all this earnest zeal and devotedness to their welfare. They made rapid advances in the path of perfection, in which they were blessed with so able and laborious a guide. Even when he was snatched from their midst, they could not soon forget his lessons, nor lose sight of his example.

We may say of him what he so ardently wished should be verified in others : that he "has brought forth fruit," and that " his fruit has remained." He has enkindled a fire in our midst, which the coldness and neglect of generations to come will not be able to quench. He has impressed his own earnest spirit on the missions served by those whom his laborious zeal has reared. Such are some of the fruits produced by this truly good man, with whose invaluable services God has pleased to bless our infant diocese.

But these were . not all, nor even one-half, of the fruits which he brought forth, and cultivated till they were ripe for Heaven. His zeal was not confined to the seminary, the labor of superintending which would have sufficed for any one man. He devoted all his moments of leisure to the exercise of the holy ministry among the Catholics living in the neighborhood of St. Thomas. He was for several years the pastor of this congregation ; and, besides the church, he attended to several neighboring stations, on Thursdays, when his duties did not require his presence at the seminary. He also visited the congregation at Bardstown once a month. Constant labor was the atmosphere he breathed, and the very element in which he lived. He was most happy, when most occupied. During his long life, he, perhaps, spent as few idle hours as any other man that ever lived.

Besides attending to the seminary and to the missions, Father David set about laying the foundation of another institution which was afterwards to become the ornament and pride of the diocese, and which was admirable even in its rude beginnings. We allude to the establishment of the Sisters of Charity in Kentucky, who justly look up to him as their father and founder.

The foundation of the Sisters of Charity in Kentucky dates back to the year 1812; one year and a half after the arrival of Bishop Flaget in his new diocese, and about twelve months after the Theological Seminary, under charge of Father David, had been removed from St. Stephen's to the farm of St. Thomas. At this time, the excellent superior of the seminary, with the advice and consent of Bishop Flaget, conceived the idea of founding a community of religious females, who, secluded from the world, might devote themselves wholly to the service of God and the good of their neighbors.

So soon as the intentions of the bishop were known in the congregations of his diocese, there were found several ladies who professed a willingness to enter the establishment and to devote their lives to the objects which its projectors proposed. In November, 1812, two pious ladies of mature age, Sister Teresa Carico and Miss Elizabeth Wells took possession of a small log house, contiguous to the church of St. Thomas. Their house consisted of but one room below and one above, and a cabin adjoining, which served as a kitchen. They commenced their work of charity by manufacturing clothing for those belonging to the seminary of St. Thomas, then in its infancy.

On the 21st of January following, 1813, another member was added to the community, in the person of Sister Catharine Spalding. On the same day, the superior, Father David, presented to them the provisional rules which he had already drawn up, unfolding the nature, objects, and duties of the new society. On the same occasion, he also read, and fully explained to those present, an order of the day, which he had written out, for the regulation of the exercises of the community; and this was still further organized by the temporary appointment of the oldest member as superior, until the society should be sufficiently numerous to proceed to a regular election, according to the provisions of the rule.

In June of the same year, the sisters, being then six in number, made a spiritual retreat of seven days, under the direction of Father David; and at the close of it, proceeded to the election of a superior, and of officers, of their own body. Sister Catharine Spalding was chosen the first Mother Superior, Sister Harriet Gardiner, Mother's Assistant, and Sister Betsey Wells, Procuratrix. At this first election ever held in the society, there were present, Bishop Flaget, Father David, and Rev. G. I. Chabrat. On that occasion the bishop made the sisters a very moving exhortation on the nature of the duties they were undertaking to perform, and on the obligations they contracted in embracing the religious life. The ceremony was closed with the episcopal benediction.

For two years the sisters continued to observe their provisional rule, patiently awaiting the decision of their bishop, and of their reverend founder, as to what order or society they would associate themselves.

At length it was determined that they should embrace the rules of the Sisters of Charity, founded in France nearly two centuries before, by St. Vincent of Paul. A copy of these rules had been brought over to the United States, from France, by Bishop Flaget, at the request of Archbishop Carroll; and they had been already adopted, with some modifications to suit the country, by the religious society of Sisters of Charity, then lately established at Emmittsburg, Maryland. Upon mature reflection, it was decided that the regulations of this excellent institute were more conformable than any other to the views and intentions of the bishop and of Father David, as well as to the wishes and objects contemplated by the members of the new society.

Father David continued to be the superior of the society for twenty years, when age and infirmity compelled him to retire from its management. He had watched over the infancy, and he lived to be cheered by the rapid growth and extended usefulness of the sisterhood.

Bishop Flaget cultivated so intimate a friendship with Father David, and found his services so indispensable for the welfare of his diocese, that he suffered the greatest anguish of soul whenever he had reason to fear that his old and tried friend might be taken away from him. The episcopal sees of Philadelphia and of New Orleans had been successively offered to Father David, who declined them. But the bishop resolved to put, at once, an end to all apprehensions of this sort, and supplicated the Holy See to appoint Father David his coadjutor. This prayer met with the approbation of Rome. The bulls, constituting John Baptist David *Bishop of Mauricastrum, in partibus infidelium*, and Coadjutor of the Bishop of Bardstown, were dated July 4th, 1817, and reached their destination on the 25th of November. But whilst Bishop Flaget was rejoicing,

Father David was distressed and dejected. He considered himself not only unworthy of so high a distinction, and unfit for the episcopal office, but his tender conscience presented to him also other obstacles, which did not allow him to accept the offered dignity. The bulls assigned, as reasons for giving the bishop a coadjutor, his age and infirmities, which applied still more strongly to Father David—being both older and of weaker health than the bishop. He communicated his doubts to the Cardinal Prefect of the Propaganda, who answered in the name of the Holy Father, and earnestly advised him to accept, alleging that those clauses were a mere formality, and not to be interpreted in their strictest sense; and that, moreover the Pope healed whatever deficiencies might be supposed to exist in the premises.

His consecration, however, did not take place till August, 1819. Bishop Flaget, meanwhile, made an excursion to Michigan and Canada; from which he returned only after an absence of nearly fourteen months. But, besides these, there were other reasons which caused the delay. Father David was blessed with so much of that holy poverty which he was in the habit of extolling to others, that he had not wherewith to make the necessary preparations for his consecration.* He had no means of procuring the episcopal habiliments, or other necessary articles for furnishing his episcopal chapel. His bishop was scarcely able to succor him in this emergency; and he was compelled patiently to await the arrival of the necessary assistance from France.

The ceremony of his consecration took place in the new cathedral, in the presence of a vast concourse of people, on the Feast of the Assumption of the Blessed Virgin, the 15th

---

* He loved his poverty even unto death: he left no property behind him, and could bequeath nothing to his friends but his virtues.

of August, 1819, the octave of the consecration of the cathedral. Bishop Flaget was the consecrator; and, having been unable to procure the attendance of any other prelate, he was assisted, on the occasion, by two among the oldest clergymen of the diocese.

After his consecration, Father David changed in nothing his former manner of life. He was still the plain, humble, and mortified man of prayer; the same regular, zealous, and indefatigable minister of God. From this time his zeal seemed to have received a new impulse; he now belonged more entirely to God, and his whole energies were to be consecrated still more fully, if possible, to the good of religion and to the salvation of souls. Living in the midst of his seminarians and clergy, eating at the same table, and joining with them in every exercise, he was at once the father and the model of both clergy and people. Into the former he labored unceasingly to infuse the true spirit of the ecclesiastical state; in the later he spared no pains to build up the sublime edifice of the Christian life.

One thing that he inculcated with particular force on the minds of his young clergy, was a zeal for the decency of divine worship. He was very fond of the *rubrics*, in which he was thoroughly versed. He trained the seminarians to an exact observance of all the ceremonies prescribed in the Roman missal, ceremonial and ritual, as fully explained in the copious and admirable decisions of the Roman Congregation of Rites. He employed every effort to promote this exact observance; and his zeal was aroused at the omission or improper performance of the least ceremony. In his instructions to the seminarians, he often dwelt in great detail on this branch of ecclesiastical education.

From his earliest youth, he had cherished and cultivated the natural taste for music with which he had been blessed.

He loved the grave severity of the venerable Gregorian chant, and could not brook the slightest departure from it in the Church of God. He spared no labor to form the choir of the cathedral; and for many years, he himself acted as organist and leader of the choir. His greatest delight seemed to be to unite with others in singing the praises of God, in that simple and soul-stirring melody, handed down to us by our fathers in the faith.

After he had been consecrated bishop, he discharged, for many years, the office of chief pastor of the cathedral; although he even then would not refuse to perform the humble functions of organist and leader of the choir on solemn occasions, when Bishop Flaget officiated pontifically. The ceaseless labors required by this triple charge of superior of the seminary, superior of the Sisters of Charity, and coadjutor bishop of the diocese, did not prevent him from devoting much of his time to the exercise of the holy ministry in the congregation of St. Joseph's. He visited the sick and the poor, he preached, he heard confessions, he gave spiritual instructions, he administered the sacraments, with indefatigable zeal. He lost not a moment of his precious time.

As a preacher, though not naturally very eloquent, he was eminently successful in imparting his own ideas and spirit to his hearers. His sermons were plain, solid, well connected, closely reasoned, and full of wholesome instruction. Every one saw, in the plain earnestness of his manner, that he was himself fully convinced of, and deeply imbued with, the holy truths and maxims which he unfolded.

But it was in the confessional that his zeal abounded most; and it was there that his success was most signalized. He there made an impression which time and the oblivious tendency of poor human nature could not soon obliterate.

His numerous penitents yet remember and profit by the
instructions which they there received. And long and grate-
fully will the congregation of St. Joseph's treasure up the
lessons enforced by the example of their oldest and most
warmly cherished pastor.

He manifested as much zeal for the maintenance of the
faith, as for the preservation of morals. As a controvertist,
he was clear, solid, logical, learned, thorough, and convincing.
These characters appeared both in his sermons and in his
controversial writings.

Shortly after he had been consecrated bishop, a Presby-
terian preacher by the name of Hall, who then resided in
Springfield, was in the habit of visiting Bardstown for the
purpose of attacking the Catholics, whose numbers were
then greatly increasing, while their institutions were spring-
ing up about this town. He was a man of strong frame and
of stentorian lungs, and as bitter and violent in his denun-
ciations, as he was confident and reckless in his assertions.
He was gifted with a certain stormy eloquence, which made
an impression on those with whom declamation passes for
argument, and assertions for proof.

Father David had been explaining, in the cathedral, in a
series of discourses, various points of Catholic doctrine, and,
among others, that which regards the use of and relative respect
paid to relics and images. The bitter attacks of the preacher
on Catholic doctrines, had induced him to undertake this
course of explanatory and *defensive* lectures on the various
points impugned or misrepresented. Preacher Hall gave out
that, on a certain day, he would preach in the court-house
of Bardstown, on this same subject of images, and would
prove the Catholic Church guilty of gross idolatry.

Though much averse to oral discussion, which seldom
ends in any thing except a widening of the breach, and the

greater imbittering of prejudice, yet Father David felt compelled, under all the circumstances of the case, to meet the reverend preacher, and to answer his objections. Bishop Flaget took so lively an interest in the movement, that he ordered public prayers to be offered up in the cathedral, to obtain victory for the truth, and also as some reparation for the blasphemies which would, no doubt, be uttered by the preacher against holy persons and things, especially against the Blessed Sacrament. A large concourse of people were in attendance on the appointed day ; and Mr. Hall opened the discussion with a discourse of two hours in length, in which he gave full play to his lungs, and a wide range to the subject he brought up as matter of accusation against Roman Catholics.

When he had concluded, Father David arose, and in a calm, solid, temperate, and argumentative discourse of about the same length, answered the minister's objections, and laid down the grounds of the Catholic faith and practice on the subject of images. His discourse made a deep impression on his hearers, which was not destroyed by the declamatory rejoinder of the preacher. Father David wished to bring him to close quarters, and to reduce the discussion to a simple and logical form; but the preacher refused this, and also another request—to reduce his objections to writing, that the bishop might be able to answer them in the same way. After having tired out the audience in his long rejoinder, Mr. Hall abruptly dismissed the meeting.

There was, of course, a diversity of opinion as to the merits of the discussion, according to the respective religious tenets or prejudices of the hearers. But many intelligent Protestants were heard to praise the calm manner and solid reasoning of Father David : and a very talented Protestant lawyer, on being asked his opinion of the debate, remarked, quaintly and pointedly: "That while Bishop David was preaching, the admirers of Mr. Hall looked like owls when the sun was shining."

Circumstances not having allowed him fully to answer the objections made in the second discourse of Mr. Hall, Father David resolved to give, in writing, a plain statement and a temperate defence of the Catholic doctrine on the subject of images and relics. Another motive for this publication was the wish to spread before the whole reading community, most of whom had not been able to attend the discussion, the whole matter in controversy. This he did in a pamphlet of sixty-four pages, entitled "Vindication of the Catholic Doctrine concerning the Use and Veneration of Images, the Honor and Invocation of Saints, and the Keeping and Honoring of their Relics."

This pamphlet exhausted the subject, and presented an unanswerable array of evidence on the articles in controversy. Mr. Hall published a "Reply," which drew forth from Father David another pamphlet of a hundred and six pages, entitled, "Defence of the Vindication of the Catholic Doctrine concerning the Use and Veneration of Images, etc., in Answer to the 'Reply' of Rev. Nathan Hall." The minister did not attempt a reply to this publication, which accordingly closed the controversy, leaving Father David master of the field.

About the same time Father David published his celebrated "Address to his Brethren of other Professions, on the Rule of Faith," a pamphlet of fifty-six pages, remarkable for its clear and logical method, its temperate spirit, and its unanswerable reasoning. Preacher Hall had delivered a discourse on the same subject in the court-house at Bardstown; and Father David had sent him, by a young divine, a series of questions on the subject, which he had declined answering. In the "Address," these questions are taken up and discussed with the thoroughness which marks every thing from the pen of Father David. It is, in a brief compass, one of the best arguments we have ever seen on the subject; and we may here express a hope, that this and other controversial writings will be shortly republished.

Controversy was not the only subject on which Father David wrote. He had already composed and published in Baltimore, the "True Piety," one of the best of our books of devotion.* In 1815 he published a "Catholic Hymn Book," which was followed, ten years later, by the "Catechism of the Diocese of Bardstown, printed by authority of the Right Rev. Benedict Joseph Flaget, Bishop of Bardstown." It was considered one of the best books of the kind ; and, like every thing that came from the pen of Father David, enjoyed great popularity, especially among the Catholics of Kentucky. Being rather more comprehensive than most other catechisms, it is well calculated to impart a thorough instruction to lay persons. At a later period in life, he wrote several very solid articles for the Metropolitan Magazine, published in Baltimore ; and when old age and infirmity compelled him to retire from the active duties of the ministry, he employed his time in translating various spiritual works of Saint Liguori, and of Bellarmine. The last translation he made, was that of Bellermine's beautiful little work "On the Felicity of the Saints." This was a foreshadowing, in his own mind and heart, of those blessed realities of heavenly bliss which he was soon to taste.

During all the time of which we are treating, the bishops

* This Prayer Book, like many other works, has since been *improved* for the worse ; and Father David was wont to call the new editions, with a smile, the *false* "True Pieties."

lived in common with their seminarians, and, on every Sunday and festival, appeared at the head of their clergy in all the services of the cathedral. We can not recall those happy days without a feeling of pride and of happiness. No one, who has seen the venerable patriarch of the West officiating in his cathedral, can ever forget the impression then made on his mind.

For more than sixteen years he continued to be the superior of the theological seminary which he had founded, and over the welfare of which he had watched with sleepless vigilance. His declining years and increasing duties now compelled him to resign this charge, and to commit the destinies of the institution to younger hands. Still, he continued to manifest an interest in its welfare, and to devote to the spiritual benefit of the seminarians all the time he could spare from his other duties. He delighted to give retreats; and he had written out an admirable course of meditations for this purpose. His coadjutorship he resigned in the year 1833, when he was succeeded by the Right Rev. Dr. Chabrat.

He continued faithful to all his spiritual exercises, as well as laborious and indefatigable in his duties, to his last breath. The evening of his life was spent in constant preparation for death. As when in the evening the sun, after sinking below the horizon, tinges with beautiful and varied colors the clouds which hang over the western sky, so also, in the evening of his life, the gathering clouds of sickness and of death were lighted up by the sun of another world, which faith opened to his view!

He died as he had lived. On the 12th of July, 1841, he quietly breathed his last, at Nazareth, the sisters of which institution had watched over him with tender solicitude during his last illness. He was interred in their cemetery.

He had reached the eighty-first year of his life, the fifty-sixth of his priesthood, and the twenty-second of his episcopacy.

It is not necessary for us to pronounce his eulogy. To those who knew him, this were unnecessary: and to those who were not personally acquainted with him, the facts contained in this sketch will suffice to give some insight into his character.

Sincerity and candor in all things, were, perhaps, the most distinctive traits in his character. He was what he appeared to be. He had less of human respect than is usually found among men. He always told you plainly what he thought; and you might rely upon the sincerity of his opinion, as much as on the soundness of his judgment. He was also, as we have already remarked, entirely consistent with his own principles. If he taught prompt obedience to others, he always practiced it himself, no matter how much pain it cost him; and this even after he had been consecrated bishop. If he was somewhat rigid towards others, he was much more stern to himself. He never sought to impose upon others a burden which he did not cheerfully bear himself.

Of the severe discipline to which he subjected his nature, we have an instance which is too precious to be here omitted. We find it recorded in the manuscript journal of Bishop Flaget. In August, 1823, the Bishop of Bardstown held a synod, in which all his clergy took part, and discussed different points of ecclesiastical discipline. By an excusable oversight, Bishop Flaget forgot to ask, at the debate of the first question, the opinion of Bishop David, who, being naturally of a hasty temper, was, by this seeming neglect, so much offended, that he, when consulted on a subsequent question, refused to have any thing at all to do with the business before the synod. Bishop Flaget apologized, and begged, publicly, pardon for the want of respect that was imputed to him. But Father David unfortunately let the sun go down upon his anger, to the great mortification of his old friend. But the next morning brought better counsel : "We had hardly sat down to begin the second session, when Bishop David came up, threw himself on his knees before me, and in this humble posture begged my pardon for the scandal which he had given the day before. The sight of this learned and venerable old gentleman, kneeling before all the clergy and his bishop, to repair, with such edification, a slight, indeliberate fault, filled me with admiration, and made me nearly forget to request him to rise. All the priests who were present entered into the same sentiments, which animated me, and were now so much more edified, as they had considered him incapable of an act of such heroic humility. Bishop David has since told me, that it was Rev. Mr. Derigand who had the courage and charity to inform him that his conduct during the first session had been a great scandal to all who witnessed it. Convinced of the happy results of this greatest of virtues, I thanked God for having permitted these aberrations in the two bishops, in order to let his glory shine with greater brightness, and to procure in the clergy of Kentucky, an example of the greatest edification."

Father David was laborious, and always occupied in doing something useful. He never lost a moment in idleness. He was as regular in all his habits, and as punctual to all his exercises and appointments, as he was industrious and indefatigable. Regularity became a second nature to him. And this accounts for the great labors he was able to undergo, and the immense good he was the instrument of effecting. We can, in no other way, explain how he was able to fulfill so many seemingly incompatible duties, and how he could find time for all his employments.

Gifted in an eminent degree with the spirit of prayer, he was always united with God, in all his actions. He labored not for men, but for God; not for earth, but for Heaven. His ambition aspired to a heavenly crown of unfading glory— he spurned all else.

In one word, he was the faithful fellow-laborer of Bishop Flaget, the founder of the seminary and of the Sisterhood of Charity in Kentucky, and the FATHER and model of our clergy and people. In their memory and in their hearts is his monument reared, and his epitaph written in indelible characters—he needs none other !

EIGHT DAYS' RETREAT.

BY THE LATE

RIGHT REV. BISHOP DAVID.

INTRODUCTION.

ON THE NATURE AND OBJECTS

OF THE

SPIRITUAL EXERCISES,

AND THE

MANNER OF PERFORMING THEM WITH FRUIT.

ST. IGNATIUS OF LOYOLA, the author of the Exercises and the founder of Spiritual Retreats, describes their nature and objects in the following compendious, but comprehensive words, placed as a title at the head of his golden little book:

"EXERCITIA SPIRITUALIA, per quæ homo dirigitur ut vincere seipsum possit, et vitæ suæ rationem, determinatione a noxiis affectibus libera, instituere — SPIRITUAL EXERCISES, by which a man is directed how he may conquer himself and may establish his manner of life, with a determination free from noxious affections."

Under the guidance of the Holy Ghost, in the lonely grotto of Manresa, the late soldier of an earthly monarch went successfully through his own training as a soldier of the Cross; and in his Book of Exercises he sets forth, with great simplicity and unction, the leading points of this spiritual drill, by which himself was converted from a sinner into a saint. Those who would wish to attain his generous self-devotion and his sanctity, should weigh well his words, and carefully mark the different stages of the spiritual combat through which he so triumphantly passed. From the words of the title above given we may readily infer the real nature and the true objects of a spiritual Retreat, according to his ideal so strongly inforced by his own example.

I. THE NATURE AND OBJECTS OF THE SPIRITUAL EXERCISES.

1. The very term *Spiritual Exercises* implies, that *active exertion* of the mind and heart belongs to the nature and the very essence of a Retreat. This consists in a series of spiritual operations, by which all the faculties of the soul and affections of the heart are brought into

active and healthy play, for a specific spiritual object. They comprise meditation, contemplation, and rigid self-examination, followed by corresponding affections and resolutions. The understanding, as the nobler faculty, leads the way, and, by meditation on the eternal truths and on the law of God, sheds a flood of heavenly light on our darksome pathway; the heart follows, with its corresponding emotions and affections; and the will terminates the process, by suitable resolutions firmly and strongly made. Man thus struggles on in the spiritual way, with all his powers and faculties on the alert; but man is weak and of himself powerless; and God accordingly cometh to his succor in his hour of conflict, and by throwing around his struggling infirmity the panoply of His omnipotent strength, completeth the work, and giveth to him the victory. Thus the divine element is happily combined with the human, and the result is, a lifting of weak man above himself, thus assuring him the victory over his perverse nature and headlong passions.

Exercise is as essential to the health of the soul as it is to that of the body. A condition of habitual quiescence and stagnation were fatal to the health of both. And as in bodily exercise, we sometimes walk slowly and wearily,

dragging our members along; sometimes step
forth with cheerful alacrity, traversing the ground .
with rapid movement, unmindful of interposing
obstacles; and sometimes even run forward
eagerly towards the goal to be attained: so it is
with those who perform their Spiritual 'Exercises. Some enter upon and perform them with
weariness and reluctance, with a sensible aversion to all mental and spiritual exertion, which
they feel almost too faint-hearted to overcome;
others undertake them with cheerful generosity,
distrusting themselves, but firmly relying on
God's help, by the aid of which they walk forward rapidly and with alacrity in the way of the
divine commandments; while others, finally,
forgetting the past and extending themselves
forward to that which is before them, gird themselves, like giants, to run the race, and fixing
their eyes steadily upon the goal, think no exertion and no sacrifice too great, provided they
can but bear away the prize and win the crown
of immortality. At the very outset of these
holy Exercises we must decide, to which of these
three classes we wish to belong. Upon this
preliminary determination the whole fruit of
our Retreat will in a great measure depend.

2. The object of these exercises is twofold:

1. To conquer ourselves; 2. To establish and enter upon a new rule of life for the future.

Our nature, tainted in its very origin by the sin of our first parents, is averse to good and prone to evil. It is constantly drifting down the current of evil inclinations towards the gulf of perdition. In the spiritual combat, then, we must constantly labor and toil to stem the current, if we would ascend and not descend. We can not lie idly by our oars; the moment we cease to struggle and toil, we will be borne downwards; not to advance is to fall back. Hence the necessity of conquering ourselves, if we would be victorious in the constantly recurring war of the spirit against the flesh. Says our blessed Lord: "If any one will come after Me, let him *deny himself*, take up his cross, and follow Me." Whosoever hath not well studied this lesson of self-denial, whosoever hath not learned in the school of the Crucified to conquer himself, is unworthy to be even called a disciple of Christ: he is no soldier of the Cross; he is faint-hearted, a craven, and a coward. The one who makes a Retreat, without earnestly seeking to conquer himself, will either lose his time or spend it with very slight profit.

After having effectually labored to overcome our evil nature, we must seek to adopt such practical means as the Spirit of God will indicate to us to be the more suitable for the practical reformation of our lives. We must walk in newness of life, after having risen from the tomb of darkness, sin, and spiritual death. To conceive sentiments of sorrow for sin and of love for virtue, to be filled with holy affections, and goodly purposes for the future, is all well enough so far as it goes; but mere emotions of the heart and general resolutions of amendment are not sufficient to accomplish the object of the Retreat, which is a solid and thorough reformation of our lives. Our resolutions must be definite and specific, not vague and general. We must lay the axe at the root of the tree of our evil nature, and sternly lop off its branches, or even cut it down, if it will not bring forth fruit worthy of penance. By diligent and unsparing self-examination, we must, with God's aid, discover our predominant passion, with the occasions or causes which have induced our repeated falls; and having found it out, we must cast to the winds all human respect, rid ourselves of all "noxious affections," and sternly take such resolutions as will be the most effectual to avert danger in the future, and to insure a solid amendment.

The Exercises of St. Ignatius are admirably

adapted for the accomplishment of this blessed result of spiritual reformation. They run in a series, with more than human connexion, sequence, and logic, and they all tend towards the same end — to reform our lives by first enlightening our understanding. The light of God shining broadly and brightly on the conclusions of human reasoning; the grace of God giving strength to human purpose, and the whisperings of the Comforter in the saddened heart, filling it with sweet consolation and making it sigh after heavenly things: these are admirably combined divine and human elements in the great work of man's reformation.

Like a wise architect, St. Ignatius begins with the foundation of the spiritual edifice, which he plants deeply and solidly; then he proceeds with the super-structure, which he works out in all its elaborate harmony of detail; nor pauses, till the temple of the Holy Ghost has been completed and secured against the rains and storms of temptation, and till it lifts its graceful pinnacles towards the heavenly Jerusalem. The work is begun amid tears and with wearing labor and fatigue; it is prosecuted with assiduous toil, relieved by the refreshments of divine grace; it is perfected in divine love, which sweetens and crowns all — as the complement and fulfillment of the law.

The work on the spiritual structure is divided into four Stages, or Weeks, each having its appropriate duties and objects. During the first Week, we lay the foundation, by meditating on, and deeply impressing on our minds, the great fundamental truth or *principle*, that we were created by God and for God, who is thus our first beginning and our last end; which once attained, all is gained, once lost, all is lost, and lost forever! All other things placed on this earth are, therefore, to be esteemed or rejected precisely and only in proportion as they lead us towards the great end of our creation, or turn us away from its attainment; and looking singly to the end, we are to school our minds and hearts to a state of holy indifference as to all else.

The only real and unmitigated evil, because the only one which can deprive us of our only real good, and last end, is *sin :* hence, we must detest and abhor sin, and fly from its very shadow, as from the hissings of the serpent, who seduced our first mother. To aid us in conceiving this holy horror of sin, not merely in general, but also particularly, as it exists in our own souls, blighting them by its pestilent breath, we next meditate on the eternal truths, on death, judgment, and hell, thus seeking to strike terror into our own hearts in view of the awful chastisements awaiting our manifold sins, unless they be pardoned by the divine mercy. The fruit, then, of this first Week's exercises, is a firm determination to labor earnestly for our last end, and to abhor and avoid sin as the only obstacle to its attainment. This is the *way of purification* — the *Via Purgativa*.

Having advanced thus far, we are prepared to enter upon the way of enlightenment in the second Week — the *Via Illuminativa*. After we have been purified from sin, Jesus Christ, our blessed Saviour, comes to us to set up His holy Kingdom in our hearts, to teach us the principles of humility, meekness, mortification, and disengagement from the world, upon which it is founded, and to make us know and *feel* in our inmost souls, that He is for us truly, "the Way, the Truth, and the Life." We are enlightened, and we are moved, by the appeals and by the example of so great and so good a Leader, and in the fullness of our hearts we cry out: "O Lord! I will follow Thee whithersoever Thou goest!" This is the practical fruit of the exercises of the second Week.

In the third, we advance still another stage. We enter upon the way of strength—the *Via*

Confirmativa. Meditating upon the passion
and death of Christ, whom we have already
chosen for our Leader and King, we endeavor
to catch somewhat of that superhuman devotedness, heroism, and love, which made Him a willing Victim for our sins, made Him die, that we
might live. Can we look upon that meek and
patient Sufferer — for our sakes — without conceiving some sentiment of the noble generosity
which prompted Him, for the love of us, to be
obedient even unto death, the death of the
Cross! Can we consent to be over dainty and
delicate members under a Head crowned with
thorns? Can we weakly and ingloriously give
away to the blandishments of the world and of
the flesh, when He spurned the world and gave
up His flesh to the bloody executioners, for the
love of us? Courage, then, generosity, willingness to suffer and to die, if need be, for Christ
who died for us, a determination to cast away
all softness and luxury and to enlist henceforth
as willing and generous soldiers of the Cross:
these are the fruits we must gather during the
third Week of the Exercises.

This frame of mind and heart prepares us
for the glorious termination and consummation
of the Exercises in the fourth Week, wherein
we enter upon the highest, the holiest, and the

sweetest way, the way of Union with God by Love — the *Via Unitiva*. After meditating on the glorious Resurrection of Christ, by which He left all His sorrows in the tomb, and entered upon a new life which should know death no more forever, we contemplate His triumphant Ascension into Heaven, and view Him sitting there in glory at the right hand of His Father, surrounded by millions of Angels and of ransomed souls; and then we exultingly break forth into those sweet emotions of that divine love, which is the chief joy of Heaven, as it is the chief duty of earth. *Sursum Corda* — Lift up your hearts! It is a happy, a glorious consummation! Jesus entered Heaven, that He might therein prepare a place for us! He is our Head, we are His members; where He is, there shall we also be forever more! Sweet and consoling thought! What are the sorrows and sufferings of this fleeting life, when compared with the cumulative glory, the abounding happiness, and the eternal bliss which await us in Heaven! I will then bear all the ills of life with cheerfulness and love, buoyed up by this blessed hope! I will do all for the divine love, knowing that God will requite me more than a hundred fold. The love of God — a love to pervade all my actions on earth and to be blissfully consummated in Heaven—this is the practical fruit of the Exercises of this fourth and last Week of the Retreat.

A learned and pious Jesuit father, who, some thirty years ago, gave more than one Retreat to the students of the Propaganda College in Rome, was in the habit of illustrating the nature and practical fruit of each Week's Exercises by phrases borrowed from the schoolmen, more remarkable for their terse significance than for their elegant Latinity. They are given here without commentary, as from what has just been said, they speak for themselves, and may besides be hereafter referred to in the proper places:

I. DEFORMATA REFORMARE — to *reform* what is *deformed* (by Sin).

II. REFORMATA CONFORMARE — to *conform* (to Christ's example) what has been *reformed.*

III. CONFORMATA CONFIRMARE — to *confirm,* or strengthen (by the Passion of Christ) what has been *conformed.*

IV. CONFIRMATA TRANSFORMARE — to *transform* (by divine love) what has been *confirmed.*

Though according to the original plan of St. Ignatius, four full Weeks were to be employed in the Exercises by those who wished to perform them thoroughly, yet they may be, and they usually are contracted into a much shorter space of time. Some now make a Retreat of ten, some of eight, and some of only seven or even six full days. In such cases, the Director will distribute the Exercises according to the time and circumstances. But, however short may be the time employed, the fruit of each successive Week may and should be gathered before passing on to the next. The first Week, comprising, as it does, the foundation, and the rising of the soul from the darkness of sin to the light of grace, is the most important, and its exercises are therefore less susceptible of abridgment than those which follow; all of these, however, as we have seen, are important for the completion of the edifice of Christian virtue and perfection. The Director will settle all these details, according to circumstances and persons. We must pass now to the second part.

II. HOW ARE WE TO PERFORM THE EXER-CISES WITH FRUIT.

To accomplish this object, which should be so very desirable to all who make a Retreat, the following practical rules, laid down by the masters of the spiritual life, should be carefully and scrupulously observed:—

1. The first disposition necessary for performing the Exercises with fruit is, to persuade ourselves of their importance and necessity *for us.* The more we penetrate ourselves with this conviction, the better will we perform this Retreat, to which God has called us in His mercy for our own spiritual profit, and perhaps for our salvation; which without it may be greatly endangered. Perhaps this is the last Retreat we may ever be allowed to make; therefore we should not fail to make it well, with our whole hearts and souls, with undivided attention and unflagging interest.

2. In entering upon our Retreat, we should be fully impressed with the true nature and real objects of the holy Exercises, as above set forth, in order that we may adhere strictly to the plan of salvation which they unfold, may not lose our time by efforts foreign to them, and may thus, with God's help, attain the great object which they contemplate — the reformation of our own lives. The more we understand and adhere to the letter and spirit of the Exercises, the more fruit we shall derive from them.

3. "The person in Retreat will find every thing easy, and himself wonderfully assisted by grace, if from the beginning he brings to God

A LARGE AND GENEROUS HEART; if he abandons himself, with all his wishes and all his liberty, to the action of his Creator; if he is disposed to allow his Sovereign Lord to order him, and all that concerns him, according to His good pleasure."

4. To make our Retreat well, we should employ two weapons essential to victory in the spiritual combat — distrust of ourselves, and confidence in God. Each of these sentiments should be carried to the furthest possible limits; there is no danger of exaggeration or excess in either, as it is impossible to trust too little in ourselves or too much in God.

5. We should be careful to let each Exercise, as it comes up, stand for itself, neither dwelling upon the past nor anticipating the future. *Age quod agis* — do what you do — should be our motto. By concentrating our entire attention upon the particular exercise before us, we shall be disposed to receive its full impression upon our minds and our hearts; and thus derive from the entire series that cumulative fruit which God designs to bestow upon the generous one who makes his Retreat well and thoroughly, and with a single eye to his own improvement.

6. Remembering that the chief object of the Retreat is the effectual reformation of our lives,

we should be careful to make well our daily examinations of conscience, both general and particular, according to the method laid down by St. Ignatius, which will be found in the proper place in this compilation. The more strictly we adhere to this method, the more fruit will we derive from our Retreat.

7. For the same end, we should be particular in preparing ourselves to make a good confession, including a review of our conduct since our last Retreat, or a general confession of our whole life, if our spiritual Director advise us to do so. This confession should be completed at the close of the first, or in the beginning of the second Week of the Exercises.

8. Another most important point is, to make proper resolutions for the amendment of our lives. These should be definite and to the point, not vague and general. They should strike at the root of our predominant vice, which the Spirit of God has enabled us to discover during the Retreat. In general, it is advisable that they be few in number, in order that the attention to our reformation may not be weakened or rendered ineffective by being divided among too many objects. It is also recommended, that they should be written out, as a memorial of the Retreat, and to enable us to renew them at

stated times. In cases of doubt as to the particular resolutions to be taken, we may profitably consult our Director.

9. We should peruse attentively and study thoroughly the Ten Additional Recommendations of St. Ignatius, which will be found in the proper place. They contain practical advice and minute details, dictated by the Spirit of God, which will be of great service to us in making the Retreat well.

10. The Exercises of each Week, as has been already intimated, should be continued until the proper fruit will have been gathered therefrom. The length of time employed and the number of Exercises performed are not so important, as the impression to be made on the mind and heart, and the practical fruit to be derived for the emendation of our lives. For those who make a Retreat of only six full days, the Director must decide which of the Meditations in the first and second Weeks, can best be omitted; but we would suggest that, in all cases, those on the Following of Christ, the Two Standards, and the Prodigal Son should be retained. The Meditations of the third and fourth Weeks, embracing, as they do in the following series, but one day each, can not well be omitted or even abridged.

11. Finally, we should, at the beginning and during the continuance of the Retreat, fervently invoke our Guardian Angels, our Patron Saints, and particularly the Immaculate Virgin, our tender, sweet, and holy Mother in Heaven, under whose powerful patronage we should place the entire fruit of the Exercises. God will not fail to crown with His most abundant blessing whatever we will undertake under the auspices of Mary, whom He loved and honored so highly as to make her the Mother of His Only Begotten and Well Beloved Son. The *Memorare* of St. Bernard, recited frequently and fervently, will fill us with great consolation, and bring down into our souls the most precious graces. We can scarcely exceed in the confidence we may repose in the intercession of the Holy Virgin.

METHOD OF MENTAL PRAYER.

BY BISHOP DAVID.

CHAPTER I.

OF MENTAL PRAYER IN GENERAL.

QUESTION. What is Mental Prayer?

ANSWER. Mental Prayer is a raising up and an application of our mind and heart to God, in order to render Him our homage and adoration; to ask His aid in our necessities, and to improve ourselves in virtue for His honor and glory.

Q. Is Mental Prayer necessary?

A. Yes, as necessary as it is to render God homage and adoration, and to beg His assistance in our wants.

Q. How many parts are there in Mental Prayer?

A. Three parts, viz.: The Preparation, the Meditation, and the Conclusion.

CHAPTER II.

OF THE PREPARATION.

Q. How many kinds of preparation are required?

A. Two kinds; viz.: The Habitual and the Actual.

Q. How are we to be habitually prepared for Mental Prayer?

A. First, by purity of heart; second, by interior and exterior recollection; and, third, by purity of intention.

Q. What do you mean by purity of heart?
A. I mean, first, to be clear of all mortal sin; second, to be free from all affections to venial sin; and, third, to be disengaged from all irregular attachment to creatures.

Q. What do you mean by interior recollection?
A. I mean an habitual attention to God and a facility for self-consideration.

Q. What do you mean by exterior recollection?
A. I mean the love and practice of silence and retirement, and a great care to avoid the causes of dissipation.

Q. What are the chief causes of dissipation?
A. A vain curiosity, liberty of the senses, idle conversation, frequenting the world, etc.

Q. What do you mean by purity of intention?
A. I mean a sincere desire of seeking in Mental Prayer singly the glory of God, and our own advancement in virtue.

Q. In what does the actual preparation consist?
A. The actual preparation is either remote or immediate.

Q. What is the remote preparation?
A. It consists in preparing beforehand the subject of the Meditation, by reading or hearing it read, and disposing in our mind the points on which we are to meditate, the principal affections we are to conceive, the petitions we are to make, and the resolutions we are to form.

Q. What is the immediate preparation?
A. It is that which immediately precedes Meditation.

Q. In what does it consist?

A. In three things: first, in placing ourselves in the presence of God; second, in acknowledging ourselves unworthy of appearing before him; third, in acknowledging ourselves incapable of praying as we ought.

Q. How must we place ourselves in the presence of God?

A. By two acts: first, of faith, believing that God, being everywhere, is in the place wherein we pray, and in our very hearts; second, of profound adoration of His infinite Majesty, before whom we are nothing.

Q. What must we do in acknowledging ourselves unworthy of appearing before God?

A. Three things: first, we must humble ourselves at the sight of our sins; second, detest them by an act of sincere contrition; third, unite ourselves to Jesus Christ in order to appear before His Father, and put up our prayer to Him in His name.

Q. What must we do in acknowledging ourselves incapable of praying as we ought?

A. We must distrust our own understanding, renounce our own will, and all distractions, and beg the light and grace of the Holy Ghost; for which we may implore the intercession of the Blessed Virgin Mary, and of the Saints to whom we have the most devotion.

CHAPTER III.

OF THE MEDITATION.

Q. What is Meditation ?

A. By Meditation we here understand the exercise of the powers of the soul on some pious subject.

Q. Which are the powers to be exercised ?

A. Memory, understanding, and will.

Q. How is the memory to be exercised ?

A. By recalling to our mind the subject we have prepared, and making a representation of it by means of the imagination, which is a kind of corporal memory.

Q. How is that representation to be made ?

A. By imagining that the thing we meditate upon is actually passing before our eyes.

Q. Explain this by example.

A. If I meditate on the Nativity of Jesus Christ, I must imagine myself to be in the stable, to see the manger, the Infant Jesus, etc., etc. If I meditate on Death, I must fancy myself on a death-bed, surrounded by friends in tears, ready to give the last gasp, etc.

Q. What is to be done when the subject is not a fact but a truth, a virtue or a vice ?

A. We must then recall to our mind some passage of the life or passion of Jesus, where he teaches that truth, gives an example of virtue, or condemns that vice.

Q. What is the use of this representation ?

A. To fix our attention, to prevent distractions,

and to make good use of our imagination, which has been given us by Almighty God for that purpose.

Q. What must we do when the subject is present to our imagination?

A. We must adore, praise, thank, and love our Blessed Saviour, with relation to the subject; and beg of Him the fruit we wish to draw from the present Meditation.

Q. How is the understanding to be exercised?

A. In seriously considering the subject.

Q. How is the subject to be considered?

A. Under two respects; viz.: in itself, and in its relation to us.

Q. How is the subject considered in itself?

A. By considering the different circumstances of it, and reasoning upon them, in order to convince our minds of the reasons and motives we have to shun vice and to embrace virtue.

Q. How do we consider the subject in relation to ourselves?

A. By making a comparison of our past conduct and actual dispositions with that which we have discovered to be our obligation, so that knowing our vices and imperfections, we may more easily reform ourselves.

Q. Is this point of great importance?

A. Yes; and without it Meditation would afford but very little profit.

Q. How is the will to be exercised?

A. In forming affections, resolutions, and petitions.

Q. What are the affections to be formed ?

A. Chiefly three : first, sorrow for our past sins; second, confusion at the sight of our present imperfections; and, third, a desire of doing better for the future.

Q. May we not occupy ourselves in some other affections ?

A. Yes; according to the interior motions of the Holy Ghost, and to the nature of the subject; such as affections of joy, compassion, fear, hope, love, hatred, aversion, contempt, etc.

Q. What do you mean by resolutions ?

A. I mean a sincere and firm determination to shun vice and to practice virtue.

Q. Is it necessary to make resolutions ?

A. Yes; for on them entirely depends the fruit of Mental Prayer.

Q. What must be the qualities of our resolutions ?

A. They must be : first, prudent; second, particular; third, present; fourth, humble; and, fifth, generous.

Q. How prudent ?

A. That is to say, they must be proportioned to our necessities which we have discovered in Meditation.

Q. How particular ?

A. By pointing out the particular vices and sins to be avoided, and the particular virtues or good works to be practiced.

Q. How present ?

A. They must be for the present day, and the immediate occasion.

Q. How humble?

A. They must be accompanied with a great distrust of ourselves, and a great confidence in God.

Q. How generous?

A. They must move us to surmount all obstacles, and to pursue the most proper means for rooting out all vicious habits, and planting virtue in our hearts.

Q. What do you mean by petition?

A. The resolution of doing better, naturally leads us to ask of Almighty God, His grace to execute our good purposes, as being incapable of any good without it.

Q. What must be the qualities of our petitions?

A. They must be accompanied with humility, fervor, confidence, and perseverance.

Q. What are the means of rendering our petitions more efficacious?

A. We must present them to Almighty God, through Jesus Christ, our Saviour and Mediator; and implore the intercession of the Blessed Virgin Mary, of the Angels and the Saints.

CHAPTER IV.

ON THE CONCLUSION.

Q. How must we conclude our prayer?

A. By spending a little while after it in reviewing in what manner the whole of it has been performed.

Q. To what purpose?

A. First, to encourage ourselves to continue, the next time, that which we find to have been rightly performed, and to correct that which has been faulty and deficient; second, to thank God for the graces which He has bestowed upon us during the time of prayer, and to beg Him to pardon the faults committed during its performance; and, third, to make choice of some of the thoughts or affections which moved us the most, in order to recall them from time to time, during the day, to our remembrance. This is commonly called the Spiritual Nosegay.

CHAPTER V.

OF SOME ADVICES CONCERNING MENTAL PRAYER.

Q. Is it necessary to follow this method?

A. Yes, unless God should call us to some other manner of prayer.

Q. What must we do when we feel ourselves attracted to some other manner of prayer?

A. We must propose it with simplicity to our director and follow his advice.

Q. Is it necessary to make many considerations?

A. No; only as many as are requisite to excite in us pious affections and resolutions, which are the chief part of Mental Prayer.

Q. Is it necessary to conceive many affections?

A. No; when we are actually employed in forming some good affection, making some petition, or making some good resolution, we must not leave it, under the pretense of passing to another.

Q. Must we, in producing these acts, confine ourselves scrupulously to the order prescribed in the method ?

A. No; if we find ourselves moved to produce them from the beginning, or out of the place pointed out by this method, we must follow that attraction without delay.

CHAPTER VI.

OF THE IMPEDIMENTS TO MENTAL PRAYER.

Q. What are the chief impediments to Mental Prayer ?
A. The chief impediments to Mental Prayer are distractions and dryness.

Q. What is distraction ?
A. It is a wandering of the imagination or of the mind towards objects foreign to the subject of Meditation.

Q. What should we do to avoid distractions ?
A. We must endeavor, before prayer, to prevent them; during prayer, to banish them; after prayer, to find out and cut off the root of them.

Q. How are we to prevent distraction before prayer ?
A. By faithfully observing what has been said of the preparation to Mental Prayer.

Q. How are we to banish them during prayer ?
A. By gently and quietly recalling our mind to our subject, as soon as we perceive ourselves to be distracted, without troubling ourselves on account of the distraction, or reflecting upon it.

Q. How are we to find out and cut off the root of them after prayer?

A. In the conclusion of our prayer, we ought to examine what has been the source of our distractions, and having found it out, we must endeavor to amend it so far as we can.

Q. What do you mean by dryness?

A. I mean the state of a soul that finds herself, as it were, incapable of reflection or affections, to which sometimes-is joined an interior disgust and desolation.

Q. How comes a soul to fall into that state?

A. It is either a punishment or a trial.

Q. What faults bring this punishment?

A. Deliberate venial sins, voluntary imperfections, seeking after human comforts, etc.

Q. What must the soul do in this case?

A. She must, by repentance and amendment, strive to regain the favor of her God, and bear willingly the punishment as long as He may choose to inflict it, acknowledging its justice.

Q. How is this state a trial?

A. God sometimes withdraws His light and consolation from His dearest friends, to perfect their humility, to purify their love, and to prepare them for greater favors.

Q. What must be the conduct of the soul in these states?

A. She must humble herself, submit to the Divine will, persevere in prayer, and wait with patience for the return of grace.

Q. What helps can she make use of in the mean time?

A. It is proper she should have recourse to some lively ejaculations, to the reciting of some

short and devout vocal prayer, to the reading of
something out of a pious book, to some exterior
act of devotion, etc., etc.

TEN ADDITIONAL RECOMMENDATIONS,

IN THE FORM OF RESOLUTIONS, WHICH WILL ASSIST US
IN MAKING THE EXERCISES WELL, AND OBTAINING FROM
GOD WHAT WE ASK OF HIM.

1. On lying down, before going to sleep,
during the short time which will suffice for
repeating the "Hail Mary," I will fix the hour
of my rising, and review in my mind the points
of my meditation.

2. On awaking, immediately excluding all
other thoughts, I will apply my mind to the
truth on which I am going to meditate; at the
same time I will excite in my heart suitable
sentiments. For example, before the Exercise
on the "triple sin," I will say to myself while I
dress, "And I, loaded with so many graces, the
object of predilection to my Lord and King, I
stand convicted of ingratitude, of treason, of
rebellion, before His eyes and those of His whole
court." Before the Exercise on personal sins,
"Behold me, a criminal deserving death, led
before my Judge loaded with chains." These
sentiments must accompany the act of rising,

and will vary according to the subject of meditation.

3. Standing a few paces from the spot where
I am going to make my meditation, I must recollect myself, raise my mind above earthly things,
and consider our Lord Jesus Christ as present
and attentive to what I am about to do. Having
given to this preparation the time required to
say the "Our Father," I will offer the homage
of my soul and body to our Saviour, assuming
an attitude full of veneration and humble
respect.

4. I will then begin my meditation, if I am
alone in my chamber or elsewhere without witnesses, in the posture most suitable to the end
I propose to myself, sometimes with my face
bowed to the earth, sometimes standing, sometimes sitting; only observing that if I obtain
what I seek kneeling, or in any other attitude,
I ought to remain so without seeking any thing
better. In the same way, if any particular point
causes me to experience the grace which I am
seeking, I must remain there calmly until my
devotion is satisfied, without caring for any thing
more.

5. After having finished the Exercise, I will
either walk about or sit still, and examine how
it has succeeded. If it has not, I will ascertain
the cause, sincerely repent, and make firm resolutions for the future. If the success has been
satisfactory, I will make acts of thanksgiving,
and resolve to follow the same method for the
future.

6. I will lay aside during the first week all joyful thoughts, such, for instance, as the glorious resurrection of Jesus Christ. This thought would dry up the tears which I ought at this period to shed over my sins. I must rather call up thoughts of death and judgment, in order to assist my sorrow.

7. For the same purpose, I will shut out the daylight, only allowing sufficient light to enter my room to enable me to read and take my meals.

8. I will carefully avoid all laughter, or any thing which can lead to it.

9. I will not look at any one, unless obliged to salute them or say adieu.

10. I will add to these practices some exercises of penance, both *interior*, exciting in myself sentiment of self-humiliation, and sorrow for my innumerable sins, and *exterior*, curbing my appetite and carefully guarding my senses against distraction from external objects.

CONTEMPLATION,

OR MANNER OF MEDITATING ON SENSIBLE OBJECTS.

In this Exercise, where the mysteries of our Saviour are the object, we fix on persons, listen to words, consider actions; and from each of

these we endeavor to draw some fruit for the
soul.

I. BEFORE THE CONTEMPLATION.

The same thing is to be observed as in the
meditations, only adding a prelude. It is a sort
of representation of the mystery intended to be
meditated upon, and which consists in recalling
the history in brief. This prelude should be
placed after the preparatory prayer, and before
the construction of place.

II. DURING THE CONTEMPLATION.

1. Consider first, the persons, with whatever
they present in themselves of good or bad.

2. The words, interior or exterior; the thoughts,
the affections.

3. The actions, praiseworthy or blamable,
going back to their cause in order to draw more
spiritual profit from them.

Each of these points we must consider as
regards ourselves, and apply the reflections sug-
gested by the different objects contemplated.
We may also meditate on the mysteries, reflecting on all the circumstances, the causes, the end,
the effect, the time, the place, the manner of
their accomplishment.

[End by one or more colloquies and the *Pater*.]

III. AFTER THE CONTEMPLATION.

The same review as after the meditation.

OF DIVERS MANNERS OF PRAYING.

FIRST MANNER.

This is less a prayer than a spiritual exercise, which assists the soul, and renders its prayer more agreeable to God. It consists in reflecting on the commandments of God, the capital sins, the three powers of the soul, the five senses of the body, as follows:

1. Before beginning, think a few minutes of what you are about to do.

2. Ask of God the grace to know the sins you have committed against His commandments, and to accomplish the obligations of His law with more fidelity henceforth.

3. Thinking over, one after another, the commandments of God, see how you have fulfilled or violated them. Ask pardon for the sins you can recall, and say the *Pater*. It is sufficient to dwell the length of three Paters on each precept; but this space of time must be abridged or prolonged according as the faults are few or numerous on each precept.

4. After having thus run through all the commandments, humble yourself, accuse yourself; ask for grace to observe them better for the future; and end by a colloquy addressed to God, suitable to the state and the dispositions in which you find yourself.

If you wish to take for your subject the capital sins, the three powers of the soul, the five senses, etc., you have only to change the matter

of the examination; the rest will be the same
as for the commandments.

Let us observe that the Christian who wishes
to imitate our Lord Jesus Christ in the use of
his senses, must ask the grace of God the Father
to enable him to do so, and, glancing at each
of his senses, examine how far they approach or
depart from his Divine Model. Before passing
from one sense to another, recite a *Pater*.

If it is proposed to imitate the Blessed Virgin,
we must ask her to obtain this grace from her
Divine Son, and after the examination of each
sense recite an *Ave*.

SECOND MANNER.

This consists in reciting some vocal prayer,
and resting successively on the words composing
it as long as we feel taste and devotion.

1. Before beginning recollect yourself.

2. Address yourself to the person to whom
you are going to pray.

3. Begin the prayer — the *Pater*, for example;
dwell on these words, Our Father; meditate on
them as long as they furnish you with thoughts,
affections, etc., and then pass to the following
words, which you will consider in the same
manner.

4. When the time comes to conclude, recite
the rest of the prayer without stopping, and
address yourself in a short prayer to the person
to whom you have been praying, to ask the
grace or the virtue which you require.

Remark. [(1.) All vocal prayers, the *Credo*, the *Salve Regina*, the *Anima Christi*, etc., may be recited in this manner. (2.) If one single word of the prayer we are reciting in this way suffices to occupy the mind and the heart all the time destined to prayer, we must put off to another day the meditation of the rest. The following day we must commence by reciting, without stopping, what was meditated on the day before, and then continue the consideration of the rest of the words of the prayer.]

THIRD MANNER.

This consists in pronouncing a vocal prayer, and, if we choose several prayers successively, only stopping the interval of a breathing between each, thinking either of the sense of the word, or of the dignity of the person to whom we pray, or of our own unworthiness, or of the distance between the two. Let us take the *Ave Maria* for an example.

1. Think of the action you are going to perform.

2. Beginning with "Hail, Mary," think for a moment what these words signify, or of the dignity of the Blessed Virgin whom you salute, or of your miseries, which place so great a distance between you and the Mother of God.

3. Then you pronounce the other words, dwelling on each one, as we have said, only the time of a breathing.

METHOD OF PARTICULAR EXAMINATION.

There are two kinds of examination (or examen), general and particular. The object of the first is to discover all the faults we have committed. The second, or particular examination, has for its object one single fault or bad habit which we have resolved to correct. It is made every day in the following manner:

1. In the morning, on rising, resolve to avoid this sin or defect.

2. Towards noon ask of God the grace to remember how often you have fallen into it, and to avoid it for the future. Then examine, thinking over the time passed since your rising to this time, the number of faults committed, marking them by so many points in the first line of a figure like the following.

DAYS OF THE WEEK.

First   day

Second day

Third   day

Fourth day

Fifth   day

Sixth   day

Seventh day

This done renew your resolutions for the rest of the day.

3. In the evening, after supper, a new examination like the first, marking the faults on the second line.

OBSERVATIONS.

1. At each fault against the resolution you have taken, put your hand on your heart and repent of your fall. This may be done without being perceived.

2. At night, count the points of the two examinations, and see if, from the first to the second, you have made any amendment.

3. Compare, in the same way, the day or the week which is ending with the preceding day or week. The lines diminish in length, because it is reasonable to expect, that the number of the faults should likewise diminish.

4. The subject of the particular examination should be ordinarily the predominant passion — that is, the one that has been the source of the greatest number of faults that you commit, and which, consequently, is the great obstacle to your sanctification.

5. This examination on the predominant passions should be continued until it is entirely overcome, or at least notably weakened.

7

METHOD OF THE GENERAL EXAMINATION,

TO BE MADE EVERY DAY.

The first point is an act of thanksgiving to the Lord for the benefits we have received.

The second is a prayer to know our faults, and to correct them.

The third is an exact discussion and examination of the sins we have committed during the day. We must demand a rigorous account from our souls of what we have thought, said, and done hour by hour. The same order and method must be followed as has been already given for the particular examen.

The fourth consists in asking pardon of God for the sins into which we have fallen.

PRAYER OF ST. IGNATIUS, "ANIMA CHRISTI,"

WHICH IS OFTEN USED DURING THE EXERCISES.

Anima Christi, sanctifica me.
Corpus Christi, salva me.
Sanguis Christi, inebria me.
Aqua lateris Christi, lava me.
Passio Christi, conforta me.
O bone Jesu, exaudi me :
Intra tua vulnera absconde me :
Ne permittas me separari a te :
Ab hoste maligno defende me ;
In hora mortis meæ voca me,
Et jube me venire ad te,
Ut cum sanctis tuis laudem te
In sæcula sæculorum.　Amen.

Soul of Christ, sanctify me.
Body of Christ, save me.
Blood of Christ, inebriate me.
Water out of the side of Christ, wash me.
Passion of Christ, strengthen me.
O good Jesus, hear me ;
Hide me within Thy wounds ;
Suffer me not to be separated from Thee.
Defend me from the malignant enemy ;
Call me at the hour of my death,
And bid me come unto Thee,
That with Thy saints I may praise Thee
For all eternity. Amen.

PRAYER OF OBLATION AND DIVINE LOVE,

BY ST. IGNATIUS.

Suspice, Domine, universam meam liberta-
tem. Accipe memoriam, intellectum, et voluntatem omnem. Quidquid habeo vel possideo,
tu mihi largitus es: id tibi totum restituo, ac
tuæ prorsus trado voluntati gubernandum.
Amorem tuî solum cum gratia tua mihi dones,
et dives sum satis, nec aliud quidquam ultra
posco.

Take and receive, O Lord, my entire liberty.
Accept my whole memory, my whole understanding, my whole will. Whatsoever I have
or possess Thou hast bounteously bestowed it
upon me; I restore it all to Thee, and deliver
it up to be governed entirely according to Thy
will. Vouchsafe to give me Thy love with Thy
grace and I am rich enough; nor do I ask for
aught else but this priceless boon.

THE MEMORARE,

BY ST. BERNARD.

Memorare, O piissima Virgo Maria, non esse auditum a sæculo quemquam ad tua cùrrentem præsidia, tua petentem suffragia, tua implorantem auxilia esse derelictum. Ego tali animatus confidentia ad te, Virgo virginum, Mater curro, ad te venio, coram te gemens peccator assisto.　Noli, Mater Verbi, verba mea despicere, sed audi benigni et exaudi.

Remember, O most compassionate Virgin Mary, that it is unheard of, through all ages, that any one flying to thy protection, asking thy prayers, and beseeching thy help, ever was abandoned.　Animated with such confidence, I run to thee, O Virgin of virgins, as to my sweet mother, I come to thee and cast myself, a weeping sinner, at thy feet.　Do not, O Mother of the Divine Word, despise my words, but graciously hear them, and obtain for me what I so humbly and so confidently ask.

[Here state your petition.]

PRAYER OF UNION WITH JESUS IN ALL OUR ACTIONS.

[Found in Bishop David's handwriting, in an old Diurnal.]

Quidquid agam auspice Jesu agam.—Visitabo? In oculis Jesus erit. Dormiam? Jesum somniabo. Ambulabo? Jesus comes ibit. Sedebo? Latus claudet Jesus. Studebo? Jesus erudiet. Scribam? Calumum cum manu Jesus ducet, et Jesus Jesum scribet. Orabo? Verba Jesus formabit, animabit Jesus. Fessus ero? Recreabit Jesus. Esuriam, sitiam? Jesus pascet, potabit. Œgrotabo? Amor aderit medicus Jesus. Moriar? Jesu immoriar meo, Jesus oculos claudet, Jesu sinus mihi tumulus, tumuli inscriptio Jesu nomen erit.

Whatever I will do, I will do it under the auspices of Jesus. Will I visit? Jesus shall be before my eyes. Will I sleep? I will dream of Jesus. Will I walk? Jesus will be my companion. Will I sit down? Jesus will be by my side. Will I study? Jesus will teach me. Will I write? Jesus will guide my hand and pen, and Jesus will write JESUS. Will I pray? Jesus will form and will animate my words. Will I be tired? Jesus will repose me. Will I hunger — thirst? Jesus will feed and give me to drink. Will I be sick? Jesus, my love, will be my physician. Will I die? I will die with my Jesus, Jesus will close my eyes, the bosom of Jesus will be my tomb, and the inscription will be the name of JESUS.

***

UNION WITH JESUS AND MARY.

O Jesu, vivens in Maria, veni et vive in famulis tuis, in spiritu sanctitatis tuæ, in plenitudine virtutis tuæ, in perfectionem viarum tuarum, in communionem mysteriorum tuorum; dominare omni adversæ potestati in Spiritu tuo ad gloriam Patris, Amen.

O Jesus, living in Mary, come and live in Thy servants, in the spirit of Thy holiness, in the plenitude of Thy power, in the perfection of Thy ways, in the communion of Thy mysteries; overrule every adverse power in Thy Spirit for the glory of the Father. Amen.

PREPARATORY EXERCISE.

[*Veni Creator. Ave maris stella. Invoke St. Joseph, your angel guardian, and your patron saints. Then read attentively the subject of meditation which is to open the Exercises.*]

MEDITATION ON RETREAT.

FIRST CONSIDERATION.

What God has prepared for you in retreat.

God has prepared for you a superabundance of His graces in this Retreat. It is the same in retreat as in the great solemnities of religion and in certain privileged sanctuaries of Mary. Jesus Christ has graces for every day; but He reserves His choicest ones for the days on which the Church celebrates the great mysteries of His life on earth. Mary is always our benefactress and our mother; but she has favorite sanctuaries, to which she attaches her greatest blessings and miracles. The privilege of a retreat is to draw down upon us all the graces of God in their greatest plenitude. "Behold, now is the acceptable time: behold, now is the day of salvation." (2 Cor. vi. 2.)

Consider, with St. Bernard, that it has been in retreat that God has always pleased to signalize His greatest mercies towards men. It was in retreat on Sinai that Moses received the tables of the law; it was in the retreat of Carmel that Elias received the double spirit which animated him; it was in the retreat of the desert that John Baptist received the plenitude of the Spirit of God; it was in retreat that the Apostles received the gifts of the Holy Ghost; it was in retreat that God converted the most illustrious penitents, that He raised up the most fervent apostles of the new law, that He inspired the founders of religious societies; in fine, it was in the retreat of Nazareth that Mary became the Mother of God; and it may be said that all the life of Jesus Christ was a retreat. "Solitude was witness of the vigils of Jesus; solitude heard the prayers of Jesus; solitude saw Him come into the world, preach, be transfigured, die, rise from the dead, ascend into Heaven." (P. de Celles.)

Believe, then, and rest assured that all the graces of God await you in this retreat.

Who are you who this day begin these holy Exercises? *Who are you?* A soul established in virtue? You need renewing. The most solid virtue is a perfume which evaporates, a mirror which tarnishes, a water which becomes impure in the midst of the world. "Bless the Lord, O my soul, ... who satisfieth thy desire with good things; thy youth shall be renewed like the eagle's." (Ps. cii. 1, 5.) To you the grace of a retreat will be one of renovation.

Who are you? A soul divided in the service of God — a soul embarrassed by a multitude of human affections? You have now to detach your heart from creatures. "How long do you halt between two sides? If the Lord be God, follow Him." (3 Kings xviii. 21.) For you the grace of retreat will be a grace of detachment.

Who are you? A soul given to worldly pleasures — one who does not pray, or prays badly? You must return to yourself and to God. "Return, ye transgressors, to the heart." (Is. xlvi. 8.) "We ought always to pray." (Luke xviii. 1.) For you the grace of retreat will be one of recollection and prayer.

Who are you? A soul struggling with long and violent temptations? You need strength to resist. "If you return and be quiet, you shall be saved: in silence and hope shall your strength be." (Is. xxx. 15.) For you the grace of retreat will be one of firmness and perseverance.

Who are you? Lastly, are you a guilty soul? perhaps a soul grown old in sin, perhaps an impenitent soul, perhaps a soul struck with blindness and hardness? And if this question alone does not make you tremble, certainly you are a hardened soul. Ah! you require nothing less than all the graces of God; and this retreat offers them to you — the grace of light on your state, on the enormity of your faults, on the greatness of your losses for eternity, on the judgments of God which menace you; the grace of compunction; the grace of firm resolution; the grace of a real and solid conversion.

SECOND CONSIDERATION.

What God asks of you in this Retreat.

God requires two things of you, on which depend all the graces of the retreat.

1. *Recollection of spirit.* You are in retreat to listen to God. "I will hear what the Lord God will speak within me." (Ps. lxxxiv. 9.) But the voice of God only makes itself heard in the repose and silence of the soul. It is true, that the voice of God, having once fully penetrated the heart, becomes strong as the tempest and loud as the thunder; but before reaching the heart, it is weak as a light breath which scarcely agitates the air. It shrinks from noise, and is silent amid agitation. "The Lord is not in the earthquake." (3 Kings xix. 11.) Retire into your heart with God, to meditate, to pray, to weep, to speak to the Lord and to listen to Him. You will not be alone when you are with Him. "How can he be alone who is always with God?" says St. Ambrose. If you are deprived of the

conversation of men, you will enjoy that of the saints, of the angels, of Jesus Christ.*

2. *Perfect docility of heart.* This comprises three things: fidelity to rules; application to the exercises; obedience to all the movements of grace. Be afraid of refusing any thing to God: however small the sacrifice may be, perhaps our conversion, our salvation, may depend on it. A single word of the Gospel converted St. Anthony; a word from a sermon converted St. Nicholas Tolentino; a fact of history, a reading, a conversation, began the conversion of St. Augustine, of St. Ignatius, of St. Francis Xavier. Can you tell to what sacrifice God may have attached the change of your heart? Enter, then, into the disposition of the prophet: "My heart, O Lord, is ready." (Ps. lvi. 8.) Do not fear to be too generous with God, and do not be afraid of the sacrifices He may ask of you; this sweet experience will force you to cry out with St. Augustine, "How sweet has it been to me to be deprived of the miserable delights of a frivolous world! and what incomparable joy have I felt after a privation once so dreaded!" Cast yourself, therefore, at the feet of Jesus Christ, and say to Him, "Lord, Thou hast given me a soul capable of knowing and loving Thee; I return it to Thee, not adorned with the grace and virtue that Thou bestowedst on it in baptism, but covered with the scars and wounds of sin;

---

* "I call to me whom I will: I possess the society of saints; a troop of angels accompany me : I enjoy converse with Jesus Christ Himself." (St. Jerome.)

cure it, O heavenly Physician, and restore to it its pristine life and beauty.

"Lord, I offer Thee my understanding; enlighten it with Thy brightest light. 'Enlighten my eyes, lest I sleep in death.' (Ps. xii. 4.)

"Lord, 1 offer Thee my memory; blot out from it the remembrance of the world, and leave in it only the memory of Thy mercies to bless them, and of my sins to weep for them.

"Lord, I offer Thee my heart; change it by Thy grace. 'Create a clean heart in me, O God, and renew a right spirit within me.' (Ps. l. 12.)

"Lord, I offer to Thee the senses of my body, the powers of my soul, my whole being; dispose of them for my salvation and for Thy greater glory. 'I have put my trust in Thee, O Lord; I have said Thou art my God; my lot is in Thy hand.'" (Ps. xxx. 15.)

Pater.   Ave.

EIGHT DAYS' RETREAT.

FIRST WEEK.

VIA PURGATIVA.
THE WAY OF PURIFICATION.

THE object of this Week's Meditations is, to purify our souls from the defilements of sin, by earnestly meditating on the eternal truths and bringing them home to our own souls. By applying this touchstone of divine truth to our own special case, we will be enabled, by the divine assistance, to see and feel our own manifold sins and deficiencies, and to reform our own conduct, which is the principal end of this Retreat. DEFORMATA REFORMARE — *to reform whatever is deformed* — this is the practical fruit of this Week's Exercises. If we should be so happy as to accomplish this, we will have made a good Retreat; if not, we will have lost our time. If we should confine ourselves to mere speculation and generalities, how much soever we may be moved for the moment, we will derive but little solid fruit from these Exercises. Let us impress this truth deeply on our minds and hearts.

God has, then, called me to this holy Retreat to give me an opportunity to *reform* my conduct by being *enlightened* in my relations and duties towards Him, and comparing these with my own conduct in the past as unfolded to me by a diligent self-examination. To accomplish this, I must look to myself alone, not to others; and I must propose to myself as my rule for making this Retreat, the following motto:

INGREDI TOTUS; MANERE SOLUS; EXIRE ALIUS — TO ENTER WHOLLY, TO REMAIN ALONE, TO COME OUT ANOTHER PERSON.

I must enter on this Retreat with my *whole* heart, with my *whole* soul, and with my *whole* attention; I must remain in it *alone* before God, as if there were no other person in the world but myself; I must come out of it *reformed* and *changed* in my life and conduct—a new man in Christ Jesus.

During this first Week I must seek to emerge from darkness into light, to rise from sin unto grace. I must propose to myself: first, to study diligently my last end, and to penetrate myself thoroughly with this great truth, that I was made for God, and that, therefore, I must live and labor for God alone; second, to persuade myself that sin alone is the real obstacle in the way of my attaining this last end, and that sin is therefore the only real evil, because it alone can deprive me of my only real good; and, third, by meditating on death, judgment, and hell, I must seek to strike a holy terror into my own guilty soul, and thus to arouse it from its iniquities and prepare it to be enlightened by Almighty God, my first beginning and my last end. *Surge! Illuminare!* — Arise! be enlightened, O my soul! "*Doce me, Domine, finem meum, ut sciam quid desit mihi!* — Teach me, O Lord, my Last End, that I may know what is wanting to me!"

FIRST DAY.

FIRST MEDITATION.

ON THE END OF MAN.

First prelude. Imagine yourself in the midst of this universe *alone*, before the Majesty of God; as Adam coming out of the hands of his Creator.

Second prelude. Adore His infinite Majesty, and beseech Him to enlighten you on the great END of your creation.

FIRST POINT.

Man is made to serve God.

The world had lasted nearly six thousand years before I had existence. Who placed me in this world? 'Tis God, who made me! 'Tis He who framed this body of mine, made of vile materials, it is true, but wonderful in its structure. 'Tis He, who created my immortal soul, made it to His own image and likeness, and united it to this mortal body. But for what end did He make me? Were there a greater Being than God, He would have made me for that Being: but no; Himself is the Supreme Being, the source of all being. It is therefore impossible that He should have made me for another. Therefore, I am His own property. His right in me is certain; it is inalienable. Therefore, if I have an understanding, it can be but to know Him. If I have a heart, it can be but to love Him. If I have a body, strength, health, etc., it can be but to serve Him. Therefore, to serve God is the END of my creation; it is my important, nay, my only business upon earth.

Make an act of faith on this fundamental truth. Give thanks to God for so noble a destination. Examine whether your past conduct has corresponded with the great END of your creation. Be confounded and grieve for having served the world and your passions instead of God. Conceive an ardent desire to lead, henceforth, a life conformable to that END. Offer yourself to God, to be His for the future.

SECOND POINT.

How far man is obliged to serve God.

I am from God. I am God's; therefore, I must serve God. This is evident. But I am from

8

God alone; therefore, I belong to Him alone; therefore, I must serve Him alone: no other has a right to my services; I can not divide my heart. Moreover, I am wholly from God; therefore, I am wholly His; therefore, I must employ my whole self in His service, both soul and body; thoughts, desires, words and actions — no exception, no reserve. Again; I am always from God. He not only created me, but He also preserves me at every instant of my existence; and that, by the same act and omnipotent operation of His will by which He first brought me into existence. "In Him we live, we move, and we are." But thus to preserve me, is in some measure creating me every instant. Therefore, I am always God's. Therefore, every moment of my life must be employed in His service. All the time employed in any thing else, is time lost. Finally, God created and He preserves me, out of pure love, being in no need of me. Therefore, I ought to serve Him out of pure love, even if I had nothing either to fear or to hope for from Him.

Compare your past life with these extensive obligations. See the deformity. Grieve for the past. Embrace those precious duties. Despise the world. Offer yourself to God, etc. Resolve, etc.

THIRD POINT.

What man may hope for from his fidelity in serving God.

He may hope, he may rest fully assured, that God will be his, in the proportion as he will be God's: God wholly his, if he will be wholly God's: God always his, if he will be always God's: God as perfectly his as if he possessed him alone, and gave no part of his affections to creatures. God Himself my reward! my happiness, the happiness of God Himself! To possess God! To enjoy God! What a recompense! And that, forever! Even in this life, God dwells in the hearts of His servants. He reigns there with all graces and consolations; His eyes are on them; His providence protects them, watches over them, heaps graces and favors on them. They are the objects of His tender love and complacency.

Thank Him for having prepared for you so immense a reward. Grieve for your past insensibility. Stir up in yourself a desire of being a child of God, a friend, a favorite of God. Resolve to neglect nothing for this END.

VERSES OF ASPIRATIONS.

1. "I am Alpha and Omega, the beginning and the end." (Apocalypse i.)

2. "Every one who invoketh my name, I have created for my glory; I have formed him and made him." (Isaias xliii. 7.)

3. "Behold O Lord! they who go far away from Thee shall perish. Thou hast destroyed all those who forsake Thee, to love creatures." (Ps. lxxii. 27.)

4. "Thou hast made us for Thyself, O Lord, and our hearts are restless until they rest in Thee!" (St. Augustine's Confessions.)

Read the "Following of Christ," book iii. chaps. 9 and 10.

CONSIDERATION.

THE PRINCIPLE OF THE EXERCISES.

The end of man.

Text of St Ignatius: *Man was created for this end: to praise, reverence, and serve the Lord his God, and by this means to arrive at eternal salvation.*

This meditation comprises three great truths which are the foundation of all the exercises;

I come from God; I belong to God; I am destined for God. That is to say, God is my first principle, my sovereign Master, my last end.

First Truth: *I come from God.*

CONSIDERATIONS.

1. Where was I a hundred years ago? I was nothing. If I look back a hundred years, I see the world with its empires, its cities, its inhabitants; I see the sun which shines to-day, the earth on which I dwell, the land which gave me birth, the family from which I sprung, the name by which I am known: but I—what was I, and where was I? I was nothing, and it is amidst nothingness I must be sought. Oh, how many ages passed during which no one thought of me! For how can nothing be the subject of thought? How many ages when even an insect or an atom was greater than I? for they possessed at least an existence.

2. But now I exist. I possess an intellect capable of knowing, a heart formed for loving, a body endowed with wonderful senses. And this existence, who gave it me? Chance?— Senseless word!—My parents? They answer in the words of the mother of the Machabees: "No, it was not I who gave you mind and soul; it was the Creator of the world." (2 Mach. vii. 22.) Lastly, was I the author of my own existence? But nothingness can not be the cause of existence. It is to God, then, that I must

turn as my first beginning. "Thy hands, O Lord, have made me and formed me." (Ps. cxviii. 73.) "Thou hast laid Thy hand upon me." (Ps. cxxxviii. 5.) Thou hast taken me from the abyss of nothing.

3. Consider, O my soul, the circumstances of thy creation.

(1.) God created me out of His pure love. Had He any need of my existence, or could I be necessary to His happiness? "I have loved thee with an everlasting love." (Jer. xxxi. 3.)

(2.) God created me, and the decree of my creation is eternal like Himself. From eternity, then, God thought of me. I was yet in the abyss of nothingness, and God gave me a place in His thoughts! I was in His mind, and in His heart. "I have loved you with an everlasting love."

(3.) God created me, and in creating me preferred me to an infinite number of creatures who were equally possible to Him, and who will for ever remain in nothingness. O God, how have I deserved this preference! "I have loved you with an everlasting love."

(4.) God created me, and by creation made me the most noble of the creatures of the visible world. My soul is in His image, and all my being bears the stamp, the living stamp of His attributes.

(5.) Lastly, God created me and He has continued His creation during every moment of my existence. As many as are the hours and moments of my life, so often does He make me a fresh present of life.

AFFECTIONS.

Sentiments of *humility* at the sight of our nothingness. "My substance is as nothing before Thee." (Ps. xxxviii. 6.)

Sentiments of *admiration.* "What is man, that Thou shouldst magnify him? or why dost Thou set Thy heart upon him?" (Job vii. 17.)

Sentiments of *gratitude.* "Bless the Lord, O my soul, and let all that is within me bless His holy name. Bless the Lord, O my soul, and forget not all He hath done for thee." (Ps. cii. 1, 2.)

SECOND TRUTH: I belong to God.

CONSIDERATIONS.

1. I come from God; hence I belong to God. God is my creator; hence, He is my Lord and my Master. To deny this consequence would be to deny my reason.

2. The Lord enters into judgment with me, and deigns to argue His rights at the bar of His creature. Is it not true that the master has a right to the services of his servants or his slaves? Is it not true that the king has a right to the obedience of his subjects? the father, to the submission as well as respect of his children? Is it not true that the workman has a right to dispose of his work as he chooses? And I, the

creature of God, do I not belong more to God than the slave to his master, than the subject to his sovereign, the child to his father, the picture to him who painted it, or the tree to him who planted it? Does not God possess over me all the rights of men over the creatures, and in a higher degree, and by more sacred titles? What is there in me that does not belong to Him, and is not the fruit, so to say, of His own capital, and therefore His property? "What have you that you have not received?" (1 Cor. iv. 7.) What would remain to me if God took back all that He has given me? If God took back my mind what should I be?—On a level with the brute animals. If He deprived me of life and motion, what should I be?—A little dust and ashes. If He took away my substance and my whole being, what should I be?—A simple nothing. O my God! all I have comes from Thee; it is just that all in me should belong to Thee. "O Lord, just art Thou, and glorious in Thy power, and no one can overcome Thee. Let all creatures serve Thee: for Thou hast spoken, and they were made; Thou didst send forth Thy spirit, and they were created." (Jud. xvi. 16, 17.)

3. Consider, O my soul, the characteristics of the dominion of God.

(1.) *Essential dominion.* It was not necessary that God should draw me from nothing. But since God has created me, it is necessary that I should be His. He would cease to be God if, being my creator, He ceased to be my sovereign and my master.

(2.) *Supreme dominion.* I belong to God before every thing, and above every thing. Properly speaking, I belong to God alone, and men have no other rights over me except such as God has given them. Their rights, then, are subordinate to the rights of God; and their authority must be always subjected to the authority of God.

(3.) *Absolute dominion.* God can dispose of me according to His pleasure: He can give or take from me fortune, health, honor, life; my duty is to receive every thing from His hand with submission and without complaint.

(4.) *Universal dominion.* Every thing in me is from God; therefore all in me belongs to God. The dominion of the Lord extends to all the stages of my life, to all the situations in which I may be placed, to all the faculties of my soul, all the senses of my body, to every hour and moment of my existence.

(5.) *Eternal dominion.* The dominion of God is immortal, like myself; it begins with time, and continues through eternity; death, which deprives men of all their rights, is unable to do any thing against the rights of God.

(6.) *Irresistible dominion.* We may escape the dominion of men; but how escape the dominion of God? Willing or unwilling, we must either live under the empire of His love, or under that of His justice; either glorify His power by free obedience, or glorify it by inevitable punishment.

"O man who art thou that repliest against

9

God? Shall the thing formed say to him who formed it, why hast thou made me thus?" (Rom. ix. 20.)

AFFECTIONS.

1. *Adoration.* "Thou art worthy, O Lord our God, to receive glory and honor and power; for Thou hast created all things." (Apoc. iv. 11.) "Come, let us adore and fall down before the Lord that made us; for He is the Lord our God." (Ps. xciv. 6, 7.)

2. *Regret.* "Is this the return thou makest to the Lord, O foolish and senseless people? Is not He thy father, that hath possessed thee, and made thee, and created thee? Thou hast forsaken the God that made thee, and hast forgotten the Lord that created thee." (Deut. xxxii. 6, 18.)

3. *Submission.* "O Lord, I am Thy servant; I am Thy servant, and the son of Thy handmaid." (Ps. cxv. 16.)

THIRD TRUTH: *I am destined for God.*

CONSIDERATIONS.

1. God is not only my creator and my master, He is also my last end. A God infinitely wise must have proposed to Himself an end in creating me; a God infinitely perfect could only have created me for His glory; that is to say, to know Him, to love Him, and to serve Him.

2. O my soul! dost thou wish for a proof of this great truth?

(1.) *Ask thy faith;* it will tell thee that God made all for Himself: "The Lord hath made all things for Himself;" (Prov. xvi. 4.) That He is the beginning and end of all things: "I am the beginning and the end;" (Apoc. i. 8.) That the greatest of the commandments is to adore, to love, and to serve God: "Thou shalt love the Lord thy God;" "Thou shalt adore the Lord thy God, and Him only shalt thou serve." (Matt. xxii. 37; iv. 10.)

(2.) *Ask thy reason;* it will tell thee that there must be some proportion between the faculties of man and their object. Hence there is nothing but the infinite perfections of God which can be the objects of a mind and heart craving with an intense desire to know and to love.

(3.) *Ask the creatures;* they will tell thee, by their imperfection, their inconstancy, their weakness, in a word, by their nothingness, that they are far too insignificant to be the end of thy being. "Vanity of vanities, and all is vanity, except to love God and to serve Him alone." (Imit. of Christ, i. 1.)

(4.) *Ask thy heart;* it will tell thee that thou art formed for happiness, and that thou requirest happiness without alloy, happiness without limits, an eternal happiness; that is, that thou requirest nothing less than God Himself.

(5.) *Ask thy own experience;* it will tell thee why it is that, when thou hast been faithful in serving God, peace has dwelt within thy breast; why it is that, when thou hast separated thyself from Him, thou hast felt nothing but disgust, emptiness, and remorse. Peace of heart is the fruit of order faithfully kept, faithfully observed. "We were made, O Lord, for Thee, and our heart is restless until it finds peace in Thee." (St. Aug.)

3. Thus my end is to know God, to love God, to serve God; this, therefore, is all my duty, all my greatness, all my happiness.

(1.) *All my duty:* Yes, I must know, love, and serve God. I must understand well this word, O my soul. I must be convinced that it is a real *necessity.* It is not necessary that I should possess talents, fortune, pleasures, an honorable position in society; it is not necessary that I should have a long life; it is not necessary that I should exist; but, supposing that I do exist, it is necessary that I should serve God. An intelligent creature that does not serve God is, in the world, what the sun would be if it ceased to shine, what our body would be if it ceased to move. It would be in the order of intelligence what a monster would be in the order of the bodily frame.

(2.) *All my greatness.* I am not made for a mortal man; I am not made for myself; I am not made for an angel. An intelligent and immortal being, I am too great for a creature, however noble, to be my end. My end is that of the angel; is that of Jesus Christ; is that of God Himself. God does not exist, could not exist, except to know Himself and to love Himself; and I only exist, or could exist, to know and to love God.

(3.) *All my happiness.* I can not serve God in time without possessing Him in eternity. I can not give myself wholly to God without His giving Himself wholly to me. "I am thy exceeding great reward." (Gen. xv. 1.) His glory and my happiness are inseparable. It is, then, a question of my eternal destiny, and I myself am the arbiter of it. O my soul! picture to thyself on one side Heaven, with its ineffable delight; on the other, Hell, with its fires and its despair; one or other will be thy eternal heritage, according as thou shalt have served or offended the Lord on earth. It is for thee to choose. "I call Heaven and earth to witness this day that I have set before you life and death, blessing and cursing. Choose, therefore, life, ... that thou mayest love the Lord thy God, and obey His voice, and adhere to Him, for He is thy life." (Deut. xxx. 19, 20.)

AFFECTIONS.

1. *Sorrow for the past.* "O God, Thou knowest my foolishness, and my offenses are not hidden from Thee." (Ps. lxviii. 6.)

2. *Contempt for creatures.* "All those that go far from Thee shall perish: Thou hast destroyed all those that were disloyal to Thee. But it is good for me to adhere to my God." (Ps. lxxii. 27, 28.)

3. *Love of God.* "What have I in Heaven? and beside Thee what do I desire upon earth? Thou art the God of my heart, and my portion for ever." (Ps. lxxii. 25, 26.)

SECOND MEDITATION.

ON THE END OF CREATURES.

First prelude. Imagine yourself *alone*, in the midst of the whole Creation, before the Majesty of God.

Second prelude. Adore that Infinite Majesty, and beseech Him to enlighten you on the use you are to make of creatures, to attain your last END.

FIRST POINT.

"All the things that are upon earth have been given to Man as a means to attain his last END."—ST. IGNATIUS OF LOYOLA.

By the things which are upon earth, are here understood not only heaven and earth and all that is therein, but also many accidental appendages thereof, which without being precisely the creatures of God, yet are intended by Him to be the companions of man's existence on earth; as health and sickness; riches and poverty;

pleasures and suffering; honor and contempt,
etc. From whatever side these things come, it
is the intention of God, that man should make
them serve for the glory of his Creator and for
his own sanctification. Creatures lose, as it
were, their being in our regard, when we view
them in another light; or, to speak more properly, they subsist still, but for our damnation;
because, then, we make creatures our last end,
and substitute them for God; which is a kind of
idolatry. Creatures thus perverted from their
proper destination, groan, says St. Paul, under a
kind of bondage and violent state: "Every
creature groans and is in labor until now." But
the day will come, when it shall be delivered
from bondage, and then, by the order of the
Creator, creatures will avenge on guilty man
the criminal abuse he has made of them. "He
shall arm," says the wise man, "the creation for
the vengeance of His enemies."

Let us deplore our past blindness and the
strange disorder in which we have hitherto
lived. Let us invite all creatures to bless His
name; or rather, let us bless Him and give Him
thanks, for having given them to us. Let us
resolve to make use of them according to the
design of the Creator.

SECOND POINT.

What rules we have to observe in the use of creatures.

All creatures, with regard to us, may be divided into two classes. There are some, the use of which is necessary. There are others, which we are left at liberty to use, or not to use, at least, to desire or not to desire. The former are of two kinds. The first are those which are necessary for the support of our life, health, and strength, such as food, clothing, lodging, rest, and some diversion. The rule to be followed in the use of these creatures, is to take of them what is necessary and sufficient; to give God thanks for them, and to make to His Divine Majesty a generous sacrifice of whatever is superfluous. How many disorders would be cut off by a diligent observance of this rule! The other kind of necessary objects, consists of such as we can not help seeing, hearing, feeling, etc.: as heaven and earth and the various objects they contain, as also other men with whom we live. The rule we are to follow in the use of these, is to make them all serve, as the Saints did, to raise our thoughts and affections to God.

As to those things, the use, or at least the desire, of which is left to our free choice, such as this or that state of life, this or that employment; riches or poverty, etc.; the rule is, that we should remain, with regard to all these things, in a state of perfect indifference; we should carefully consider the relation they bear to the service of God, who is at the same time their last END and ours. We should invariably embrace that which leads us to that END, and reject, with horror, whatever removes us from its attainment.

Examine whether you have followed these rules; see what has hitherto prevented you from serving God as you ought. Grieve for the faults you have committed in the use of creatures. Embrace these rules, and resolve to conform your life to them in the future.

THIRD POINT.

How necessary and advantageous these rules are.

First, Necessary: For unless we comply with them, we can never fulfill the promise we have made to God in the preceding meditation, to be His, to serve Him alone, to be wholly His, and always His, as justice and gratitude require: the greatest obstacle, and for many the only obstacle to this duty, being their disorderly affection to some created object. Whatever we can do for God, without observing these rules, will be reduced to an esteem and preference, of mere speculation. We shall love and serve God with our tongues, not with our hearts. "Ah! my little children," says St. John, "let us not love in words, or in tongue, but indeed and in truth!"

Second, Advantageous: In them we find the safety of our innocence; sin being nothing else besides an attachment to creatures, against the design of the Creator. We are thereby elevated above earthly things and all the vicissitudes of human life; we enjoy tranquillity of mind; all things turn to our profit. "To those who love God," says St. Paul, "all things work together unto good." These rules are an abridgment of Christian wisdom. By them man is restored, in some measure, to the liberty and independence of his former origin. He acquires a sort of empire over all created things.

Attach yourself, therefore, to these rules. Resolve to embrace with more zeal such of them as you have hitherto transgressed. Beg of God to disengage and separate your heart from all that is not Himself, and to give you the grace never to depart from these holy rules.

1. "Great are the works of the Lord; exquisitely fitted to all His purposes." (Psalms.)

2. "Grant, oh Lord! that we may so pass through temporal goods, that we may not lose those which are eternal; and that amidst the variety of worldly objects, our hearts may be there fixed, where eternal joys are found." (Prayer of the Church.)

Read "Following of Christ," Book III., chaps. 31 and 34.

THIRD MEDITATION.

On the difference between attaching ourselves to God, and attaching ourselves to creatures.

First prelude. Imagine yourself placed between God and creatures, each calling for your affection, and, as if you were deliberating to which side you should turn yourself.

Second prelude. Beg of God not to permit you to be so blind, as to give the preference to creatures over the Creator.

FIRST POINT.

First difference.

It is a great honor to attach one's self to God; it is a great disgrace to attach one's self to creatures.

Our heart transforms itself into the object of our love. In attaching itself to God, it becomes in some measure divine; it becomes earthly if we love the earth. And what have we to do with the world? We who are so much greater than the world. Creatures are made for our use, and we only for God. The world shall pass away, but we shall not pass away. Can I forget the nobility of my first origin? I am the offspring of God. God is my Father, I am His child and the heir of His kingdom; destined to see Him face to face, and enjoy Him for eternity: therefore, to attach myself to what is not God is debasing, degrading myself.—What! Men esteem it a great honor to serve kings, and behold, God will have me to be His servant! What do I say? To be His child, His friend, His favorite! And should I receive His offer with indifference, with insensibility? "He will long be little and lie groveling to the earth," says the pious A'Kempis, ' who shall esteem any thing great, except the Sovereign, Immense, Eternal Good; and whatsoever is not God, is nothing, and ought to be counted as nothing."

Let us leisurely consider and relish these two great words: God is ALL; Creatures are nothing.

SECOND POINT.

Second difference.

In attaching ourselves to God, we become happy; in attaching ourselves to creatures, we become miserable.

This we have already many times experienced. All our troubles arise from our attachment to creatures. Before we possess them, we are tormented by unceasing desires. When we have obtained them, we are not contented, because our hearts remain empty. A little that is wanting seems to poison all that is already possessed. The fleeting nature of these objects, the fear of losing them, the grief of having lost them, the necessity of being separated from them by death, all contribute to embitter the possession of them; and the greater our attachment is, the greater also becomes our torment.

The words of St. Augustine are an oracle for all such as are not entirely blinded by passion.

10

"Thou hast made us for Thyself, O Lord, and our hearts are restless until they rest in Thee!" Yes, our hearts will be a prey to trouble, uneasiness, agitation, and remorse, until forsaking all affection to created things, they seek their rest in God alone. God has so ordained it, and His orders are executed. Every disorderly affection becomes its own first punishment. But if I once fix my affections on God alone, if I sincerely attach myself to Him, I begin to enjoy rest and contentment; because, then, my heart rests in its center, and has found an object capable of filling the vast capacity of its desires. And this advantage I can enjoy this moment, if I please. I can, this moment, become the friend of God, and begin to enjoy the possession of my sovereign Good. To be the friend of God! To have God Himself for my Friend! What happiness! He is a Friend whom no one can take from me. He is not inconstant and will not forsake me, if I do not forsake Him first.

THIRD POINT. .

Third difference.

In attaching ourselves to creatures, we become criminal. In attaching ourselves to God, we preserve our innocence; we sanctify and perfect ourselves.

Let us recall to mind so many sins, perhaps so many crimes, we have been guilty of; the imminent danger of damnation to which we have been exposed; so many sinful habits which we have contracted, and which have been a fruitful source of disorderly actions; whence did all this proceed, but from our irregular and multiplied attachments to created objects? We would still enjoy our first innocence, if we had carefully preserved our hearts from such attachments. In vain do we hope to divide ourselves between God and His creatures, and to satisfy both at the same time. No; he who seeks to please creatures, shall never please God. Ah! how innocent is the heart, that seeks to please God alone! How innocent, how holy! In pleasing God, he may even content creatures; because God commands us to render to creatures, whatever is truly due to them. As the servant of God advances in sanctity, he becomes more just, more zealous, more meek, more condescending, more disinterested, more exact in the observance of every duty. All, then, is vanity, besides knowing, loving, and serving God. I say too little: All is baseness, trouble, and affliction of spirit; all is a snare, all is danger, all is a frightful precipice; besides attaching and devoting ourselves to God alone.

After forming your good resolutions, finish by reciting slowly the Lord's Prayer, and applying every petition of it to your subject, in a fervent colloquy.

VERSES OF ASPIRATIONS.

1. "What is there for me in Heaven? And besides Thee what do I desire upon earth? Oh thou God of my heart! Oh God! my portion forever." (Psalm lxxii. 25, 26.)

2. "It is good for me to adhere to my God; and to put my hopes in the Lord, my God." (Psalm xvi. 28.)

> Go, world, with all thy pompous train,
> I care nothing for thee :
> Thy joys, wealth, glory I disdain ;
> My God is ALL to me !

Read "Following of Christ." Book III. chaps. 16—21.

SECOND DAY

FIRST MEDITATION.

ON THE ENORMITY OF MORTAL SIN FROM THE PUNISHMENT THEREOF.

First prelude. Imagine yourself to be in the place, where you consider the punishment of sin, and behold the awful scene.

Second prelude. Beg of God to enlighten you, that you may know the greatness of the guilt, by the greatness of the chastisement.

FIRST POINT.

Sin in Heaven.

Let us recall to mind what faith teaches us on the fall of the angels. God had created beautiful spirits, and endowed them with most precious graces and gifts. They suffered themselves to be puffed up with pride, and refused to their Creator the tribute of adoration they owed Him. In an instant, they were hurled down into a place of torments, where they burn, and where they shall burn eternally, in an inextinguishable fire. Terrible judgment! Let us draw consequences from it. First. Therefore, damnation may be incurred in the most holy places, in the most sublime state. No secure situation in this life.

Second. Therefore, neither past innocence, nor the gifts of nature or grace can make us secure.

Third. Therefore, one single sin, a first sin, the sin of a moment, is sufficient to associate us with devils.

Fourth. Therefore, the goodness of God and His mercy do not always put a stop to the strokes of His justice.

But let us turn our eyes on ourselves. The angels had committed but one sin; and I have committed so many. It was a sin only of thought, or at most of desire, and my conscience reproaches me with so many sinful actions. They never were forgiven, and I have so many times obtained pardon of my sins. Give thanks to God for His patience and mercy towards you. Fear the rigor of His justice. Detest sin, the object of the horror and vengeance of your God. Grieve for those you have committed. Resolve to cleanse your soul from them, and carefully avoid them for the future.

SECOND POINT.

Sin in the earthly Paradise.

Eve, seduced by the devil, under the form of a serpent, eats of the forbidden fruit. Adam, by her persuasion, eats also of it. By this transgression, they both lose the grace and friendship of their Creator; they forfeit the privilege of immortality; they are driven out of the earthly Paradise. God is not yet satisfied. Their unfortunate posterity shall be infected with the contagion, and disgraced with the stain of that sin; millions shall be deprived, on that sole account, of the happiness of Heaven; even those, who will be cleansed from that stain shall groan under a flood of miseries. Adam himself, after being forgiven, shall be condemned to nine hundred years of a most rigorous penance; viz. to eat his bread in the sweat of his brow, to see murder in his own family, and to hear himself reproached until his death by his children, with his being the first author of their disorders and of their misfortunes. Now, compare your own sins with that of Adam. His was only one sin, and yours are multiplied over the hairs of your head. His was punished even in those who are not personally guilty of it: what, then, do mine

deserve, which are personally my own?   In fine,
if God sometimes punishes without mercy, as
He did the angels, He never forgives without
requiring a rigorous satisfaction.

THIRD POINT.

Sin in Hell.

Behold in spirit that multitude of reprobate
souls, now condemned to the flames of Hell, suffering there inexpressible, unrelenting, and everlasting tortures.   Ah! if Hell were now opened
to your view, how many souls would you find
there, who were cast into these fiery dungeons
for one single mortal sin?   How many of the
same profession, of the same age, of the same
natural dispositions, as yourself?   How many
for abusing the same graces, for committing the
same sins, as you do?   How many for sins much
less than yours?   You should have been with
them long ago, had God treated you in the rigor
of His justice.   They are the creatures of God,
and in that quality are dear to Him.   He is
goodness and mercy itself; He never punishes
but when provoked to it, and, as it were, with
regret.   What a monster, then, mortal sin must
be in His sight!   Conceive a new horror of it.

Efface yours by a timely repentance. Renounce them forever.

FOURTH POINT.

Sin on Mount Calvary.

Place yourself at the foot of the Cross, and behold the Son of God expiring on an ignominious gibbet; bleeding and dying in the most excruciating torments, for the expiation of sin. Sin is, then, so horrid an evil, so enormous an offense of God, that His justice would be satisfor its expiation with nothing less than the death and blood of His own beloved Son! Hence, conclude that sin must be an infinite evil, since a life of infinite value, and a blood infinitely precious, are actually required to atone for it. Oh, how eloquently do the blood, the sufferings, the gaping wounds of my Jesus, speak to me of the enormity of my crimes! Oh, what a monster must I appear in my own eyes, when I consider that, by my repeated treasons and ingratitudes I have crucified my Jesus, covered Him with wounds, spilt His sacred blood to the last drop, and been the murderer of my God! How hard my heart must be - if this sight does not move me to repentance! If, beholding my Saviour covered with wounds and blood, and dying for my sins,

I can not be prevailed on, at least to minglo
the tears of my sorrow with the streams of
precious blood, that flow from every part of
His sacred body.

Recite "Our Father," "Soul of Christ," etc.

VERSES OF ASPIRATIONS.

1. "Fly from sin, as from the face of a serpent." (Eccles. xxi. 2.)

2. "I have hated and abhorred iniquity."
(Ps. cxviii. 163.)

3. "He has been wounded for our iniquities;
He has been bruised for our sins; we have all
strayed as sheep, the Lord has put on Him the
iniquities of us all." (Isaias, liii.)

4. "He has carried our sins in His body, on
the wood." (St. Peter.)

Read "Following of Christ," book i. c. 21; book iii. 4.

CONSIDERATION.

The effects of mortal sin on the soul of the sinner.

Preparatory Prayer.

First prelude. Present yourself before God
like a criminal loaded with chains, brought from

the dungeon of a prison and placed before the tribunal of his judge.

Second prelude. Beg of our Lord that He will vouchsafe to show you the sad state of a soul which has been so unhappy as mortally to offend God: "Give me, O Lord, that I may see." (Luke xviii. 41.)

FIRST CONSIDERATION.

By mortal sin we forfeit the friendship of God.

When you were in a state of grace, God dwelt in your soul: "If any man love Me, My Father will love him, and We will come to him, and will make Our abode with him." (John xiv. 23.) The most august bonds united you to Him. He called you His people: "Thou art My people." (Osee ii. 24.) His friend: "I have called you friends." (John xv. 15.) His spouse: "Thou hast wounded my heart, my sister, my spouse." (Cant. iv. 9.) His children: "Behold what manner of charity the Father hath bestowed upon us, that we should be called, and should be, the sons of God." (1 John iii. 1.) Another self: "I have said ye are gods." (Psalm lxxxi. 6.) But what a change since mortal sin entered into your soul! That moment God left your heart: "Woe to them, when I shall depart from them." (Osee ix. 12.) To his friendship has succeeded hatred: "Thou hatest all the works of iniquity." (Psalm v. 7.) You have ceased to be His people: "Ye are not My people, and I will not be yours." (Osee i. 9.) In His eyes you are now an enemy

on whom He has sworn vengeance: "I live for
ever; I will render vengeance to my enemies."
(Deut. xxxii. 40, 41.) He no longer recognizes
you as His spouse: "I know you not." (Matt.
xxv. 12.) In you He no longer sees any thing
but the child of Satan: "Ye are of your father,
the devil." (John viii. 44.) He has no longer
any thing for you but maledictions: "If thou
wilt not hear the voice of the Lord thy God,
cursed shalt thou be in the city, cursed in the
field, cursed shall be the fruit of thy womb.
And all these curses shall come upon thee, and
shall pursue and overtake thee, until thou perish." (Deut. xxviii. 15–17, 45.) He arms every
scourge against you: "Death and bloodshed,
strife and the sword, oppressions, famine, afflictions, scourges: all these things are created for
the wicked." (Eccles. xl. 9, 10.) O guilty soul,
consider what thou hast been, and what thou
now art in the eyes of thy Lord; and sigh
deeply at the sight of thy misery. "Thou wast
the spouse of Christ, the temple of God, the
sanctuary of the Holy Ghost; and as often as I
say 'thou wast,' I must needs groan, because
thou art not what thou wast." (St. Augustine.)

SECOND CONSIDERATION.

Mortal sin deprives us of all the gifts of grace.

1. *It destroys the beauty of the soul.* A soul
in a state of grace attracts the looks and ravishes the heart of God: "I will fix my eyes
upon thee." (Psalm xxxi. 8.) "Behold, thou art

fair, O my love." (Cant. i. 14.)   But mortal sin destroys all traces of this beauty: "All her beauty is departed," (Lament. i. 6;) and covers the soul with a hideous leprosy, which makes it an object of horror to God and His angels.

2. *It deprives the soul of all merit.*   Even if you united in yourself all the merits of all the saints together, all their alms, all their prayers, all their austerities, all their sacrifices — a single mortal sin would be enough to destroy all: "If the just man turn himself away from his justice, and do iniquity, all his justices which he hath done shall not be remembered." (Ezech. xviii. 24.)

3. *It deprives the soul of all power of meriting.*   Yes; if you are in mortal sin, all your good works are useless to obtain Heaven. Spend all your goods in alms; embrace the most rigorous austerities; convert the whole world, if it be possible; give your body to the flames — St. Paul assures you that all this is useless for salvation if there be a single sin in your heart: "If I have not charity I am nothing." (Cor. xiii. 2.)   To what can I compare you, O unhappy soul?   "To what shall I compare thee, or to what shall I liken thee, O daughter of Jerusalem?" (Lam. ii. 13.)   To a vine loaded with fruit suddenly destroyed by the storm; to a temple unexpectedly overthrown; to a ship that the tempest suddenly sinks with all her treasures; to a rich city which fire has reduced to a heap of burning ashes: "To what shall I equal thee, that I may comfort thee?.... Who shall heal thee?" (Lam. ii. 13.)

11

THIRD CONSIDERATION.

Mortal sin deprives us of our liberty.

When you are in a state of grace, you are
free: "Where the Spirit of the Lord is, there is
liberty." (2 Cor. iii. 17.) You enjoy the sweetest, the most honorable liberty; the only liberty
that no power in the world can deprive you of,
liberty conquered for you by the blood of Jesus
Christ: "The freedom wherewith Christ has
made us free," (Gal. iv. 31;) which consists in
freedom from every yoke except that of God,
which we can not lose without degrading ourselves. But have you had the unhappiness to
sin mortally? You have become a slave: "Whosoever committeth sin is the servant of sin."
(John viii. 34.) You are given over to sin:
"Sold under sin." (Rom. vii. 14.) The devil
reigns as master in your heart, which is your
prison: "He hath built against me round about,
that I may not get out." (Lam. iii. 7.) Each
day he tightens his chains about us: "He hath
made my fetters heavy." (Lam. iii. 7.) Every
thing within you is enslaved: your faculties,
your senses, your talents, your fortune. Is it
not true that, in this sad state, you have often
wished to return to God, to pray, to confess, to
avoid the occasions of sin, to break through the
habit of sin? Did the devil permit it? Has he
not treated you as the centurion in the Gospel
treated his soldiers: "I say to one, Go, and he
goeth; and to another, Come, and he cometh;

and to my servant, Do this, and he doeth it."
(Luke vii. 8.) Has he not always said to you,
" Bring, bring," (Prov. xxx. 15:) — again this
passion; again this sin. Has he not always
been obeyed? Finally, is it not the story of
your slavery that St. Augustine tells with so
much force when he describes the servitude of
his own passions: " I sighed, chained as I was,
not by iron, but by my own will, stronger even
than iron. My own will held me bound; and
it was of it that the enemy of salvation made
use to enchain me, and surround me on all sides
by inextricable bonds." (Conf., book viii. c. 5.)

FOURTH CONSIDERATION.

Mortal sin robs us of peace of heart.

A soul which belongs to God knows no trouble or fear: "The just is bold as a lion." (Prov.
xxviii. 1.) The heart of the just is like an eternal festival: "A secure mind is like a continual
feast." (Prov. xv. 15.) Even in the midst of
tribulations he tastes ineffable joys: "I exceedingly abound with joy in all my tribulations."
(2 Cor. vii. 4.) But how different is it with the
sinner; every where he carries a trembling
heart, a heart a prey to sorrow: "If, you will not
hear the voice of the Lord, He will give thee a
fearful heart, and a soul consumed with pensive-
ness." (Deut. xxviii. 15, 65.) Tribulation and
anguish penetrate the depths of his soul: "Tribulation and anguish upon every soul of man

that worketh evil." (Rom. ii. 9.) Remorse is in the conscience like an arrow which lacerates it: "I am turned in my anguish whilst the thorn is fastened." (Psalm xxxi. 4.) And his life is like the waves of the sea tossed by a storm: "The wicked are like the raging sea." (Isa. lvii. 20.) God has no need to arm the hand of man against the sinner; his conscience pursues him incessantly, and is at once witness, judge, and executioner; it accuses, condemns, and tortures him. Sometimes it pursues him in the midst of serious occupations, like David — "I walked sorrowful all the day long, there is no peace for my bones because of my sins," (Psalm xxxvii. 4, 7;) sometimes amidst pleasures, like Baltassar; sometimes amidst the pain of sickness, like Antiochus; almost always in silence and solitude, like Cain. To some it reproaches the pleasure of a moment purchased by a long repentance: "What fruit, therefore, had you then in those things of which you are now ashamed?" (Rom. vi. 21.) To others it shows all the bitterness of iniquity: "Know thou, and see that it is an evil and a bitter thing for thee to have left the Lord thy God." (Jer. ii. 19.) To some it recalls incessantly the ingratitude and malice of their sin: "Thy own wickedness shall reprove thee, and thy apostasy shall rebuke thee." (Jer. ii. 19.) To others it shows the sword of God's justice suspended over their heads: "Looking round about for the sword on every side." (Job xv. 22.) It causes cries of vengeance to be heard around them: "The sound of dread is always in his

ears." (Job xv. 21.)   It disturbs their sleep
with threatening visions: "Thou wilt frighten
me with dreams, and terrify me with visions."
(Job vii. 14.)   "O sinner, what misery is yours!
How much are you to be pitied if your conscience thus pursues you!   Yet you are still
more so if your conscience leave you in peace."
(St. Aug.)   For this peace of a guilty conscience
is the certain sign of the great wrath of God.

FIFTH CONSIDERATION.

Mortal sin destroys the soul.

The soul is the life of the body, and God is
the life of the soul.   Thus sin kills our soul in
separating it from God: "The soul that sinneth,
the same shall die." (Ezech. xviii. 20.)   Look
at the man who has mortally offended the Lord;
he walks, he sees, he speaks, and you think he
lives.   Ah! what lives in him is the body, the
soul has ceased to live.   "The most noble part
is extinct; the house stands, but the inhabitant
is dead.   O Christian, there is no longer any
feeling of piety in your heart; if you weep over
the body from which the soul has departed, and
yet shed no tear over the soul from which God
hás departed." (St. Aug.)

And what difference is there between a corpse
and a soul in mortal sin?   A corpse has lost the
use of all its senses.   Is not this a faithful image
of the sinner?

1. *A dead man no longer sees.*   Every thing
ought to strike the eyes of the sinner;—the

state of his soul, the grave ready to open for him — judgment, hell, eternity; and the sinner sees nothing!

2. *The dead no longer hears.* Every thing speaks to the sinner; —conscience, grace, events, ministers of religion; and the sinner hears nothing!

3. *The dead are insensible.* Neither insults nor honors, neither the attentions of men nor their contempt, can touch them. God moves Heaven and earth to touch the sinner; He endeavors to rouse him, sometimes by benefits, sometimes by afflictions; and the sinner remains insensible!

4. *The dead exhale an infectious odor.* A corpse if not placed in the grave, spreads around it a fatal contagion. The sinner exhales an odor of corruption; the contagion of his scandals spreads death around him, and the infection of his vices makes him an object of horror to just men, to angels, and to God.

O fatal death! O death which deprives us, not of the life of nature, but of the life of grace; that is to say, of the life of God! Who will give us tears to bewail thee? "Who will give water to my head, and a fountain of tears to my eyes? and I will weep day and night for the slain of the daughter of my people." (Jer. ix. 1.)

AFFECTIONS AT THE FOOT OF THE CROSS.

"Bless the Lord, O my soul, and forget not all that He hath done for thee; . . . . . who healeth

all thy diseases; who redeemeth thee from destruction." (Psalm cii. 2, 4.)

Pater.   Ave.

SECOND MEDITATION.

ON OUR OWN SINS.

First prelude.   Represent to yosurelf your
own soul, under the figure of a criminal, bound
hands and feet, lying in a dark dungeon, covered
with filth and ulcers.

Second prelude.   Earnestly beseech the
divine Goodness, for some rays of light to know
the number and enormity of your sins.

FIRST POINT.

How enormous our sins are, both by their number and grievousness.

1. Recall to your mind, that unhappy time,
when, being in the forgetfulness of God, you
abandoned yourself to your disorderly passions.
How numerous and how enormous your sins
were! Alas! You sinned perhaps as soon as
the use of reason rendered you capable of sin-
ning. Almost every day brought out new irregularities. You sinned by all the powers of your

soul, and all the senses and members of your body. See if you can find many of the commandments of God, or of the Church, which you have not violated; any of the Seven Deadly Sins, which you have not been guilty of, etc. And were not many of your sins very enormous, either by their nature or their circumstances; because of the scandal which arose from them, or the sanctity of your state, or the particular favors which you have received from the divine Goodness?

2. Ever since your conversion to God, could you truly say that you have not been a great sinner? Judge yourself impartially. Have you been free from all mortal sins? Have you not reason to fear that you have been guilty of many? Consider how little respect and love you have had for God, how ungrateful you have been for His benefits, how slothful and ignorant in His service; how full of human respect; how little charity you have had for your neighbor; how much you have been attached to your own will, and to your own judgment; how much you still love your flesh, your honor, your interest; always proud, ambitions, passionate, vain, envious, a lover of your ease, inconstant, sensual, etc. Let us not look at each of these sins in particular; they would perhaps

appear to us of little consequence. Let us look at their multitude, at their continuance, at that long series of infidelities, of ingratitudes, of abuse of graces. Let us admire the goodness of God, who has borne with us so long. Let us give Him thanks for it. Let us confound ourselves and grieve at the sight of iniquities so multiplied and so enormous.

SECOND POINT.

How much we ought to fear at the sight of the multitude and enormity of our sins.

God might have punished us, after the first mortal sin we committed, as He did the rebellious Angels. He has not done it; we are still living, and it is perhaps, what makes us so unconcerned. However, it is certain from the Sacred Scriptures, that there is a certain measure of sins, which being filled up, the mercy of God gives place to His avenging justice. Our measure is perhaps, well nigh full; perhaps the very first sin which we shall hereafter commit, may draw down upon us the stroke of God's avenging hand. Moreover, there are sins that cry to Heaven for vengeance, either by their nature, heinousness, and malice, by the great evils they produce, or by the character of the sinner, who profanes either the sanctity of his state, or the dignity of his functions. Do we not find some sin of this kind among those which we have committed.

Let us conceive a salutary fear. Let us resolve to renounce even the smallest offenses.

THIRD POINT.

What penance so many and so grievous offenses require.

God is willing to forgive when we repent, but His justice does not give up all its rights. The penitent must punish himself, if he wishes not to fall into the hands of the Living God. What, then, ought to be our penance, after so many and so grievous offenses? The Church formerly prescribed several years of penance for one single sin. Sin does not now deserve less punishment than it did then. According to this calculation, had we many ages to live, alas! perhaps, we should scarcely have time enough fully to satisfy the justice of God. Therefore, if we are wise, and understand our own true interest, we shall devote ourselves to a life of penance. We shall forbid ourselves every pleasure, every diversion, however innocent, which is not necessary. Labor, austerity, afflictions,

solitude, works of charity, etc., will make up
the series of our life.

Let us humble ourselves before God. Let
us be little in our own eyes. Let us humble
ourselves at the feet of all men; voluntary
humiliation is our only resource. Let us beseech God to grant us the spirit of penance.

VERSES OF ASPIRATIONS.

1. "I know my iniquity, and my sin is always
against me." (Psalm l. 4.)

2. "I will confess against myself my iniquity,
to the Lord, and thou hast forgiven the impiety
of my sin." (Psalm xxxi. 5.)

3. "Bring forth fruits worthy of penance."
(Matt. iv. 8.)

Read "Following of Christ," book iii. c. 52; book iv. c. 7.

THIRD MEDITATION.

ON HELL.

First prelude. Represent to your imagination an immense abyss, full of fiery waves and of
millions of reprobate souls, imprisoned in fiery

bodies, devoted to the action of those everlasting flames.

Second prelude. Beg of God to give you a lively feeling and apprehension of the pains which are suffered by the damned; to the end that, if love does not as yet restrain you from sin, at least, the fear of those pains may produce that salutary effect.

FIRST POINT.

The pain of loss.

As the possession of God is the sovereign happiness of Heaven; so the privation of God is the sovereign misery of Hell. That privation is not severely felt by the sinner in this life, because he is distracted and led away by thousands of objects and amusements, to which he gives all his attention. But in Hell such distractions are impossible. A profound solitude, a forced recollection, do not permit the soul of the reprobate to be for one instant distracted from the thought of what she has lost. She clearly sees that God is her sovereign good; for which she was created, and in which alone she can find her true happiness. Hence she is drawn towards Him with inexpressible force ; she makes the most violent efforts to fly from the midst of the flames to the bosom of God; but she finds herself repulsed with as much violence, and confined with invisible chains, to those fiery dungeons. For an increase of her misery, she is made a witness of the bliss, joy, and transports of the blessed, whom she beholds, from the place of her torments, in the bosom of God, as the rich reprobate "saw Abraham afar off and Lazarus in his bosom." (Luke xvi. 23.) "The wicked shall see," says the Royal Prophet, (Psalm cxi.) "and he shall be angry; he shall gnash his teeth and pine away: The desire of the wicked shall perish." I have lost my God, and lost Him by my own fault! Lost Him for vain and perishable goods! And lost Him forever!

Adhere now to God, if you would not lose Him for all eternity.

SECOND POINT.

The pain of sense.

In Hell all the senses are most cruelly tormented; each of them has its peculiar torture. The sight is afflicted by the horrid darkness of the dismal place; which, however, is such as to allow a sort of gloomy light, that discovers to the reprobate the most frightful objects. The hearing is tormented by the howlings of devils, the shrieks of the damned, the continual out-cries, curses, blasphemies, and oaths, with which those dismal vaults perpetually resound. The smell is afflicted by the most noisome scent and intolerable stench. "The taste is embittered with the gall of dragons," says the Holy Scripture, "and the incurable venom of asps;" to which are joined a most tormenting hunger and excruciating thirst. Witness the rich reprobate, above mentioned. The feeling is of all the senses the one most cruelly tortured. "There a fire is kindled," says the Prophet, "by the breath of the wrath of God," as by a torrent of sulphur, having the property of burning even souls; endowed with a kind of discernment to proportion its rigor to the guilt of the criminal; and like salt, having the property of preserving bodies incorrupt and always fresh for suffering. Re-present to yourself a reprobate, plunged soul and body into this devouring fire. Fire is the bed on which he is stretched. Fire is his covering. Fire is his food. Fire is the air he breathes. Fire penetrates into his very bowels, into the marrow of his bones! What a situation! Oh, pleasure of sin, whither do you lead? "Which of you," exclaims the Prophet Isaiah, "will be able to dwell in a devouring fire? Who shall abide with everlasting burning?"

Fear those dreadful torments; detest your sins, which have exposed you to them. Thank God for having spared you, when you provoked His wrath by your repeated insults. Suffer any pains, rather than fall into those of Hell.

THIRD POINT.

The worm of conscience.

"Their worm dieth not," says the Gospel. It preys on their hearts with everlasting rigor. This worm is composed of the following ingredients: First, Of their own sins, which during life they would not see, but which are now continually present to their minds, in all their hideous shapes, like so many enraged torturers; Second, Of the sins of others, which either they caused to be committed, or encouraged by their example, or connived at by their silence; Third, Of the graces they have received and abused; here, it is the blood of Jesus Christ, which called a long time for mercy, but now calls for vengeance against them. The mercy of God, the love of their Redeemer now torment them more than all the rigor of His justice or the rage of their executioners. Fourth, Of the presence and reproaches of their companions, formerly in crime, now in suffering. Hell is a place of strife and discord. To all this, add the rage, anguish, and despair, which continually rack those unhappy wretches, at the thought, ever present to their minds, of the eternity of their torments. The feeling sense of that eternity forms an ingredient which seasons every suffering they endure.

Repent now, if you are not willing to repent fruitlessly forever. You will prevent the eternal and unavailing remorses of Hell, by now listening and yielding to the seasonable remorses of a guilty conscience. Abhor and renounce sin, the parent of this never dying worm.

VERSES OF ASPIRATIONS.

1. "O Lord, cast me not away from Thy face!" (Psalm l. 12.)

2. "O Lord, rebuke me not in Thy fury, nor chastise me in Thy wrath!" (Psalm vi.)

3. "Knowest thou not, that the benignity of God leadeth thee to repentance, but according to thy hardness, and thy impenitent heart, thou treasurest unto thyself treasures of wrath unto the Day of Wrath!" (Rom. ii. 4, 5.)

Read "Following of Christ," book i. c. 24.

THIRD DAY.

FIRST MEDITATION.

ON DEATH.

First prelude.   Imagine yourself to be on your death-bed, informed that your last hour is at hand, surrounded by your friends in tears, and upon the point of expiring.

Second prelude.   Beg of God, that you may experience now the same sentiments as you will have then.

FIRST POINT.

The certainty and circumstances of Death.

"It is decreed for all men to die once." (Heb. ix. 27.)   No one can escape the execution of that decree.   But what is Death?   A separation from the world, and whatever is most dear in the world.   Why then would you attach yourself to creatures?   What is Death?   A separation of the soul from the body.   The soul returns to God in order to be judged.   The body is committed to the grave, falls into rottenness,

12

and becomes the food of worms. Why would you then take so much care of your body? Why would you sacrifice to its appetites the dearest interests of your soul? What is Death? It is the end of time. For the man that dies, time shall be no more. No more time to do penance, to receive graces, to do good works. "Ergo dum tempus habemus, operemur bonum — Therefore, whilst we have time, let us do good." What is Death? It is the beginning of Eternity, a two-fold Eternity, of bliss, of torments. If you are wise, you will lay up treasures for the former, and secure yourself against the latter.

SECOND POINT.

The uncertainty of death.

First. Uncertainty of the time. "You know neither the day nor the hour." Neither youth, nor health, nor riches can avert the blow. Therefore "be ye ever ready!" Second. Uncertainy of the manner. It may be violent; it may be sudden; it may be such, in fine, as to leave you neither time, nor power to prepare yourself. Be, then, always ready: Watch at all times. It is not a sudden death that is to be feared; but an un-provided one. Third. Uncertainty of the state. You know not whether death will surprise you in the state of grace, or in the state of sin. If you spend a good part of your life in sin, you have great reason to fear lest you die in sin. Were you but one hour in mortal sin, you have reason to dread lest you should be overtaken by death in that state. Strive, then, to remain always in a state of grace.

THIRD POINT.

Two different sorts of death.

First. The death of the sinner. How dismal it is! "The death of sinners is very evil — Mors peccatorum pessima." If he turn his thoughts on the past, what painful recollections! All his pleasures vanished; all his labors vain; a numerous train of sins that press heavily upon him. If he look at present objects, all is distressing. He is surprised; he must part from the dearest objects of his love. The scene is now dreadfully changed; objects now appear to him in a very different light from what they appeared during his life. If he cast an eye on futurity, it offers to him most terrifying objects: An angry God, before whom he is going to appear, a Heaven which he has slighted, and for which he has done nothing; a Hell which he is conscious of deserving; an eternity of torments, to which he justly fears he is going to be condemned.

Second. The death of the just. "Precious in the sight of the Lord is the death of the Saints — pretiosa in conspectu Domini mors Sanctorum ejus." Subjects of consolation offer themselves to him on every side; a retrospect of his past life brings to his remembrance, either a preserved innocence, or an innocence recovered and repaired by a sincere repentance, and works of penance: together with a series of good works worthy a happy eternity. The present causes no surprise; he is prepared: no painful separation; he is disengaged: no change of scene; he has always viewed everything in the same light as he does at this moment. The future presents to him a God, whom he loves; a heaven, for which he has labored, and which he hopes to possess; a happy eternity, for which he has endeavored to provide.

"Oh, may my soul die the death of the just, and my end be made like unto theirs!—Moriatur anima mea morte Justorum, et fiant novissima mea horum similia."

VERSES OF ASPIRATIONS.

1. "Oh Death! how bitter is the remem-

brance of thee, to a man who has peace in his possession!" (Eccle. xli. 1.)

2. "Oh! how great confidence a dying man will have, whom no affection to any thing detains in this world!"

Read "Following of Christ," book iii. c. 53; book i. c. 23.

CONSIDERATION.

ON THE PUNISHMENT OF THE DAMNED.

Preparatory Prayer.

First prelude. Imagine to yourself the height, the breadth, and the depth of hell.

Second prelude. Ask of God a lively fear of the pains of hell, so that, if ever you are so unhappy as to lose the grace of the love of God, at least the fear of punishment may deter you from sin.

FIRST CONSIDERATION.

The habitation of the damned.

It is hell. But what is hell? The Holy Spirit calls it the place of torments. (St. Luke xvi. 28.) A prison, where the condemned shall be imprisoned by the justice of God, to be tormented through ages of ages: "They shall be shut up there in prison." (Isaiah xxiv. 22.) A region of misery, a darkness where an eternal horror dwells: "A land of misery and darkness, where the shadow of death and no order, but everlasting horror dwelleth." (Job x. 22.) A lake of fire and brimstone: "They shall have their portion in the pool burning with fire and brimstone." (Apoc. xxi. 8.) A deep valley, where a torrent of sulphur rolls, lighted by the breath of the Lord: "For Topheth is prepared from yesterday, prepared by the King, deep and wide; the nourishments thereof are fire and much wood; the breath of the Lord, as a torrent of brimstone, doth kindle it." (Isaias xxx. 33.) A burning furnace: "Thou shalt make them as an oven of fire," (Psalm xx. 10.) The depths of an abyss: "He opened the bottomless pit," (Apoc. ix. 2;) the smoke from which darkens the sun like the smoke from a vast furnace; "And he opened the bottomless pit; and the smoke of the pit arose as the smoke of a great furnace." (Apoc. ix. 2.) Finally, the anger of the Almighty is like a wine-press, in which an angry God will trample upon and crush His enemies: "And He treadeth the wine-press of the fierceness of the wrath of God the Almighty." (Apoc. xix. 15;) "I have trampled on them in My indignation, and have trodden them down in My wrath." (Isaias lxiii. 3.)

SECOND CONSIDERATION.

The company of the damned.

In hell a triple society will form the torment of the condemned.

1. The society of his body, which, to the infectious corruption of a corpse, will unite all the sensibility of a living frame, and every member of which will have its torment and its pain.

2. The society of devils. "There are spirits that are created for vengeance, and in their fury they lay on grievous torments." (Ecclus. xxxix. 33.) Damned themselves, they have no other occupation but to torture the damned. Not being able to revenge their reprobation on God, they revenge it on man, His image; they pursue God in the condemned, and they pursue Him with all the hate and fury that can enter the hearts of demons.

3. The society of an infinite number of wretched creatures damned like himself. Represent to yourself an assembly so hideous, that even in the galleys and prisons of human justice you could not find any thing like it; an assembly of all that the earth has borne of licentious men, of robbers, of assassins, of parricides. Imagine to yourself all these wretches bound together, according to the expression of the Holy Spirit, like a bundle of thorns—"As a bundle of thorns they shall be burnt with fire," (Isaias xxxiii. 12;) or a heap of tow cast into the midst of the flames—"The congregation of sinners is like tow

heaped together, and the end of them is a flame of fire." (Ecclus. xxi. 10.) Represent to yourself in this horrible reunion the accomplices or the victims of the damned, bound and chained with him to burn in the same fire: "They themselves being fettered with the bonds of darkness, and a long night." (Wis. xvii. 2.) What torment for the unhappy man, not to be able to separate himself from the companions of his reprobation, who never cease to accuse him of their misfortune, and who find a horrible consolation in tearing him to pieces! "They have opened their mouths upon me, and reproaching me they have struck me on the cheek; they are filled with my pains." (Job xvi. 11.)

THIRD CONSIDERATION.

The punishment of the reprobate through the powers of his soul.

1. *Torment of the imagination.* The imagination of the damned presents his misery to him with incredible clearness. It represents to him all the pleasures of his past life. See how happy thou wert on earth; thy life was but one tissue of delight and joy; all that is passed and can never return: "All those things have passed away." (Wis. v. 9.) It shows him all he has suffered, all that he has yet to suffer. Oh, what years thou hast burnt in hell, and yet thy eternity is not begun! Oh, what ages and millions of ages will pass, and thou wilt have no other occupation but to burn! It shows him heaven,

with all its felicity. How happy thou wouldst be near Mary, near Jesus Christ. Listen to the songs of the blessed; behold those souls which love and possess God for all eternity. All that is lost for thee. "The wicked shall see, and shall be angry, he shall gnash with his teeth and pine away; the desire of the wicked shall perish." (Psalm cxi. 10.)

2. *Torment of memory.* The memory of the damned will recall all his sins: "What fruit, therefore, had you in those things of which you are now ashamed?" (Rom. vi. 21.) It recalls all the trouble taken for advancement in this world: "What doth it profit?" (Wis. v. 8.) It recalls all the graces received—faith, a Christian education, the example of so many virtuous persons, the instructions of the ministers of Jesus Christ, the Sacraments of the Church. "And have been able to show no mark of virtue," (Wis. v. 13.) It recalls the warnings that were given on earth. How often has he not heard that it is terrible to fall into the hands of the living God, that there is no mercy in hell! Why didst thou not 'listen to these wise warnings? "Did I not protest to thee by the Lord, and tell thee before?" (3 Kings ii. 42.)

3. *Torment of the understanding.* The understanding of the reprobate never ceases to show him the deformity of sin, the greatness and beauty of God, the justice of the punishment of hell. Thou wert made for God; why hast thou refused Him thy heart? God is so great, He is so perfect, He is so good; who

13

deserved thy love and service as He did? Ungrateful! thou hast abandoned thy benefactor. Perjured! thou hast dared to break thy oaths. Parricide! thou hast wished to kill thy Father. Begone! suffer for all eternity; an eternal hell is not too much to punish thy crime. "Thou art just, O Lord, and Thy judgments are right." (Psalm cxviii. 137.)

4. *Torment of the will.* Represent to yourself how the condemned soul is tormented. *By its regrets:* It was so easy to save myself. Oh, why did I abuse the time and the grace of God? *By its remorse:* Woe to me! I was mad, a wretch; I am lost through my own fault. *By its jealousy:* Why was such a one saved? He had committed greater sins than I; he had received fewer graces than I; he is happy in heaven, and I burn in hell. *By its desires:* Oh, that I might return to the earth, that I might receive a few years of life; I would frighten the world by the rigors of my penance. *Its reaching after God:* Oh, that I might yet see Thee, Lord; that I might love, that I might possess thee! *Its imprecations:* My prayer, then, is useless. Malediction upon me! perish the day of my birth! destruction fall on my body, on my soul, which the anger of God pursues! perish this unpitying God, who has nothing but vengeance for me! "The wicked shall gnash his teeth and pine away; the desire of the wicked shall perish." (Psalm cxi. 10.)

FOURTH CONSIDERATION.

The torment of the damned in all his senses.

1. *Torment of sight.* The aspect of this dreary prison—of the damned, the companions of his misery—of the demons, the executioners of the vengeance of God—of the cross of Jesus Christ printed on the vaults—of these terrible words engraved on the gates of hell, "*ever, never*"—of those flames which roar around him.

2. *Torment of hearing.* The groans of so many millions of the damned—the howls of their despair—their blasphemies against God and against the saints—their imprecations on themselves—their cries of rage as they invoke death or annihilation—the reproaches they address to themselves—the maledictions with which they load their accomplices—the noise of the flames devouring so many victims.

3. *Torment of smell.* The horrible infection which exhales from so many bodies, which preserve in hell all the corruption of the grave: "Out of their carcasses shall rise a stink." (Is. xxxiv. 3.)

4. *Torment of taste.* A maddening hunger—"they shall suffer hunger like dogs," (Psalm lviii. 7,)—the violence of which shall compel the damned to devour his own flesh: "Every one shall eat the flesh of his own arm." (Is. ix. 20.) A devouring thirst, and not one drop of water to refresh his parched tongue, no drink but wormwood and gall: "Their wine is the gall of dragons

and the venom of asps, which is incurable." (Deut. xxxii. 33.) For refreshment, a chalice which the anger of God has filled with fire, with sulphur, and the spirit of tempests: "Flames and brimstone and storms of winds shall be the portion of their cup." (Psalm x. 7.)

5. *Torment of touch.* The damned will be enveloped in flames as in a garment. The fire will penetrate all the members of his body—and what a fire! Not a fire like that on earth, which is a gift of the divine bounty, but a fire created by justice to punish sin; not a fire lighted by men—and yet what terrible power in a fire which calcines marble, melts metals!—but a fire lighted and kept up by the breath of God, who avenges His offenses, and avenges them without mercy, and avenges them according to the extent of His justice and His power; a fire which does not consume the victim, but which at one and the same time exhausts and renews that sensibility, and thus renders the pain eternal; a fire armed with the attributes of God; His anger to punish, His knowledge to distinguish the senses which have been the most guilty, His wisdom to proportion the chastisement to the degree of crime; a fire so penetrating that it in a manner so identifies itself with its victim that it boils in the veins and in the marrow, that it escapes and reenters by all the pores, that it makes of the damned a burning coal in the midst of the furnaces of hell; a fire which unites in itself every torment and every pain, which infinitely surpasses any thing man can suffer from sickness,

all that tyrants ever made the confessors of Christ to endure: "Which of you can dwell with devouring fire, which of you can dwell with everlasting burnings." (Is. xxxiii. 14.)

FIFTH CONSIDERATION.

Torment of eternity.

How many years or centuries will the damned be chained in this prison? *Forever.* How many years or centuries will he groan in tears of regret and despair? *Forever.* How many years or centuries will he be condemned to the society of demons? *Forever.* How many years or centuries will he burn in flames. *Forever.*

Will God, then, never have pity on his misery? *Never.* Will there not be any interruption of his torment? *Never.* Will he not at any time receive any mitigation of his pains? *Never;* always, *never.* Stretch your imagination, add years to years, ages to ages; multiply them like the leaves of the forest, the sand of the sea-shore, the drops of water in the immensity of the seas; you will not yet conceive the meaning of those two words, *ever, never.* "What number of years can equal eternity, since it is without end?" (St. Aug.)

COLLOQUY.

Cast yourself at the feet of Jesus Christ. Represent to yourself this innumerable multitude of souls that sin has precipitated into hell.

Return thanks to our Saviour, who has preserved you from this dreadful eternity, and has hitherto followed you with His mercy and His love.

Pater. Ave.

SECOND MEDITATION.

ON THE PARTICULAR JUDGMENT.

First prelude. Place yourself in spirit at the bar of the judgment-seat, before Jesus Christ.

Second prelude. Beg grace to discover how you may now gain over your Judge, whilst he is flexible, and effectually to determine upon it.

FIRST POINT.

Who shall be my Judge?

Jesus Christ; no longer in His debased and humble state, but arrayed in all the brightness of His glory and majesty. Jesus Christ an all-knowing God and Judge, from whose piercing sight nothing can be hidden. Jesus Christ, an inflexible Judge, who can neither be bribed nor moved by tears, nor prevailed on by prayers, to reverse His sentence. Jesus Christ, a Judge infinitely just, who will render to every one according to his works. Jesus Christ, an allpowerful Judge, from whose hands no one shall be able to wrest the impenitent wretch who has incurred His displeasure.

Fear that awful Judge. Make haste to appease. Endeavor to become His child, His friend, His spouse.

SECOND POINT.

What shall be the rule of my judgment?

The books shall be opened, says St. John: and what books? On one side the *book* of the law of God, the Gospel of Jesus Christ, containing His doctrine, His maxims, His examples. On the other side, the book of my life. My actions shall be compared with those divine rules; and approved of or condemned, according to their conformity or opposition to them. The maxims, customs, and laws of the world shall be then counted for nothing.

Grieve at seeing so little conformity between your life and the great rules on which you are to be judged. Resolve to learn these rules, and to regulate every part of your life by them.

THIRD POINT.

What will be the matter of my judgment?

First. All the sins I have ever committed, from the first use of reason to my last breath; not only my open sins, but also those that have been covered with the shades of darkness; not only my exterior sins, of words or actions, but even my most secret thoughts and desires. Second. All omissions of those duties, which the law of God or my state of life imposed upon me. Third. All the graces, exterior and interior, which I have received and neglected or abused. Fourth. The sins of others, to which I have been any ways accessory. Fifth. Even my best actions shall be nicely examined and sifted, with my intentions in doing them, and all the circumstances which accompanied them.

Tremble at the thought of so rigorous an account. Resolve to prepare for it by judging yourself before hand, accusing yourself, condemning and punishing yourself, and amending your life.

FOURTH POINT.

What will be the sentence?

An eternal and irrevocable one, either to

bliss or damnation. To eternal salvation, if my life be found conformable to the law of God; if the heavenly Father discovers in me a resemblance to His Son. "Come thou, beloved of my Father, possess the kingdom prepared for thee!" To eternal damnation, if my life be found contrary to the law of God and in opposition to the life of Jesus Christ. "Depart from me, thou cursed, into everlasting fire!" What a joy to hear the former; what a fright, what a consternation to hear the latter!

Let us suppose ourselves successively in each one of these two conditions, and imagine what would be our feelings. Let us resolve to omit nothing to procure to ourselves a favorable sentence.

VERSES OF ASPIRATIONS.

1. "O Lord! pierce my flesh with Thy fear; for I have feared Thy judgments!" (Ps. cxviii.)

2. "Enter not into judgment with Thy servant, O Lord, for no man living shall be justified in thy sight!" (Psalm cxlii. 2.)

3. "I will search Jerusalem with lamps." (Soph. i. 12.)

Read "Following of Christ," book ii. c. 5; book iii. c. 14.

THIRD MEDITATION.

ON THE PRODIGAL SON.

First prelude. After recalling to your mind the chief circumstances of the parable, represent to yourself Jesus Christ relating it to the Jews, and depicting Himself in it.

Second prelude. Beg grace to be converted to God, and from this time forward to serve Him most perfectly.

FIRST POINT.

The disorders of the prodigal son.

Consider, first, the sources of his disorders, namely, youth and a want of experience — he is the younger of the two; presumption — he thinks he can govern himself and his goods; the love of liberty — he can bear no longer with the control of a superior. Do you not find herein the sources of your own disorders?

Second. The progress of his disorders. First step; he leaves his father's house, and goes to a far country. How far from God is the country of sin? Second step; he associates himself with evil companions. Oh evil company, the chief source of the corruption of youth! Third step; he abandons himselfs to debauchery and carnal pleasures. Oh sensual pleasures, the fatal grave of innocence, and the fruitful nursery of sins!

Third. The effects of his disorders. First; the wasting of his substance; precious innocence, gifts of nature and grace, what becomes of you when sin takes possession of a soul? Second; a distressing poverty, a raging famine, ensued. Nothing but spiritual indigence, distressing want, horrid famine, is to be found in the region of sin. Third; the basest and most cruel servitude is his last resource. The basest; it is a herd of unclean swine he is obliged to feed. The most cruel; he is left in such a want of all things, that he envies the food of those vile animals, and is not allowed to touch it! Sinner! acknowledge here the cruel tyrant, who is become thy master, Satan, thy implacable enemy! Acknowledge the baseness of thy bondage. He employs thee in feeding thy impure and filthy passions. Acknowledge his cruelty.

SECOND POINT.

The return of the prodigal son.

First. Reduced to an entire solitude, he enters into himself. Happy solitude! Blessed recollection! Ye are the sources of every good. Second. He remembers he has a father, and

what abundance of good is found in his house.
Third. He resolves to quit the place, where he
lives so miserably, and to return to his father.
"I will arise and go to my father." Fourth.
He disposes himself to obtain his pardon by a
sincere repentance of his fault. "I will say to
him, father, I have sinned against Heaven and
before thee; I am not worthy to be called thy
son; make me as one of thy hired servants."
Fifth. He puts his resolution into immediate execution, and rising up he goes to his father.
Sixth. He falls on his knees, and, bathed in tears,
he expresses the most profound and the most
unfeigned grief.

Sinner, remember the abundance of good you
formerly enjoyed in your Father's house, in the
state of grace; and which is still enjoyed by His
faithful servants. Will you remain in a state of
miserable want and distressing hunger? Arise,
then, return without delay to thy Father; but go
to Him penetrated with that sincere and deep sorrow which is expressed in the words of the prodigal son. True repentance alone can secure you
a favorable reception.

THIRD POINT.

His reception by his father.

View with a particular attention all the actions of that amiable and merciful father. First. He descries his son coming afar off, although hardly to be known again, through the rags which cover his emaciated body. Second. His bowels are moved with a tender compassion. Third. He runs to meet his son, and throwing his arms around his neck, he tenderly embraces him. Fourth. Content with the first expressions of his grief, the sincerity of which he sufficiently reads on his countenance, he does not give him time to finish the discourse he had prepared, but commands his servants to bring forth quickly the first robe and put it on him, to put a ring on his hand and shoes on his feet. Fifth. This is not yet enough to express the joy of that tender father. He orders the fatted calf to be killed, and a splendid banquet to be prepared to celebrate the return, and, as he calls it, the resurrection of his son. "Because my son was dead, and is come to life again; he was lost, and is found."

Oh! mercy of God, with what lively colors thou art here depicted! Thus it is, O Lord, that

Thou dealest with a repenting sinner! Through the filth and deformity of his sins, Thou perceivest some remaining features of Thy disfigured image, by which Thou still knowest him to be Thy child! Thus dost Thou, oh loving Father! make the first advances towards him, by the solicitations of Thy preventing grace! Thus, as soon as Thou seest him humbled, dost Thou begin to comfort him, to caress him, to embrace him! Thus dost Thou readily forgive him, even without so much as one single reproach for his ingratitude; bring him back to Thy house, clothe him again with the robe of innocence, restore him to the liberty of Thy children, and give strength to his feet to walk in the path of Thy commandments! Thus dost Thou invite Thy saints and angels in heaven, and Thy faithful servants on earth, to congratulate Thee, and to rejoice at the return of Thy child. Thus dost Thou, oh, incomprehensible Goodness! prepare a heavenly banquet for that repenting son, in which Thou feedest his soul with the bread of angels; even with the flesh and blood of Thine only begotten Son, our Saviour Jesus Christ! Oh, goodness! oh, mercy! what sinner can despair of pardon? But what sinner beholding Thee can consent to continue to offend

Thee, to abuse Thee, and to provoke the strokes of Thy justice?

Let us deplore our past blindness, let us, full of hope and sorrow, return to our offended Father, and being once readmitted into His house, let us never forsake Him any more.

VERSES OF ASPIRATIONS.

1. "Convert us O God, our Saviour, and turn away Thy anger from us!"

2. "I have said it, now I begin: this change is of the hand of the Most High!"

3. "Many sins are forgiven her, because she has loved much."

' Read "Following of Christ," book i. c. 25.

SECOND WEEK.

VIA ILLUMINATIVA.
THE WAY OF ENLIGHTENMENT.

AFTER having diligently studied our last end, and risen from our sins, we are now prepared to be taught by Christ, "who enlighteneth every man that cometh into the world." "*Surge qui dormis, et illuminabit te Christus* — Arise thou who sleepest, and Christ shall enlighten thee!" Christ is "the way, and the truth, and the life." His example points out the way in which we are to walk; His words unfold the truth which is to guide our footsteps; and He Himself is the principle and source of the divine life, both in time and in eternity.

During this Week, then, I am called on to study and to imitate the life of Christ; to dwell on His holy example, to mark the words of heavenly wisdom which fall from His lips, to

.penetrate my whole being with the meek and humble spirit of His sacred heart; in one word, to endeavor to set up His Kingdom in my own heart, and to become His faithful, devoted, and loving subject and disciple. This is the practical fruit of this Week's exercises; and to this I should bend all the energies of my soul, with an earnest purpose and a single heart. I must regard Christ as my great Model, whom I am to copy in my own heart; and as the artist who would succeed in copying a great original painting must carefully study every light and shade, every outline and lineament, so must I study, with earnest and loving diligence, every trait in the life and character of this my divine Original and Model, if I would hope to succeed in making my life a copy of His, and in becoming "conformable to His image."

Thus may I be enabled to succeed in taking the important step in the religious life, which God proposes to me at this stage of the exercises. After having, with God's grace, corrected whatever has been deformed in my past life, I will now seek to *conform* to Christ's example

14

what has been, through His mercy, *reformed,* thereby fulfilling the motto:

REFORMATA CONFORMARE.

FOURTH DAY.

FIRST MEDITATION.

ON THE FOLLOWING OF CHRIST.

First prelude. Fix your imagination on Jesus Christ traveling through Judea, and endeavoring to draw all men by His preaching and examples to the practice of perfection.

Second prelude. Beg of Him grace courageously to yield to His imitation, and perfectly to conform yourself to His most holy life.

FIRST POINT.

Jesus Christ our Master — Ego sum veritas.

"God," says St. Paul, "spoke formerly to our fathers by the Prophets; but in these latter times, He has spoken to us by His own Son — Multifariam multisque modis olim loquens Deus

Patribus in Prophetis, novissime diebus istis locutus est in filio, etc." From the highest Heavens, He has declared Him the teacher of mankind — "This is my beloved Son, in whom I am well pleased, hear ye Him — Hic est filius meus dilectus, ipsum audite." What honor, what happiness, for us to have such a Teacher! He knows all things, He is truth itself — Ego sum veritas. He is the eternal, increated light and wisdom of God communicated to men under the veil of human flesh — Ego sum lux mundi. He not only teaches, but gives sense and understanding to those whom He instructs — Erunt omnes docibiles Dei. He is infallible, no danger of erring in following His doctrine. His doctrine is the invariable rule of our faith, of our morals, and of the whole series of our life.

Have we followed that doctrine? Have the precepts, the maxims. and counsels of Jesus Christ been the rule of our lives? Did we not in many cases give the preference to the maxims of the world, to the prudence of the flesh? Give thanks to the heavenly Father for giving you His Son for your teacher and your guide. Give thanks to the Son for having come down from Heaven to teach you. Ask Him pardon for having made hitherto so little account of His divine lessons. Resolve to be His faithful disciple for the future.

SECOND POINT.

Jesus our Model — Ego sum via.

"I have given you example," says He, "that as I have done, so you may do also." Our eternal salvation depends on that imitation. The uncertainty of our predestination is a most frightful thing to the faithful servants of God. "Man knows not whether he be worthy of love or hatred — Nescit homo utrum amore an odio dignus sit." He knows much less, whether he will persevere in the state of grace unto the end. Am I of the number of the elect, or of that of the reprobate? Who can seriously think of this, without trembling? Can nothing draw us from that uncertainty? Nothing, says the holy Council of Trent, but a particular revelation; and can we, without rashness, expect such a favor? No, but we have a general revelation, in some sense, more capable of calming our fears, than a particular one, in which illusion might be feared. This revelation is contained in St. Paul's Epistle to the Romans, and is expressed in these words: "Whom He foreknew, He also predestinated to be made *conformable to the image of*

His Son—Quos præscivit et prædestinavit conformes fieri imagini Filii Sui." In the two different ways this text is interpreted, it signifies, that to be an elect of God, it is absolutely required that we should bear the image and resemblance of His Son Jesus Christ. Hence we may form a very probable conjecture as whether we are of the number of the elect or of that of the reprobate. Does my life bespeak a conformity with that of Christ? Am I humble, obedient, meek, patient, chaste, zealous, charitable, etc., as was Christ? Then, I may reasonably·expect to be one of His elect. But is there no resemblance between Jesus Christ and myself, and do I make no endeavors to copy after that divine Model? I must tremble; it is very probable I am of the number of the damned!

THIRD POINT.

Jesus our Head — Ego sum vita.

All men were in a state of spiritual death in consequence of the sin of Adam. They were unable to restore themselves to life. God sent His own Son, whom He established the head of mankind. That divine Word has taken our nature, and restored it to the supernatural life we had lost. He first re-established that precious life in that individual humanity which He took, and which by its union with the divine nature received a perfection much superior to that of Adam in the state of his innocence. Then, by and through the merits and sufferings of that sacred humanity, he communicates His divine life to every one of us, who is willing to make use of the means He established, and to become His living member. We are made such by baptism, by penance, and by the other sacraments, which are the sources of the spiritual life. We are thereby made partakers of the life of Jesus Christ. We are united to Him as to our head. Precious life! Without it we are dead in the sight of God, and we shall be infallibly lost. With it, we become ourselves the beloved children of God, and the heirs of His Kingdom; joint heirs with Jesus Christ, destined to be forever united to Him in Heaven.

Ah! let us then, secure, as much as we can, that precious life to our souls; and be willing to lose all else, even temporal life, rather than to lose it. Let us contract here a close union with Jesus Christ our Head, that we may never be separated from Him.

VERSES OF ASPIRATIONS.

1. "I am the Way, the Truth, and the Life — Ego sum via, veritas, et vita." (John xiv. 6.)

2. "Your Master is one, Christ — Magister vester unus est Christus." (Matt. xxiii. 10)

3. "I have given you an example, that as I have done, you should do likewise — Exemplum dedi vobis, ut quemadmodum ego feci, ita et vos faciatis."

4. "I live, now not I; but Christ liveth in me — Vivo autem, jam non ego, vivit vero in me Christus." (Gal. ii. 20.)

Read "Following of Christ," book i. c. i.; book iii. c. i. ii.

CONSIDERATION.

ON THE PUBLIC LIFE OF JESUS CHRIST.

Preparatory Prayer.

First prelude. Represent to yourself our Lord Jesus Christ showing Himself to you as the apostles and inhabitants of Judea saw Him, and saying to you, "Look, and make it according to the pattern." (Exod. xxv. 40.)

Second prelude. Ask the grace faithfully to imitate your divine Model.

Third prelude. Consider our Lord as the most perfect model man can propose to himself, in regard to God, to himself, and to his neighbor.

FIRST POINT.

Conduct of Jesus Christ in regard to His Father.

To pray to God, to obey the will of God, to labor for the glory of God, are the principal obligations of man towards his Creator.

Consider how Jesus Christ accomplished these obligations in His public life.

1. *Jesus Christ obeying.* He is not subject to the law, since He is the first author of it, and comes to substitute another of a more perfect kind; yet, as He sees in it an expression of the Divine will, He observes all its rules with religious exactness. Recall what the Gospel tells us of His fidelity in coming to pray in the Temple, in sanctifying the Sabbath-day, in celebrating the Passover. He carries His respect for the law so far as to honor its ministers even in the Scribes and Pharisees: "The Scribes and the Pharisees have sitten on the chair of Moses. All things, therefore, whatsoever they shall say to you observe and do." (Matt. xxiii. 2, 3.)

2. *Jesus Christ laboring for the glory of God.* The three years of His public life were devoted to the preaching of the Gospel. Admire with what zeal He seizes all occasions to speak to men of salvation, and the obligation of serving God. Represent to yourself this God-apostle in

the midst of His disciples, and surrounded by an innumerable crowd.

With what force and with what sweetness combined does He reprove sinners! With what patience He repeats the same truths under different forms to their simple and coarse minds, which can scarcely understand them! With what abnegation of Himself and His own glory, at the price of what toils and perils, does He announce the word of His heavenly Father.

3. *Jesus Christ praying.* Although He has only three years to give to His preaching, He retrenches whole days of even this short space to devote them exclusively to prayer: "He went up into a mountain alone to pray." (Matt. xiv. 23.) "He went into a desert place, and there He prayed." (Mark i. 35.) After the fatigues of the day, instead of giving Himself up to the necessary sleep, He retires to a distance from His apostles on the mountains, or to some desert place, to pray in the silence of night. Meditate on all the circumstances of this divine prayer. It is a prayer made in solitude; a prayer accompanied by outward signs of the most profound respect — He prays kneeling, or with His face bowed to the ground; it is a prayer consisting of the purest and most heroic sentiments of charity — He offers Himself as a victim ready to immolate Himself to repair His Father's glory and to save men.

Look in upon yourself. Do you pray? Do you fulfill the precepts of your religion? Do you labor for the glory of God?

15

Learn from the example of Jesus Christ to fulfill your duties towards God in a Christian manner.

SECOND POINT.

Conduct of Jesus Christ in regard to Himself.

Consider our Lord—

1. *In the use of His creatures.* Admire His *humility*—how He hides His knowledge and His virtues; how He forbids those He has cured to publish His miracles; how He steals away from the enthusiasm of the people who wish to proclaim Him king. His *poverty*—His want is so great, that often He has not even a little bread to support His strength, and only a stone whereon to rest His head; and—oh, most admirable!—He who lavishes miracles. when required for the necessities of His neighbor, refuses them for Himself. His *continual mortifications*—He renounces, He crucifies Himself in all things; His life is a course of fatigues, of fasts, of watchings: "The whole life of Christ was but one cross and one continual martyrdom." (*Imit. of Christ*, i. 2-12.)

2. *With regard to the exterior.* Contemplate the simplicity of His garments; the gravity of His deportment; the modesty which regulates His bearing; the reserve of His words and looks; the serenity and sweetness of His looks, which draw all men to Him;—in a word, recognise in Him what the Prophets had announced; "Behold My servant, My elect; My soul delighteth

in Him. I have given My spirit unto Him. He shall not cry, neither shall His voice be heard in the streets. He shall not be sad or troublesome." (Is. xlii. 1, 2, 4.)

3. *With regard to the interior.* Penetrate into the sacred soul of Jesus Christ: study His admirable virtues; His purity of intention, which refers all to His Father; His charity, which leaves but two affections in His heart—zeal for the glory of God, and zeal for the salvation of men; His detachment in success, when the people, in raptures at hearing Him, cried out, "Never did man speak like this man." (John vii. 46.) His resignation and profound peace when His enemies wished to stone Him; His interior calm when He turned the sellers out of the Temple, or when He confounded the Pharisees.

Practical reflections and affections.

THIRD POINT.

Conduct of Jesus Christ towards His neighbor.

Consider—

1. *The reserve of Jesus Christ in His intercourse with His neighbor.* His conversations were few and short; He feared, as it were, to be in the midst of men. And yet what had He to dread from communication with them? and, on the contrary, what graces might not men draw from Him who had the words of eternal life? Yet Jesus Christ avoids mingling with them as

much as His ministry permits, and prefers silence, prayer, and solitude.

2. *The charity of Jesus Christ towards His neighbor.* He bears with divine meekness the hatred and persecutions of the Pharisees, the rudeness of His disciples, the unworthy treatment of His neighbors, who wish to bind Him as a fool and a madman. He receives with kindness, even with a sort of predilection, the ignorant and the common people: "His communication is with the simple;" (Prov. iii. 32;) with the poor: "The poor have the Gospel preached to them;" (Matt. xi. 5;) with little children: "Suffer the little children, and forbid them not to come to Me; for of such is the kingdom of Heaven;" (Matt. xix. 14;) with sinners: witness Zacheus, the Samaritan, the adulteress, Magdalen. He could not refuse miracles when they brought to Him one possessed, a paralytic, etc.; thus it is written of Him that He "went about doing good." (Acts x. 38.)

3. *The end Jesus Christ proposed to Himself in His intercourse with His neighbor.* His sole end was to instruct, to convert, to save men: thus He was never known to speak of vain or curious things: He only spoke of the kingdom of God — "Speaking of the kingdom of God," (Acts i. 3,) of the value of the soul — "What will it profit a man if he gain the whole world and lose his own soul;" (Matt. xvi. 28;) of the obligation of loving God — "Thou shalt love the Lord thy God;" (Matt. xxii. 37;) of the necessity of renouncing and conquering ourselves —

"If any man will come after Me, let him deny himself" (Matt. xvi. 24); of the happiness of suffering and poverty — "Blessed are the poor in spirit." (Matt. v. 3.)

Practical reflections and affections.

Colloquy with our Lord, to beg of Him the grace of a faithful imitation of His virtues.

Anima Christi.   Pater.   Ave.

"Paint to yourself in your heart the conduct and the whole life of Jesus Christ. What humility He displayed among men; what benignity towards His disciples; what commiseration towards the poor, to whom He made Himself like in all things, and who appeared to be the most cherished portion of His family. How He contemned not nor spurned one; how He flattered not the rich; how free He was from the solicitudes of this life, and the fears that men entertain for temporal necessities. What patience He showed under insult; what mildness in His answers. How He sought not to vindicate Himself by bitter or sharp words, but to triumph over malice by gentle and humble replies; how willing to suffer labor and poverty, and how compassionate towards the afflicted; how He condescended to the imperfections of the weak; how He avoided all scandal; how He disdained not sinners, but received the penitent with infinite clemency; how calm in all His words, in all His gestures; how solicitous for the salvation of souls, for love of whom He deigned to become incarnate and to die; how fervent in prayer;

how prompt in the service of others, as He says Himself: 'I am in the midst of you as he that serveth.' (Luke xxii. 27.)

"In all your actions, then, in all your words, whether you walk or eat, whether you speak or keep silence, whether alone or in company, lift your eyes to Him as your model. By this you will inflame your love; you will increase your confidence in Him, you will enter into a holy familiarity with Him, and you will become perfect in every kind of virtue. Let this be your wisdom, your study, your prayer, always to have something about Him in your mind, in order that you may be stirred up to a greater love and imitation of Him. For the more we conform ourselves to Him in the imitation of His virtues, the nearer we shall approach and be like to Him in His celestial beauty and glory." (St. Bonav.)

SECOND MEDITATION.

ON THE INCARNATION.

First prelude. Recall to your remembrance the chief circumstances of the mystery.

Second prelude. Imagine yourself to be in the house of Nazareth, to see the angel and our Lady, to hear the conversation, etc.

Third prelude. Adore the Word Incarnate,

and beg of Him light to know and learn the great lesson of humility, which He gives you in this mystery.

FIRST POINT.

The depth of His humility.

To form to ourselves some idea of it, let us ascend in spirit to the highest heavens, and there contemplate in a boundless eternity, before the beginning of all things, the Word of God, in the bosom of His Father, equal to Him and the same God as He is. "In the beginning was the Word; and the Word was with God; and the Word was God—In principio erat Verbum, et Verbum erat apud Deum, et Deus erat Verbum." "By Him all things were made. He is the source of life and light.—Omnia per ipsum facta sunt—In ipso vita erat, et vita erat lux hominum." Then, descending through a space of four thousand years, let us contemplate Him in the cottage of Nazareth, in the womb of the Virgin, reduced to the condition of an infant of a day, of a moment. "And the Word was made flesh and He dwelt amongst us.—Et Verbum caro factum est, et habitavit in nobis." Ah, what a strange humiliation! Let us exclaim with Isaias: "Vere Tu es Deus absconditus—Thou art truly a hidden God!" That says even too little. Thou art a

God humbled, debased, annihilated! But if for the love of us, the Son of God embraces so humble and debased a state, could we suffer ourselves to be puffed up with pride?

Let us be ashamed at seeing ourselves so subject to that vice. Let us renounce it. Let us with Jesus Christ espouse humility; to live obscure, unknown, little, in the eyes of men, ought to be the ambition of the disciple of an Incarnate God.

SECOND POINT.

The justice of His humility.

The Son of God was not obliged to become Man, nor to be the Redeemer or Model of Men. This was an effect of His pure love for us, by reason, says St. Paul, "of the exceeding great charity with which He has loved us — Propter nimiam charitatem suam qua dilexit nos." But these steps being once presupposed, it was just and necessary that He should humble Himself as much as He has done. First. As man; because human nature, even united to the Divinity, is still nothing before God, if considered in itself. "My substance," says He by the prophet, "is as nothing before Thee." Hence in the Man-God, the baseness of the humanity hides, and, in some measure, eclipses the grandeur of the Divinity.

Secondly. As Redeemer of men; because in that quality He becomes their substitute. He takes their sins on Himself; and in that character, He deserves all the shame, humiliation and punishment due to sin. Thirdly. As the Model of men; because in this quality He must give them an example, which may afford a remedy proportioned to their greatest evil, which is pride. Man had lost himself by endeavoring to become like God, his Creator. He must now save himself by endeavoring to become like God, his Redeemer.

Conclude from these reflections, how just, how necessary it is that you should be humble, you who are a mere man, a real sinner, both by the misfortune of your origin, and by the actual malice of your heart; and who can not expect a share in His redemption, unless you first have a share in His humility. Let us acknowledge that nothing can be more just, than that we should humble ourselves; and nothing more unjust than our pride. That, as men, we deserve no glory: as sinners, we deserve all sorts of humiliation and punishments: and as penitents and disciples of Christ, we are in the necessity of conforming ourselves to our humble Master. Let us, then, generously embrace both humility and humiliations.

THIRD POINT.

The glory of His humility.

The humility of Jesus Chirst has been the source of His immense and everlasting glory. God, His Father, has exalted Him in proportion to His humiliations. " He humbled Himself, being made in shape as a man, He debased Himself; therefore God has exalted Him, and given Him a name above all names," etc —Humiliavit semetipsum in similitudinem hominum factus; exinanivit semetipsum, propter quod et Deus exaltavit illum et dedit illi nomen quod est super omne nomen," etc. Let us then humble ourselves. 'T is now an essential and invariable rule in the religion of Christ. 'T is by humility alone that we can ascend to glory. " He who humbles himself shall be exalted—Qui se humiliat, exaltabitur." Pride could not fail to precipitate us, as the fallen angels, into eternal humiliation. " He who exalts himself shall be humbled—Qui se exaltat, humiliabitur." How dear, then, ought humility to be to us !

Let us therefore declare war against our pride, and neglect nothing to acquire the precious treasure of humility. Let us often beg it of God, through the humiliations of His beloved Son.

When we are tempted by pride let us look at our Incarnate God. Let us also implore the same grace by the intercession of the humblest of Virgins, the Mother of the Incarnate Word, and the most faithful imitator of His humility.

VERSES OF ASPIRATIONS.

1. "I am a worm, and not a man.—Ego sum vermis et non homo." (Psalm xxi.)

2. "Truly Thou art a hidden God.—Vere tu es Deus absconditus, Deus salvator." (Psalm xlv. 15.)

8. "From the pride of life, by the mystery of Thy holy Incarnation, deliver us, O Lord!—A superbia vitæ, per mysterium sanctæ Incarnationis Tuæ, libera nos Domine." (Litany of Saints.)

Read " Following of Christ," book i. c. 2 ; book ii. c. 2 ; b. iii. c. 8.

THIRD MEDITATION.

ON THE NATIVITY OF OUR LORD.

First prelude. Recall to your mind the chief circumstances of this mystery: the journey to Bethlehem, the search after a lodging, the rebukes, and the entrance into a stable. '

Second prelude. Imagine yourself to be in the stable of Bethlehem, to see the Infant, His Mother, St. Joseph, the shepherds, etc.

Third prelude. Adore Him, thank Him, embrace Him, and beg Him to imprint in your heart, the great lesson of His poverty.

FIRST POINT.

Painful and universal poverty. He suffers much from it.

First, Poverty in His lodging. No house to shelter Him from the inclemency of the season, nothing but an open stable, that lets in the air and the cold. Second. Poverty in His accommodations; no cradle but a manger, no bed but a handful of straw, no fire, to warm his tender limbs, no clothing, but a few coarse and swadling clothes. Contemplate your Saviour and your God in that wretched lodging, on that poor bed, in that distressing condition, shivering with cold, deprived of the common solaces of life, and in want of those necessaries which are not denied to the poorest of children.

Oh, how truly does this example condemn the abundance and luxury of worldlings! How loudly it condemns our love of riches, of the

comforts and conveniencies of life! We are not
willing to suffer the want of any thing, and, behold the Son of God is reduced, for the love of
us, to the want of the most necessary comforts
of life! Let us be ashamed and resolve to cherish and embrace His poverty.

SECOND POINT.

Humbling and ignominious poverty.

His poverty causes Him to be rebuked and
rejected from every house in Bethlehem; to be
neglected, forgotten, despised, as the outcast
of men. A few poor shepherds alone, admon-
ished by the angels, take notice of Him. He
remains unnoticed and unknown to His own
people. " He came unto His own; and His own
received Him not — In propria venit, et sui eum
non receperunt." Behold the great Messiah of
Israel, the Redeemer of the world, driven to the
corner of an abandoned stable; drinking already,
in full draught, the bitter cup of ignominy prepared for Him. Behold the supreme Lord of
the universe become a little weeping babe, de-
pendent on others for His subsistence; mani-
festing His wants by His cries; but in vain;
since those who wish to relieve them have it
not in their power, and those who have it in

their power are not willing to do it. We are
not perhaps unwilling to be poor, provided it
be an honorable poverty, a poverty that attracts,
or, at least, does not exclude the attention, the
respect, and the esteem of men. But an ignominious poverty, a poverty that excites the contempt, the reproaches, and the rebukes of men;
a poverty that keeps us unknown, unregarded,
slighted by the world, is for us an object of fear,
and perhaps of aversion and horror. How little
we resemble our Saviour!

THIRD POINT.

Voluntary poverty.

Jesus Christ is the sovereign Lord of the
universe. All the riches and glory of this world
are at His disposal. He might have been born
in the bosom of opulence, in the midst of grandeur. He might have called to His cradle the
kings and potentates of the earth. He might
have surrounded Himself with all the comforts
and conveniences of life. He might have called
His angels to wait on Him. Therefore, that He
should find no lodging in Bethlehem, that a
stable should be the place of His birth, that the
most universal, distressing, and humiliating póv-
erty should be His lot, was no effect of hazard;

but the order of Providence, for our instruction and reformation. It was to intimate to us the danger of riches; it was to inspire us with a contempt of the advantages of this world. It was to remind us that our true riches, our true glory, our solid happiness, are not in this life, but in heaven. The stable, the manger, the swaddling clothes, the tears of Jesus Christ cry aloud unto us: "Blessed are the poor in spirit." They teach us that heaven is the lot of the poor in spirit; that even if we are poor in reality, there is no heaven for us, unless we love our poverty, and despise riches; and also that if we are rich in reality, there is no heaven for us, unless we are poor in spirit, and disengaged from the riches we possess.

Let us examine how we have followed these lessons. Let us love, embrace, and practice a true poverty of spirit.

Read "Following of Christ," book i. c. 6, 7; book iii. c. 18.

FIFTH DAY.

FIRST MEDITATION.

ON THE CIRCUMCISION OF JESUS CHRIST.

First prelude. Recall to your mind the chief circumstances of this mystery.

Second prelude. Imagine that you see before you Jesus Christ, suffering that painful operation, and His blood flowing from the wound.

Third prelude. Adore Him and beg Him to imprint in your heart the lessons of mortification, which He gives you.

FIRST POINT.

Jesus Christ receives the legal Circumcision, and thereby teaches us the mortification of the body.

Jesus Christ had come into the world only to immolate Himself for our redemption. Obliged to restrain the ardent desire that burned in His heart of dying on the cross, He joyfully embraced every occasion of suffering for us. He now offers the first fruits of His blood, as a pledge of His resolution to shed it one day to the last drop. From this example of Jesus Christ, the Saints have learned to mortify their flesh. "Those who are Christ's have crucified their flesh — Qui Christi sunt carnem suam crucifixerunt." The mortification of the flesh is necessary to expiate our sins, and to preserve us from a relapse. A flesh which is unmortified will be rebellious. "He who feeds his slave delicately, shall find him obstinate — Qui delicate nutrit servum suum, sentiet contumacem." Besides the corporal penances, which we might embrace under the direction of obedience, we have frequent opportunities of mortifying the flesh. A modest and composed posture of the body, a constant restraint put on our eyes, ears, and tongue; little privations at meals, a great fidelity in taking nothing at other times without necessity, a great punctuality in rising at the appointed hour, a constant application to labor, to study, and other occupations prescribed by obedience; voluntary privations of many little satisfactions, etc., are very profitable mortifications. The general maxim followed by the Saints, is that we never can exceed in our desire of corporal mortifications, and, that the measure thereof, is not to be fixed by sloth and fear of suffering, but only by the fear of displeasing God, and of rendering ourselves incapable of a more solid good. Is

16

this our practice? Let us blush at our remiss-
ness and want of courage, and resolve to chastise our flesh and reduce it to subjection.　_

SECOND POINT.

For the legal, Jesus Christ substitutes the evangelical Circumcision.

The Circumcision of the law was only a figure
of the spiritual Circumcision of the heart, so
often recommended to the Jews by Moses and
the Prophets. "Circumcise the desires of your
heart — Circumcidite præputium cordis vestri."
This is the proper Circumcision of the law of
grace, which St. Paul calls "a Circumcision not
made by the hands, the Circumcision of the
heart, in the spirit, not in the letter — Circumcisio non manu facta, Circumcisio in spiritu non
littera;" which consists in retrenching all ungod-
liness and worldly desires, and in leading a life
of sobriety, justice, and piety. "The grace of
our Saviour-God has appeared, teaching us, that
renouncing impiety and worldly desires, we live
soberly, justly and piously in this world—Appa-
ruit gratia Salvatoris nostri Dei, erudiens nos,
ut abnegantes impietatem et sæcularia desideria,
sobrie, et juste et pie vivamus in hoc sæculo."

Let us then give great attention, during this
Retreat, and every day afterwards, in our medi-

tations and examens, to discover all our passions and vicious inclinations, not only those which are criminal and dangerous, but even such as are only defective and imperfect; and let us use a constant application in rooting out the smallest fibres of every propensity which may hinder or retard our progress in perfection. One single passion left unmortified may cause our perdition. Is it not to that cause we must ascribe our past disorders and irregularities?

THIRD POINT.

Jesus Christ in His Circumcision, receives the name of Jesus, as the reward both of the Circumcision He suffers, and of that which He establishes.

Jesus is the name of the Saviour and the great Penitent of mankind. But a name reverenced and adored by all creatures, by the devils themselves. "In the name of Jesus, let every knee bow — In nomine Jesu omne genu flectatur." Christians, ecclesiastics, and religious persons partake of the glory of that name. In the latter, it implies a particular union and resemblance with Jesus Christ. They should, like Him, be public penitents for the salvation of men. "Inter vestibulum et altare plorabunt sacerdotes, ministri Domini, et dicent: parce

Domine: parce populo tuo!" That precious resemblance to Jesus, penitent, would make them also partakers of the privileges and glory of His name. A Religious, and still more an Apostolic man, truly mortified and dead to himself, possesses a glorious empire over his own heart, over the heart of other men, over the heart of God Himself, of whom it is said: "He will do the will of those that fear Him — Voluntatem timentium se faciet." Hell trembles before such a man. He rescues multitudes of souls from the slavery of Satan. He is powerful in words and works. Whereas, the unmortified man is weak and unsuccessful. "This kind of devil," says our Saviour, "is not cast out, but in prayer and fasting — Hoc autem genus Demoniorum non ejicitur, nisi in oratione et jejunio." Let us then, by forming in ourselves a holy habit of mortification, prepare ourselves to be the coöperators of Jesus Christ in the glorious work of the salvation of souls.

VERSES OF ASPIRATIONS.

1. "Those who belong to Christ, have crucified their flesh, with its vices and concupiscences." (Gal. v. 24.)

2. "If you live according to the flesh, you

shall die; but if, by the spirit you mortify the deeds of the flesh, you shall live." (Rom. viii. 13.)

3. "I chastise my body and bring it into subjection, lest after I have preached to others, I might become myself a reprobate."

Read "Following of Christ," book i. c. 2; book iii. c. 18, 32.

CONSIDERATION.

ON VENIAL SIN.

Preparatory Prayer.

First prelude. Represent to yourself the fires of purgatory, and a soul in these fires expiating the sins it committed on earth.

Second prelude. Ask of God the knowledge and the hatred of venial sin.

FIRST CONSIDERATION.

The malice of venial sin.

Venial sin is essentially an offense against God. It is consequently a contempt of the majesty of God, an ingratitude towards His goodness, a resistance to His will, an injury to all His perfections;—a slight injury, if compared to that which mortal sin offers to God, but very serious if considered in itself; for it is an offense against Infinite Majesty by a vile creature, and for a vile motive.

Venial sin is, then, really the evil of God. Meditate well on these words: *An evil against God;* that is to say, an evil so great that it surpasses all the temporal and even eternal evils of creatures.

The destruction, or above all the damnation, of the whole human race would be a great evil; and yet it would be a sin to wish, if we had the power, to save the human race from destruction or hell at the price of one venial sin.

It is an evil so great that all the sacrifices and virtues of creatures render less glory to God than one venial sin takes from Him.

It is an evil so great that neither the mind of man can comprehend it, nor his will hate it as it deserves to be hated, nor any expiation of his suffice to repair it. For it requires nothing less than the mind, the will, and the atonement of a God.

SECOND CONSIDERATION.

The effects of venial sin.

Venial sin, it is true, does not destroy in us habitual grace; but, nevertheless, how deplorable are its effects in the soul!

1. It imprints a stain which tarnishes its beauty. It is to the soul what an ulcer is to the body.

2. It weakens the lights of the spirit and the fervor of the will; and from that arises languor

in prayer, in the use of the Sacraments, and in the practice of Christian virtues.

3. It deprives the soul of the superabundance of graces — choice graces, which God only gives to purity of heart.

4. It deprives the soul of a greater degree of grace and glory which it would have acquired by its fidelity, and which is lost by its fault. A God less glorified eternally, less loved, and less possessed — such are the consequences of venial sin to the soul.

5. It leads to mortal sin as sickness leads to death; for the repetition of venial sins insensibly weakens the fear of God, hardens the conscience, forms evil attachments and habits, gives fresh strength to the temptations of the enemy of our salvation, nourishes and develops the passions. Hence the Holy Spirit says, "He that contemneth small things, shall fall little by little," (Ecclus. xix. 1;) and that of our Saviour, "He that is unjust in that which is little, is unjust also in that which is greater." (Luke xvi. 10.)

THIRD CONSIDERATION.

The punishment of venial sin.

Even in this life God has often inflicted most rigorous vengeance for venial sin. Moses and Aaron were excluded from the promised land in punishment of a slight distrust; the Bethsamites were struck dead for an indiscreet look at the ark; seventy thousand Israelites were carried

off by a destructive scourge in punishment of
the vain complaisance of David in the number-
ing of his subjects.

But it is above all in the next life that venial
sin is punished with the most alarming rigor.
Enter in spirit this blazing prison, where the
justice of God punishes His elect, and meditate
attentively on the following circumstances:

1. *What is the victim suffering in purgatory?*
It is a predestined soul; a soul confirmed in
grace, and that can not lose it; a soul so dear
to God that He is impatient to give it the most
magnificent testimony of His love, that is to
say, the possession of Himself.

2. *What does it suffer?* Pain which man can
not conceive; that is, fires which differ in nothing
from those which devour the damned — it is the
opinion of St. Augustine, confirmed by St. Thomas,
"The same fire forms the torment of the damned
and the purification of the just;" and the privation of God, which delivers up the soul to all
that is most agonizing in regrets and desires.

3. *Why does it suffer?* For some of those
faults which almost every moment are committed
from the weakness of our will.

End by looking into your conscience. Examine the faculties of your soul and the senses of
your body. Call to mind how far divine faith
regulates the use of them with regard to God,
your neighbor, and yourself. Examine all the
venial faults you commit each day in these
different points, through ignorance, levity, or
weakness — perhaps even with malice and re-

flection.   Humble yourself before God, and say
with the prophet: "For evils without number
have surrounded me; my iniquities have overtaken me, and I am not able to see.   They are
multiplied above the hairs of my head, and my
heart hath forsaken me.   Be pleased, O Lord, to
deliver me." (Psalm xxxix. 13, 14.)

Colloquy with the blessed Virgin and our
Saviour.

Pater.   Ave.

SECOND MEDITATION.

ON THE PRESENTATION OF OUR LORD IN THE TEMPLE.

First prelude.   Recall to your remembrance
how, the days of Mary's purification being accomplished, she and St. Joseph carried the child
Jesus to the temple, presented Him to God, and
redeemed Him according to the law, and offered
a sacrifice of a couple of pigeons or turtle-doves.

Second prelude.   Join in spirit the blessed
company that met on that occasion, to pay their
homage to the infant Saviour, the Blessed Virgin
Mary, St. Joseph, St. Simeon, and St. Ann the
Prophetess.

Third prelude.   Beg your Saviour to imprint
in your heart the lesson of fidelity to His Father's
will, which He gives you in this mystery.

17

FIRST POINT.

First Example. — Fidelity in the smallest duties.

To be circumcised, to be presented in the temple, may appear considerable duties. But to be circumcised precisely on the eighth day; to be presented the fortieth day, to be redeemed by a small sum of money, to offer in sacrifice two turtle-doves does not appear to be of very great consequence. Nevertheless, Jesus Christ accomplishes every point with an equal exactness. The love He had for His Father, did not allow Him to leave one single, tittle of the law without being fulfilled. "Iota unum aut unus apex non prœteribit a lege donec omnia fiant." Such ought to be the fidelity of every true servant of God. He strictly complies with every, even the smallest duty: First. Because nothing is small in His eyes, when commanded by Almighty God: Second. Because, should the law of God contain small points, He well knows, that they become great when practiced with love: Third. Because small duties become great by their frequency and continuity. "It is not little," says A'Kempis, "to be faithful in little things—Non minimum est in minimis esse fidelem:" Fourth. Because small duties are the safeguard of great ones. "He who is faithful in small things, is also faithful in greater ones. Qui in minimo fidelis est, et in majori fidelis est:" Fifth. Because it is always great to imitate Jesus Christ.

Are we faithful in small duties? Do we not often neglect them under the pretense, that such an omission is only a venial sin? If so, we have but little love for God, and we are in imminent danger of perishing.

SECOND POINT.

Second Example.— Fidelity in all the points of God's law, how painful and difficult soever they may be.

The mystery of Christ's presentation in the temple is not confined to the bare exterior ceremony. He does not offer Himself to His Father as other children are offered. He knows that to offer Himself to His Father in His quality of our Redeemer, our security and substitute, is to put Himself into the hands of His justice, to devote Himself to a most cruel death. He hears holy Simeon foretelling this to His Blessed Mother. He is The victim of mankind, and now finds Himself in the place where victims are solemnly offered to God. He therefore here makes a prelude to His future sacrifice. He views minutely in advance all the circumstances of that cruel scene. He cheerfully accepts of all, and takes a solemn and irrevocable engagement to pay the immense debt due to the offended majesty of His Father. Thus the love of Jesus for us, makes Him undergo the most difficult and most painful labors and sufferings.

As to us, we stop at every thing. We transgress small duties, by a pretended strength of mind, and great ones, by a true weakness of courage. We would fain do great things, provided they be easy, that is to say, we will do nothing, or almost nothing. The Saints did not do so: nay, the children of this world do not so act. What difficulties, what obstacles do they not surmount, to satisfy their passions, to secure their interests, to gain a little smoke of worldly honor? Have you not often shrunk from the difficulties in the way of practising virtue? Have you not omitted essential duties, under the pretense of impossibility? Whence does your sloth come? Is it from a want of confidence in God's grace? Does He then command that which is impossible?

THIRD POINT.

Third Example. — Fidelity in all those points which, although not commanded, yet are conducive to the glory of God.

Jesus Christ was under no obligation of being circumcised, nor of being presented in the temple, nor even of dying on the cross. The glory and the wish of His heavenly Father alone were to Him equivalent to an order. We shall always be very far from perfection, nay, we shall never reach it, as long as we shall so carefully distinguish the counsel from the precept. God will not see in us His faithful and loving children; He will see in us mere slaves, who will do His will only when He commands and threatens, but who are not willing to put themselves to any great trouble to satisfy His desires and good pleasure. A loving child needs no commands. It is sufficient to him, that it will give his father satisfaction; this alone will make him perform even things that are most painful. Ah! what would become of us, had Jesus Christ done for us no more than He was strictly obliged to do?

Let us, then, never say: this is not obligatory; there is no sin in doing this, nor in omitting that; therefore I shall indulge my own inclination. But let us say: this will please my God; it will turn to His honor and glory. Therefore I shall faithfully comply with it. Lament your past negligence, your infidelities, your resistance to the divine inspirations, and resolve always to do that which will appear to you most pleasing in the sight of God.

VERSES OF ASPIRATIONS.

1. "Behold I come, O my God! I have desired it, and Thy law is in the midst of my heart." (Psalm xxxix. 9.)

2. "My food is to do the will of Him that sent me." (John iv. 34.)

3. "I do nothing of myself." (John viii. 28.)

Read "Following of Christ," book i. c. 9, 15 ; book iii. c. 13.

THIRD MEDITATION.

ON THE PRIVATE LIFE OF JESUS CHRIST.

First prelude. Represent to yourself Jesus Christ leading a retired and private life with Mary and Joseph, in their little cottage in Nazareth.

Second prelude. Beseech Him to teach you how to love solitude, and to sanctify yourself in it.

FIRST POINT.

In solitude Jesus obeyed — "And He was subject to them." (Luke ii.)

Jesus obeyed; and whom? Joseph and Mary, that is, a poor mechanic and an humble virgin. But had they, in commanding Him, any peculiar personal influence or advantage over Him? Had they more knowledge, more prudence, more virtue? No; but they were for Him in the place of His heavenly Father, and in them, He respected His authority; in Mary, as His mother, in Joseph, as the husband and superior of Mary, and in that quality His own superior, whom His Father had intrusted with the care of His conduct. Jesus obeyed; and in what? Often in things of very little consequence. What other things could they command Him to do, at least in His early years? Jesus obeyed; and how? With all the degrees of perfection that are recommended by the Saints; with submission of heart and mind; with exact, prompt, generous, cheerful obedience. No objection, no excuse, no murmur. In this He merited as much as when He was born in

Bethlehem, or when He was expiring on the cross; because God has not so much regard to the thing which is done, as to the spirit with which it is done. He used every where and in all things the same attention, the same zeal for whatever His Father prescribed to Him, by the mouth of Mary and Joseph.

Let us examine our own conduct towards our superiors and compare our obedience with His, in every respect.

SECOND POINT.

In solitude Jesus labored.

He tells us, by His prophet, that He was subject to labors from His youth. And what labors? In His childhood He waited on Himself; He served Joseph and Mary; He always acted in submission to their orders. He assisted His holy Mother in the management of her household. Oh! what a wonderful spectacle, to see the great God of the universe, under the form and in the humble garb of a poor child, employed in the mean occupations of a poor cottage; such as sweeping the floor, carrying wood, kindling a fire, fetching water, etc. These were His first labors. Then, as He grew up in years and strength, He lent His help to St. Joseph in the exercise of his trade, until He became Himself a professed workman, as the Gospel testifies. "Is not this the carpenter, the son of the carpenter?"

Let us, after this example, accustom ourselves to be always employed in useful occupations. Let us disdain no employment, however mean it may appear to our pride, when it is prescribed by obedience. Let us carefully strive to shun idleness, as the mother of all evils. An idle solitude is a very dangerous one. Let us, then, have always in hand some useful employment. "Let the devil," says St. Jerome, "always find you busy." Let us resolve to imitate that part of our Saviour's life, by a constant and assiduous application to study, to manual labor, or to other employments of our calling.

THIRD POINT.

In solitude, Jesus advanced in virtue and sanctity.

As to His interior, He could not acquire any new kind of virtue or perfection. The words of the Gospel signify, that as He advanced in age, He daily gave outwardly more marks of the virtue and sanctity that were in Him. In this our Saviour teaches the important obligations incumbent on every Christian, but still more on religious persons or ecclesiastics; to aspire to sanctity themselves, and to strive every day to advance in perfection. It is the peculiar duty of young persons, who are brought up in the solitude of their houses under the eyes of their parents, or in houses of education under the care of teachers; but still more of novices in religious solitude, under the guidance of superiors; or of young candidates for holy orders in the solitude of an ecclesiastical seminary, to advance every day, to make a continual progress towards that sanctity and perfection, which their state requires. Those who govern them, should have the consolation, as had Joseph and Mary, to discover daily in them some marks of proficiency.

Let us reproach ourselves with our backwardness. After so long a time spent in solitude, after so many instructions received, so many exercises of piety, so many graces heaped upon us, how little, how imperceptible is our progress! Do we not even, perhaps, go backwards, instead of advancing? Have we not fallen from our former fervor? Let us renew our primitive ardor, and resolve to neglect nothing, in order to repair the time lost, by a rapid advancement in recollection, in obedience, in regularity, in humility, in mortification, and in other virtues.

VERSES OF ASPIRATIONS.

1. "Who will give me wings as of a dove, and I shall fly and be at rest. Behold I have fled far away, and dwell in solitude." (Psalm liv. 6, 7.)

2. "Blessed is the man whose help is from Thee; in his heart he has disposed to ascend by steps, in the vale of tears, in that which he has set." (Psalm lxxxiii.)

Read "Following of Christ," book i. c. 26.

SIXTH DAY.

FIRST MEDITATION.

ON THE TWO STANDARDS.

First prelude. Represent to yourself, on a mountain near Babylon, Satan sitting on a throne of fire, surrounded with flames and smoke; and around him a numerous army of followers.

Then represent to yourself in a plain near Jerusalem, Jesus Christ sitting on a chair, and

surrounded by a small number of faithful followers.

Second prelude. Beg of God not to permit
you to be so unhappy, as to follow the former,
but to attract you by His grace, to a close union
with the latter.

FIRST POINT.

The difference of character between these two leaders.

Satan is a most odious and abominable
spirit, whom his pride has changed from a beautiful angel, into a hideous devil. He hides himself from the sight of his followers; or if he
ever shows himself, it is under a borrowed form,
never in his own shape. He even transforms
himself sometimes into an angel of light,
(2 Cor. xi. 14.) What an odious monster!

Jesus Christ, on the contrary, is the most
amiable, and the most beautiful of the children
of men. (Psalm xliv.) "He has shown Himself
to man, and has conversed with him — Inter
homines visus est, et cum hominibus conversatus
est." He is the only Son of God, made man for
the salvation of mankind. How amiable a
Master!

Conceive a great fear and detestation of
Satan, and a tender love and confidence in Jesus
Christ.

SECOND POINT.

The difference of views and intentions.

With whatever promises Satan may flatter men to draw them to his service, his real intention is, to make them first partakers of his pride, and by this means, partakers of his reprobation.

On the contrary, Jesus Christ has no other intention than our eternal salvation. He wishes to make us partakers of His virtues, of His sanctity, of His divine life; and by this means, partakers of His eternal felicity.

Could we hesitate one moment, in renouncing Satan with the utmost abhorrence, and in adhering irrevocably to Jesus Christ? "Abrenuntio tibi, Satana! — I renounce thee, Oh, Satan!" I renounce all thy works, I renounce all thy pomps! "Adhœreo tibi, Christe! — I adhere to Thee, Oh Christ!" I become Thy follower! Oh! receive me in the number of Thy disciples. "I will follow Thee whithersoever Thou goest — sequar te quocumque ieris."

THIRD POINT.

The difference of the means they employ.

Consider attentively this third difference, that you may not be deluded by the wiles of

Satan. Satan proposes apparent goods, worldly riches, honors, and pleasures, in order to avert the minds of men from heavenly goods, and to inspire them with pride. "I will give thee all these things if thou wilt fall down and adore me — Hæc omnia tibi dabo, si cadens adoraveris me." (Matt. iv.)

Jesus Christ proposes the contempt of all that is earthly and perishable; the contempt of temporal honor, riches, and delights; in order that we may turn all our desires to the heavénly felicity, and, by the practice of His poverty, humility, and self-denial, become partakers of His glory and happiness. If that way appears hard, He animates us to embrace it by His example; He walks before us; by His grace He strengthens and assists us.

Which of the two sides, have we hitherto followed? Which are we determined to follow in future?

VERSES OF ASPIRATIONS.

1. "If any man love not Jesus Christ, let him be anathema." (1 Cor. xvi. 22.)

2. "Who shall separate us from the love of Christ?" (Rom. viii. 35.)

Read "Following of Christ," book ii. c. 2; book iii. c. 6.

CONSIDERATION

ON THE DISCOURSE OF OUR LORD AFTER THE LAST SUPPER.

(St. John, xiii.–xvii.)

Preparatory Prayer.

First Prelude. Represent to yourself the disciple whom Jesus loved reposing on His bosom, and drawing from His heart the understanding of His sublime teachings.

Second Prelude. Ask the grace to partake with him this place of honor during your meditation.

FIRST POINT.

Jesus answers the questions of His Apostles.

1. Peter asks Him, "Lord, whither goest Thou?" Jesus answers, "Whither I go thou canst not follow Me now, but thou shalt follow hereafter." Peter replies, "Why can not I follow Thee now? I will lay down my life for Thee." Jesus answers, "Wilt thou lay down thy life for Me? Amen, amen, I say to thee, the cock shall not crow till thou deny Me thrice."

2. Thomas says to Him, "We know not whither Thou goest; and how can we know the way?" Jesus answers him, "I am the way, the truth, and the life. No man cometh to the Father but by Me. If you had known Me, you would without doubt have known My Father

also, and from henceforth you shall know Him,
and you have seen Him."

3. Philip saith to Him, "Lord, show us the
Father, and it is enough for us." Jesus saith to
him, "So long a time have I been with you, and
have you not known Me? Philip, he that seeth
Me seeth the Father also. How sayest thou,
show us the Father? Do you not believe that I
am in the Father, and the Father is in Me? The
words that I speak to you, I speak not of Myself. But My Father who abideth in Me, He
doth the works. Believe you not that I am in
the Father, and the Father in Me? Otherwise
believe for the very works' sake. Amen, amen,
I say to you, he that believeth in Me, the works
that I do, he shall also do,. and greater than
these shall he do: because I go to the Father.
And whatsoever you shall ask the Father in My
name, that will I do: that the Father may be
glorified in the Son. If you shall ask Me any
thing in My name, that I will do. If you love
Me, keep My commandments. And I will ask
the Father, and He shall give you another Paraclete, that He may abide with you for ever.
The Spirit of truth, whom the world can not
receive, because it seeth Him not, nor knoweth
Him: but you shall know Him, because He
shall abide with you, and shall be in you. I
will not leave you orphans. I will come to you.
Yet a little while, and the world seeth Me no
more. But you see Me, because I live, and you
shall live. In that day you shall know that
I am in My Father, and you in Me, and I in

you. He that hath My commandments and keepeth them, he it is that loveth Me. And he that loveth Me shall be loved by My Father: and I will love him, and will manifest Myself to him."

. 4. Judas saith to Him, not Iscariot, "Lord, how is it that Thou wilt manifest Thyself to us and not to the world?" Jesus answered him, "If any man love Me, he will keep My word, and My Father will love him, and we will come to him, and will make Our abode with him. He that loveth Me not keepeth not My words and the word which you have heard is not Mine, but the Father's who sent Me. These things have I spoken to you, abiding with you; but the Paraclete, the Holy Ghost, whom the Father will send in My name, He will teach you all things, and bring all things to your mind, whatsoever I shall have said to you."

5. The Apostles asked each other what the words signified that Jesus had just said: "A little while, and you shall not see Me; and again a little while, and you shall see Me." Jesus, knowing they wished to ask Him, said to them, "Of this do you inquire among yourselves, because I said: A little while, and you shall not see Me; and again a little while, and you shall see Me. Amen, amen, I say to you, that you shall lament and weep, but the world shall rejoice, and you shall be made sorrowful, but your sorrow shall be turned into joy. A woman, when she is in labor, hath sorrow because her hour is come; but when she hath brought forth

18

the child, she remembereth no more the anguish for joy that a man is born into the world. So also you now indeed have sorrow; but I will see you again, and your heart shall rejóice, and your joy no man shall take from you. And in that day you shall not ask me any thing. Amen, amen, I say to you, if you ask the Father any thing in My name, He will give it you. Hitherto you have not asked any thing in My name. Ask, and you shall receive, that your joy may be full."

SECOND POINT.

Jesus announces His passion; recommends charity, peace, intimate union with Him and with our brethren, constancy in persecutions: He promises the Holy Ghost.

1. *He announces His passion.* "Now is the Son of man glorified, and God is glorified in Him. If God be glorified in Him, God also will glorify Him in Himself, and immediately will He glorify Him. Little children, yet a little while I am with you." (John xiii. 31–33.)

2. *He recommends charity.* "A new commandment I give unto you, that you love one another; as I have loved you, that you also love one another. By this shall all men know that you are My disciples, if you have love one for another." (John xiii. 34, 35.)

3. *Peace.* "Let not your heart be troubled. You believe in God, believe also in Me. In My Father's house are many mansions. If not, I would have told you that I go to prepare a place

for you. And if I shall go and prepare a place for you, I will come again, and will take you to Myself, that where I am you also may be." (John xiv. 1–3.)

4. *Union with Him and with our brethren.* "I am the true Vine, and My Father is the husbandman. Every branch in Me that beareth not fruit He will take away; and every one that beareth fruit, He will purge it, that it may bring forth more fruit. Now you are clean by reason of the word which I have spoken to you. Abide in Me, and I in you. As the branch can not bear fruit of itself unless it abide in the vine, so neither can you unless you abide in Me. I am the Vine; you the branches. He that abideth in Me and I in him, the same beareth much fruit: for without Me you can do nothing. If any one abide not in Me, he shall be cast forth as a branch, and shall wither, and they shall gather him up and cast him into the fire, and he burneth. If you abide in Me, and My words abide in you, you shall ask whatever you will, and it shall be done unto you. In this is My Father glorified, that ye bring forth very much fruit, and become My disciples. As the Father hath loved Me, I also loved you. Abide in My love. If you keep My commandments, you shall abide in My love, as I also have kept my Father's commandments, and do abide in His love. These things I have spoken to you, that My joy may be in you, and your joy may be filled. This is My commandment, that you love one another, as I have loved you. Greater love than this no man

hath, that a man lay down his life for his friends. You are My friends, if you do the things that I command you. I will not now call you servants: for the servant knoweth not what his lord doth. But I have called you friends: because all things whatsoever I have heard of My Father I have made known to you. You have not chosen Me, but I have chosen you; and have appointed you that you should go and should bring forth fruit, and your fruit should remain; that whatsoever you shall ask of the Father in My name, He may give it you. These things I command you, that you love one another." (John xvi. 1–17.)

5. *Constancy in persecutions.* "If the world hate you, know ye that it hath hated Me before you. If you had been of the world, the world would love its own; but because you are not of the world, but I have chosen you out of the world, therefore the world hateth you. Remember My word that I said to you: The servant is not greater than his master. If they have persecuted Me, they will also persecute you: if they have kept My word, they will keep yours also. But all these things they will do to you for My name's sake, because they know not Him that sent Me. If I had not come and spoken to them, they would not have sin; but now they have no excuse for their sin. He that hateth Me hateth my Father also. If I had not done among them the works that no other man hath done, they would not have sin; but now they have both seen and hated both Me and My Father. But

that the word may be fulfilled which is written
in their law: They hated Me without cause.
But when the Paraclete cometh, whom I will
send you from the Father, the Spirit of truth,
who proceedeth from the Father, He shall give
testimony of Me: and you shall give testimony,
because you are with Me from the beginning.
These things have I spoken to you, that you
may not be scandalized. They will put you out
of the synagogues; yea, the hour cometh that
whosoever killeth you will think that he doth a
service to God. And these things will they do
to you, because they have not known the Father,
nor Me. But these things I have told you, that
when the hour of them shall come, you may remember that I told you." (John xv. 18 to end;
xvi. 1–4.)

6. *He promises the Holy Ghost.* "But I tell
you the truth: it is expedient to you that I go;
for if I go not, the Paraclete will not come to
you; but if I go, I will send Him to you. And
when He is come, He will convince the world
of sin and of justice and of judgment. Of sin:
because they believed not in Me. And of justice: because I go to the Father, and you shall
see Me no longer. And of judgment: because
the prince of this world is already judged. I
have yet many things to say to you; but you
can not bear them now. But when He, the
Spirit of truth, is come, He will teach you all
truth. For He shall not speak of Himself; but
what things soever He shall hear, He shall
speak, and the things that are to come He shall

show you. He shall glorify Me; because He shall receive of Mine, and shall show it to you. All things whatsoever the Father hath are Mine. Therefore I said, that He shall receive of Mine and show it to you." (John xvi. 7–15.)

THIRD POINT.

The prayer of Jesus.

1. *Jesus prays for Himself.* Lifting up His eyes to heaven, Jesus said: "Father, the hour is come; glorify Thy Son, that Thy Son may glorify Thee. As Thou hast given Him power over all flesh, that He may give eternal life to all whom Thou hast given Him. Now this is eternal life: That they may know Thee, the only true God, and Jesus Christ whom Thou hast sent. I have glorified Thee on earth. I have finished the work which Thou gavest Me to do. And now glorify Thou Me, O Father, with Thyself, with the glory which I had, before the world was, with Thee." (John xvii. 1–5.)

2. *Jesus prays for His disciples.* "I have manifested Thy name to the men whom Thou hast given Me out of the world. Thine they were, and to Me Thou gavest them: and they have kept Thy word. Now they have known that all things which Thou hast given Me are from Thee: because the words which Thou gavest Me I have given to them, and they have received them, and have known in very deed that I came out from Thee, and they have

believed that Thou didst send Me. I pray for them:
I pray not for the world, but for them whom
Thou hast given Me; because they are Thine.
And all My things are Thine, and Thine are
Mine: and I am glorified in them. And now I
am not in the world, and these are in the world,
and I come to Thee. Holy Father, keep them
in Thy name whom Thou hast given Me; that
they may be one, as We are also. While I was
with them, I kept them in Thy name. Those
whom Thou gavest Me have I kept: and none
of them are lost, but the son of perdition, that
the Scripture may be fulfilled. And now I come
to Thee: and these things I speak in the world,
that they may have My joy filled in themselves.
I have given them Thy word, and the world hath
hated them, because they are not of the world,
as I also am not of the world. I pray not that
Thou shouldst take them out of the world, but
that Thou shouldst keep them from evil. They
are not of the world, as I also am not of the
world. Sanctify them in truth. Thy word is
truth. As Thou hast sent Me into the world, I
also have sent them into the world. And for
them do I sanctify Myself: that they also may
be sanctified in truth. And not for them only
do I pray, but for them also who through their
word shall believe in Me. That they all may be
one, as Thou, Father, in Me, and I in Thee: that
they also may be one in Us: that the world may
believe that Thou hast sent Me. And the glory
which Thou hast given Me I have given to them:
that they may be one, as We also are one. I in

them, and Thou in Me; that they may be made perfect in one; and the world may know that Thou hast sent Me, and hast loved them as Thou hast also loved Me. Father, I will that where I am, they also whom Thou hast given Me may be with Me: that they may see My glory which Thou hast given Me, because Thou hast loved Me before the foundation of the world. Just Father, the world hath not known Thee; but I have known Thee; and these have known that Thou hast sent Me. And I have made known Thy name to them, and will make it known: that the love, wherewith Thou hast loved Me, may be in them, and I in them." (John xvii. 6 to end.)

Affections at the foot of the crucifix.

Anima Christi.

SECOND MEDITATION.

OF THE THREE CLASSES.

First prelude. Cast yourself at the feet of Jesus Christ, and renew the protestations of your allegiance.

Second prelude. Beseech Him not to permit you to deceive yourself in the desire you feel of following Him.

FIRST CLASS.

It is composed of those, who seem to desire their salvation, their perfection, and the glory of God; but who, at the same time, are unwilling to use the means, which are necessary to attain that end. They may be compared to a husbandman, who seems desirous to make a good crop, but is unwilling either to plant, or to sow, or to labor; or to a sick man, who says that he is willing to be cured, but is not willing to take any remedy. Can these be said to be willing? No: it may be said, that they would wish to attain the object of their desires, but they are not truly desirous for its attainment. It is a folly, a mere chimera, to will the end without willing the means.

Now is this not the case with many Christians? You will find no man, but who will tell you that he most certainly wishes to save his soul; but how many, who will not use one single means for this purpose. It is commonly and very truly said, that Hell is paved with good intentions; that is, is full of men who wished to save their souls, and who are nevertheless miserably damned. Have we not been too long in that deplorable error? Are we not still thus deluded? If not with regard to salvation, at least with regard to the perfection of our state, and the glory of God; ever desiring to advance, and never willing to take an effectual means of making a real progress in virtue.

SECOND CLASS.

The second class is composed of those who say that they are desirous of their salvation or perfection, and use some means to that effect, but use neither all, nor the best means to attain the end proposed. They are compared to a husbandman, who is desirous of a plentiful crop, and is willing to sow or to plant, but is not willing to take all the pains, nor to use all the means to promote the growth of his seed and plants. Or to a sick man, who is willing to take some remedies, but not all, nor even the most efficacious. The number of Christians laboring under this illusion, is exceedingly great. Many embrace the service of God and the way of perfection, and make use of some means for that purpose; but they devote themselves to God only by half. Their good resolutions are always made with many reserves and exceptions; they embrace some practices of devotion, but only such as are to their liking and are of easy observance. Whatever is painful to nature and repugnant to their inclination, however necessary and efficacious, is rejected. What wonder if they go back instead of advancing? Are such truly willing to save their souls? To become perfect? No: because they are not willing to use all the means necessary for that end.

Has this not been our case? Do we not yet stand in this class? Let us examine our resolutions. Are they not too full of reserves and exceptions?

THIRD CLASS.

The third class is composed of those who will their salvation, their perfection, the glory of Jesus Christ, with an absolute and determined will. This appears in their neglecting no means, let them ever be so difficult and painful to nature, to obtain their end. They are compared to a husbandman, who wishes for a plentiful harvest, and who, to effect it, spares no pains, no labors, no care, to succeed in his undertaking; or to a sick man, who earnestly wishes for a cure, and is willing to take the most bitter and disagreeable remedies, to suffer the most painful operations. A soul truly willing to sanctify herself, to become perfect, to procure the glory of Jesus Christ, spares no pains for that purpose, is ready to sacrifice the dearest things, pleasures, amusements, friends, parents, connections, goods, time, health, etc., to attain her end. Yea, even if the right hand must be cut off, if the right eye must be plucked out.

Are we in this generous disposition? Let us endeavor to acquire it, if on self-examination we find that we have not hitherto belonged to this class.

VERSES OF ASPIRATIONS.

1. "Then, said I, behold I come! I delight to do Thy will, and Thy law is in the midst of my heart." (Psalm xxxix. 9.)

2. "What is there in Heaven for me, and besides Thee, what can I desire upon earth." (Psalm lxxii. 25.)

3. "Who shall separate me from the charity of Jesus Christ?" (Rom. viii. 35.)

Read "Following of Christ," book iii. c. 5 and 6.

THIRD MEDITATION.

ON THE THREE DEGREES OF HUMILITY.

"Be zealous for better gifts, and I will yet show you a more excellent way."

First prelude. Imagine yourself to stand among the disciples of Jesus Christ, and to hear that good Master inviting you to the practice of humility and perfection.

Second prelude. Beg of Him to imprint in your heart the lesson of His humility, and to teach you the way to true perfection.

FIRST DEGREE.

Consider that the first degree of humility and perfection consists in submitting yourself so perfectly to the holy will of God, as to be ready to die, rather than offend Him. So that if it were question of transgressing a single one of God's commandments; as, to detract from your neighbor's reputation, to do him a notable injury, to profane the sacraments, etc.; and thereby to fall into God's disgrace, you had rather, after the example of the holy Martyrs and all the Saints, lose all the goods of the world, be deprived of every pleasure, suffer every torment, and the most cruel death, rather than fail in your fidelity to so holy and so powerful a Master.

Weigh the reasons which oblige you to be in that disposition; it is essential to salvation. Examine whether you are in that degree. Produce an act of this holy submission; and form on this a strong and unshaken determination.

SECOND DEGREE.

The second degree of humility and perfection, is to submit yourself so profoundly to your Creator, as to be habitually in the firm resolution to die, rather than deliberately to displease Him, even in the smallest point; were it only in a slight lie, an indiscreet expression, a little raillery, an unprofitable word; nay, rather, than commit a voluntary imperfection. In effect is it not reasonable that a beloved son should never cause the least displeasure to his father, never pass in the least, the bounds of the respect which he owes him, and never omit wilfully what is most pleasing to him? The smallest degree of the glory of God is infinitely better than your life and all the pleasures of the world, because it is your end; and the end is always preferable to the means. Now, the glory of God consists in this, that His creature should submit to His will, and endeavor to please Him. How much therefore ought His children to abhor venial sin, which offends Him, and is contrary to His honor? St. Catharine of Genoa said, that, had she been plunged into a sea of flames, and, in endeavoring to emerge therefrom, perceived on the shore the shadow of sin, she never could have dared to come out. What aversion ought not you also to have for voluntary imperfections, by which the soul prefers her own pleasure to the pleasure and the greater glory of God!

Are you not yet very far from this degree? With what facility you commit venial sin! How great is the number of venial sins that defile your soul! How easily and how often do you resist good inspirations! Confound yourself in seeing that, after so many graces, you are yet so far from perfection. Resolve to neglect nothing to reach at least this degree; that is, not to commit the smallest offense, for any consideration whatsoever, and always to choose in preference that which is most pleasing, and most glorious to God.

THIRD DEGREE.

The third degree of humility and perfection, consists in so great a disengagement and contempt for whatever the world esteems and man is naturally inclined to love, that you give always the preference to humiliation, poverty, and suffering, over worldly honors, riches, and joys; actuated thereto by this motive alone, that you wish to resemble Jesus Christ, even in the case that both should be equally conducive to the glory of God. So that, if God would choose to place you in a state of honor, and in a condition pleasing to nature, you should still cherish in your heart a secret inclination for the cross of Jesus Christ; and whenever both are left to your option, you should always turn yourself to the cross, it being your center, out of which you can never enjoy a secure and permanent tranquillity.

Is this your disposition? How far you are from it! When will you be wholly devoted to Christ, and bear in yourself a perfect resemblance to Him?

VERSES OF ASPIRATIONS.

1. "It is good for me to adhere to my God, and to put all my hope in the Lord God." (Psalm lxxii. 28.)

2. "Be ye perfect, as your heavenly Father is perfect." (Matt. v. 48.)

Read "Following of Christ," book i. c. 11 and 18.

THIRD WEEK.

VIA CONFIRMATIVA.
THE WAY OF STRENGTH.

AFTER having studied the life of Christ, and sought to conform our lives thereto, we must now during this third Week seek to strengthen our good resolutions, that we may not falter in the hour of danger, or fail through weakness while walking in the way of virtue. For this purpose we meditate on the passion and sufferings of Christ, who became weak that He might make us strong. In Him strength grew out of weakness, the life of the Resurrection out of the death of the Sepulchre.

_ So should it be with us. At this more advanced stage of these holy exercises, after having already learned the first rudiments of the science of salvation, we are to enter upon our regular training as soldiers of the Cross. Man's life is a warfare upon earth; and we are to nerve ourselves for the contest. Christ will have none that are over-nice and delicate, none that are faint-hearted, none that are cowards, in the ranks of His soldiers. The conflict will be short, but it may be sharp; it will be painful to nature, but it will be alleviated and comforted by grace. Christ is our Captain; He marches at the head of the column; He endures all the hardships of the campaign; we are called upon merely to follow Him: "If any one will come after Me, let Him deny himself, take up his cross, and follow Me!"

O my Lord and Saviour! "I will follow Thee whithersoever Thou goest!" I will cheerfully endure for Thy sake what Thou didst so lovingly endure for mine. I will say with Thy devoted soldier, St. Bernard, "It is not seemly that the member should be over-delicate under a head crowned with thorns;" and with Thyself, "The disciple is not above the Master." But, O dear Lord, my divine Captain and Leader, Thou knowest my great weakness; strengthen me by Thy holy grace; indue me with a portion of Thy divine fortitude, that through Thee I may be enabled to accomplish what through Thee I have resolved to do. Extend forth Thy hand to me amidst the billows of sorrow, that I may not be submerged! Grant, my good Jesus, that after having resolved, during the last Week of these holy exercises, to *conform* my life entirely with Thine, I may, during the present one, be *confirmed* and strengthened in this resolution of following Thee even unto death, the death of the cross; thus fulfilling the motto of this portion of my Retreat:

CONFORMATA CONFIRMARE.

SEVENTH DAY.

FIRST MEDITATION.

ON OUR SAVIOUR'S PASSION.

First prelude. Represent to yourself our Saviour in the garden of Olives, prostrate on the ground, in an agony of grief, covered with a sweat of blood.

Second prelude. Beseech Him to permit you to enter into His sacred interior, and to learn from Him, how to sacrifice for His sake your interior comforts.

FIRST POINT.

The greatness of our Saviour's sorrow.

Conclude it from the expression of the Gospel: He is sad, He trembles, He is filled with anguish. He began to be sorrowful and afflicted, says St. Matthew, and it is the first time of His life that He appears so. He utters sad complaints, He, who never was heard before to complain: and in what terms? "My soul," says He, "is sorrowful even unto death!" That is, my sorrow is such, that it would put an end to my life, did I not support it by the power of my Divinity. He can neither stop long in one place, nor quiet His afflicted mind. He prays, and His prayer, His reflections, can afford Him no relief, no rest. He goes to His disciples, and leaves them the next instant. He prays again, He desires His Father to remove from Him a bitter chalice, which He has a reluctance to drink. Yet He submissively resigns Himself to the divine will — "Thy will be done, not mine!" Even this can not appease the agitation and affliction of His mind. A second visit to His disciples proves as ineffectual as the first.

He continues to pray; but the more He advances, the more fearful become His combats. His sorrow grows into an agony. The violence of the struggle produces a profuse sweat, which covers all His limbs; when lo! the blood itself propelled from the heart, where fear had gathered it, makes itself an issue through every pore, in so great an abundance as to cover His body, bathe His garments, and trickle down in streams upon the ground — "And His sweat was made as drops of blood, running upon the ground." What affliction! What sadness!

Condole with your suffering Jesus; beg Him to disclose to you the cause of that frightful anguish.

SECOND POINT.

The causes of His sorrow.

The first cause is no other than His love. We certainly know that none of these sentiments of fear, sadness, anguish, etc., could arise in His blessed soul, without His own consent. It must then have been His choice to suffer them. This is properly the passion of His love. No torturers have yet appeared, no scourges, no thorns, no nails, no spears, present themselves; and Jesus is already covered with His blood! Admire that love, and beg it to disclose to you, the instruments it employed.   These instruments were no other than our sins, and the clear foresight of all that He was going to endure for them; and of the inutility of all He was to suffer for a great number of men.   In this awful moment, the sins of mankind, from the first to the last, were all mustered before His mind, in all their hideous shapes and deformities.   This caused His fright.   But He could not see so many offenses committed against the majesty of His Father, without the most profound grief.   His sorrow was proportionate to His love for Him, which was without bounds: nor could He see mankind, whom He so tenderly loved, fallen into such depths of misery, without the most lively sorrow and tender compassion.   This caused His sadness.

But this is not all.   He must take all those heinous monsters of sin on Himself; He must atone for them.   Oh! what a frightful moment for the pure and spotless soul of Jesus, when He saw Himself encompassed with that innumerable army of hideous crimes, and thus become the object of the hatred and vengeance of His heavenly Father!   This caused that weariness and anguish, expressed by the Evangelists.

Add to this the distinct sight of all the tortures, ignominies, insults, and ill-treatment, which were prepared for Him on the morrow; the clear knowledge He had of the malice and perverse designs of His enemies; and of the inutility of His sufferings for the greater part of mankind, who would not profit by them, but would abuse His grace, and repay His sufferings by the most shameful ingratitude. This caused the agony of grief, which would surely have put an end to His life, had He not supported it by His divine power; and the violence He offered to His natural repugnance, to submit to His Father's will, and to accept of all those horrors, caused that extraordinary sweat of blood, which bathed His whole body.

Conceive sentiments of the most lively compassion for the sorrow and anguish your Saviour endures for your sake, and thank Him for His excessive love towards you. View also the number, the enormity and hideousness of your own sins. Grieve for them. Beg of your Saviour some share in His sorrow. Offer it up to the heavenly Father, to supply the weakness of yours. Mingle the tears of your repentance with the tears of blood He sheds for you. Submit to all the sadness, interior desolation, perplexity, scruples, and anguish of mind, into which He may permit you to fall.

THIRD POINT.

Where Jesus Christ seeks for consolation.

He seeks relief to His interior pains, in God, in prayer, in communication with His Father. "Is any of you sad," says St. James, "let. him pray." But what kind of prayer?

First. A prayer of humiliation. He prostrates himself with his face to the ground. The soul must acknowledge that she well deserves all the interior pains and afflictions she endures. Second. A prayer of resignation. "Oh my Father! Thy will be done, not mine!" God is our Father even when He afflicts us. Let us submit our will to His, and be content with its appointments so long as He pleases. Third. A prayer of perseverance. "Being made into an agony, He prayed the longer." Let us persevere in prayer, notwithstanding our interior dryness, and wait patiently for the moments of grace, seeking relief only in our acquiescence in the holy will of God. We are not forbidden to have recourse to pious friends, especially to our spiritual directors; but let us not rely too much on human assistance, which our Lord could not find among His disciples.

Examine your conduct, and form your good resolutions according to this divine Model of suffering.

Read "Following of Christ," book ii. c. 9.

CONSIDERATION.

ON MARY OUR MOTHER.

Preparatory Prayer.

First prelude. See Mary at the foot of the cross; hear Jesus saying to you, "Behold thy Mother!"

Second prelude. Ask of Jesus a filial love for Mary your Mother.

Consider —

1. That Mary was given you for your Mother.

2. That she has really shown herself a Mother to you.

3. That you ought to be a confiding and devoted son to her.

FIRST POINT.

Mary has been given you for a Mother. Consider then, in your heart all the circumstances of this gift.

1. She was given to you by Jesus Christ, God and Master of all creatures, from whom emanates all power, paternal and maternal; by Jesus Christ the God-Saviour, who had already sacri-

20

ficed for you the body and lavished the blood
He derived from Mary. Having nothing more
to give you but her, He bestows her on you as
a complement of all His gifts.

2. She is given to you in the clearest terms,
the strongest, the most precise, to enable you to
realize what they signify: " Behold your Mother."
Jesus said, in showing the bread, "This is My
body; " and the bread became His body. Pointing to His Mother, He says, "Behold thy
Mother; " Mary immediately became our Mother.

3. She was given to you under the most serious and solemn circumstances. Jesus, dying,
makes His last dispositions and signifies His
last will. Alone of all the disciples the beloved
John is present to receive in the name of all
Christians the last gift which their divine Master
makes to them. Thus all the fathers and doctors
of the Church have understood it.

4. She is given you "for your Mother." Feel
these words at the bottom of your heart. Recall
to yourself that man does not live only by
bread; that his soul as well as his body has a
life to receive and support. It is in this supernatural order that Mary is your mother; if you
live to grace, it is through her. The principle
of this spiritual life is in Jesus; but Mary's is
the bosom that bore you, the milk that nourished
you, the maternal heart that always loves its
children even when ungrateful.

5. Why was a mother according to grace given
to you? and why was this mother the mother of
God? Interrogate Jesus in profound recollection

of heart. He wished to become your brother both by father and mother; He wished that all should be in common between you; He wished that if the infinite height of His divinity terrified you, a creature, His mother and yours, should serve as your advocate, your refuge, and your mediatrix with Him; He wished to encourage the most timid, open the hearts most oppressed by fear, offer to all the sweetest motive for trust, always well founded, never too great; for a mother always loves her child, and Jesus, Son of Mary, will always love His mother.

SECOND POINT.

Mary has always shown herself your mother.

1. She received you to her heart when Jesus gave you to her for her child; so the Scripture calls Jesus Christ her first-born. (Matt. i. 25.) You ought to be born in her and by her, after Him.

2. She has nourished you, not only by the graces her prayers have obtained for you, but also in a real manner, by the Body and Blood of her Son given to you in the Eucharist.

3. She has anticipated you, cared for you, loaded you with favors. All the graces you have received from the Lord have been solicited and obtained by her. So, your call to the faith, the grace of a Christian education, of a first communion; the grace of conversion and retreat,

the grace that now leads you to give yourself entirely to God — all come to you from Jesus through Mary. (St. Bernard.)

4. At need, Mary obtains for the defense and salvation of her children -extraordinary graces and wonderful miracles. What prodigies have caused, sustained, spread every where, confidence among Christian people? What striking proofs of her protection the Church recalls to our memory by solemn feasts and pious practices, enriched by precious indulgences. What titles Christians give her to testify their gratitude: " Help of Christians, health of the sick, comfort of the afflicted, refuge of sinners, gate of Heaven, our life, our sweetness, our hope!" What a concourse of people to the places where she is most honored, where she obtains the most succors to those who invoke her! What prayers and acts of thanksgiving at the foot of her altars! and in our days what conquests made by Our Lady of Victories! What favors bestowed on all hearts devoted to the heart of Mary.

5. Her protection, "strong as an army," (Cant. vi,) preserves her faithful children from all dangers; she is for them an assured pledge of predestination. So the doctors of the Church believe, who assure us "that a servant of Mary can not perish."

THIRD POINT.

1. *Love* for her who is the beloved of our
Lord; gratitude towards her who has loaded us
with benefits; filial affections for our mother.

2. *Confidence.* Her power and her title of
mother were given to her that our trust in her
might be unlimited, that we might know that
she would always be able and willing to help us.

3. *Imitation.* She expects from us this proof
of true love. Does not the child naturally resemble the mother? Let this resemblance in
us be the fruit of our efforts, of a careful study
and practice of her virtues. Sons of a virgin, let
us be pure; sons of the Mother of sorrows, let
us be faithful to Jesus, even unto the cross.

4. *Zeal* to spread her devotion. A sincere
love will produce this zeal. We must praise
and defend all the practices authorized by the
Church; her images must be venerated and distributed; we must love to bear her livery, to
visit the places where she is honored; take
pleasure in singing her praises, in preceding her
feasts by penance, and in sanctifying them by
the reception of the holy Eucharist. Let us
honor the sacred heart of Mary, and honor it
by a particular devotion.

COLLOQIUES.

Let us recite the *Magnificat* in union with Mary, or else address these words of St. Bernard to ourselves: "O thou who feelest thyself tossed by the tempests in the midsts of the shoals of this world, turn not away thine eyes from the star of the sea if thou wouldst avoid shipwreck. If the winds of temptation blow, if tribulations rise up like rocks before thee, a look at the star, a sigh towards Mary. If the waves of pride, ambition, calumny, jealousy, seek to swallow up thy soul, a look towards the star, a prayer to Mary. If anger, avarice, love of pleasure, shiver thy frail bark, seek the eyes of Mary. If horror of thy sins, trouble of conscience, dread of the judgments of God, begin to plunge thee into the gulf of sadness, the abyss of despair, attach thy heart, to Mary. In thy dangers, thy anguish, thy doubts, think of Mary, call on Mary. Let Mary be on thy lips, in thy heart, and in the suffrage of her prayers lose not sight of the examples of her virtues. Following her, thou canst not wander; whilst thou prayest to her thou canst not be without hope ; as long as thou thinkest of her thou wilt be in the path; thou canst not fall when she sustains thee ; thou hast nothing to fear while she protects thee ; if she favor thy voyage, thou wilt reach the harbor of safety without weariness."

SECOND MEDITATION.

ON THE PASSION OF JESUS CHRIST; FROM THE GARDEN OF
OLIVES TO HIS CONDEMNATION.

First prelude. Place yourself by your Saviour's side; follow Him wherever He goeth, and behold Him in all His sufferings.

Second prelude. Beseech Him to enlighten you, that you may know the greatness of His love, the moving examples He sets before you, and may perfectly imitate them.

FIRST POINT.

Sacrifice of His liberty.

Meditate how your Saviour delivers Himself up to His enemies; with what rage they rush upon Him. How they load Him with chains, how cruelly they insult Him, and how rudely they dràg Him along. Prostrate at His feet, adore your captive Saviour, and humbly kiss the chains He wears for your sake.

Consider —

First. That it is His love for you, not the power of His enemies, that has reduced Him to that captivity. He showed by the double miracle He performed in the garden, that His enemies had no power over Him, but what He was Himself pleased to bestow upon them. Be grateful for that love. Second. That He is become a captive to expiate your criminal liberties. Detest them and repent for them. Third. That He has sacrificed His liberty, to free you from the shameful bondage and slavery of sin, and to procure for you the glorious liberty of the children of God. Aspire to that blessed liberty, the only one that deserves the name, and use every means in your power to obtain it. Fourth. That He is become a captive, to win you over to the sweet captivity of His love.

Sweet captivity! Glorious bondage, which makes you a child of God, an heir of Heaven, and leads you to the possession of His Kingdom. Accept of it; thank your Jesus for His love; ask Him pardon for your sins. Beg Him to break your bonds asunder. Beseech Him to make you a captive of His love. Put on those glorious chains, and never lay them aside.

SECOND POINT.

Sacrifice of His reputation and honor.

Jesus Christ had by His holy life and miracles acquired a great reputation for power, for sanctity, and for wisdom, and had thus been an

object of veneration for the Jews. This day
He loses all this. First. The reputation of
power, by falling into the power of His enemies,
and appearing unable to rescue Himself from
their hands. Second. Of His sanctity, by appearing in chains, as a criminal, accused of most
grievous crimes, and condemned to death as a
blasphemer, a disturber of the public peace, and
a seditious man. Third. Of wisdom, by His
constant silence, never answering any thing to
the accusations brought against Him, which induced Herod to treat Him as a fool and a sim-
pleton.

He also loses His honor. First. By the ig-
nomies and insults with which He was loaded;
He received a blow on His face in the High
Priest's house. He was, during the whole night,
the sport of the guards, who blindfolded Him,
buffeted Him, spit in His face, bid Him in derision guess who had struck Him. Those mock-
eries and insults were repeated at His crowning
with thorns, and on Mount Calvary. Second.
He was compared with, nay, postponed to Bar-
rabbas, a man infamous for murder and sedition.
Third. He was condemned to suffer between two
malefactors, as the greatest of them.

Learn from all this how to despise the honors
and reputation of a vain world. How frail, how

empty, how contemptible they appear in the
eyes of a disciple of Jesus Christ, who has so .
manifestly disdained them! But how precious
and desirable must be to His true disciple, those
reproaches, insults, derisions, slanders, outrages,
and manifold ignominies, which He so cheerfully
embraced for their sakes! Acknowledge that
such a sinner as you are deserves no reputation,
no glory, no honor whatsoever, but rather shame
and ignominy. What have been hitherto your
thoughts, your judgments, your inclinations in
regard to these things? Do they bear a conformity with that of your Saviour? Are you
resolved to acquire that conformity for the
future? "Be ye of the same mind, which is
also in the Lord Jesus."

THIRD POINT.

Sacrifice of His body.

Behold your Saviour exposed naked to the
view of an insolent multitude, and tied to a
pillar. Hear the cruel and numberless blows
that are inflicted on His pure and innocent body.
Behold His numerous wounds; His flesh torn,
and the blood streaming from every part. Prostrate yourself at His feet, adore those wounds,
that blood; and acknowledge that it is your

sins, that have thus armed His torturers. "Sinners have wrought on my back, says He by His Prophet — Supra dorsum meum fabricaverunt peccatores." Hate your sinful flesh, and ask of your Saviour to give you the courage to mortify its vices and concupiscences.

But turn now your eyes to a new scene Behold the innocent Lamb of God surrounded by a band of barbarous soldiers. An old purple cloak is thrown across His mangled shoulders, long and hard thorns are entwined together in form of a royal crown, which is laid on the sacred head of Jesus; and with repeated blows sunk into His sacred brows. The thorns penetrate on every side, and open new streams of blood. Jesus bears this torment with an incredible patience, much less sensible of the cruel points of the thorns than our crimes which have placed them on His head. To this frightful torment His enemies add derision and insults. They bend in mockery the knee before Him. They repeat their blows, they sink the crown deeper into His sacred head. They add buffets on His sacred face.

Adore Him as your true King, your Saviour, and your God. Ask Him pardon for having, by your sins, put that crown of thorns on His head, and brought on Him all these ignominies. Offer Him to His heavenly Father, and beg mercy through Him. Beseech Him to grant you an utter contempt of worldly honors, and a relish for His humiliations.

Read "Following of Christ," book ii. c. 12, one half.

THIRD MEDITATION.

ON OUR SAVIOUR'S CRUCIFIXION.

FIRST POINT.

The carrying of the Cross.

Pilate, after many difficulties, prevailed upon by human respect, consents at last to the death of Jesus, and pronounces his condemnation. A huge cross is immediately brought, and Jesus is obliged to carry it Himself, exhausted as He was, to Mount Cavalry. Let us join the pious women who followed Him, but let us remember the advice He gave them, rather to weep over ourselves, who are the real causes of His sufferings, than over Him. "Filiæ Jerusalem nolite flere super Me, sed super vos et filios vestros." Let us observe the track of blood He leaves after Him; but, above all, let us enter into His sentiments with regard to His cross, which He so willingly and so tenderly embraces, as a beloved Spouse, on which He is going to regenerate the world; thus establishing it as the standard of His elect, the glorious portion of His disciples, the seal of His covenant, the instrument of the salvation of men, the terror of the powers of hell, the bulwark of His Church, the way to glory, and the gate of Heaven. Loaded, like another Isaac, with the wood of the sacrifice, carrying in His heart the fire and the sword, that is, His immense love, He ascends Mount Calvary, and reaches the top of it after a most painful march, and there He lays down His painful burden.

Let us venerate that saving cross. Let us thank Jesus for having carried it for our sake. Let us beg Him to give us a place under that standard of salvation; but let us also lovingly embrace it, and remember, that He has said: "If any man will come after Me, let him take up his cross, and follow Me;" and, "He who carries not his cross, can not be my disciple."

SECOND POINT.

The crucifixion.

Jesus is scarcely arrived at the place of execution, when His enemies hasten to prepare the instruments of His death.　He is again stripped of His clothes; they had by this time stuck to His wounds, which were thereby all re-opened. Oh! Innocent Victim, in how pitiful a state thou appearest to my eyes!　How are not the hearts of Thy torturers moved with compassion?　Oh! Eternal Father!　Oh! God, just and terrible! Behold the limbs already mangled and bleeding, of Thy beloved Son, which are to be substituted for the ancient victims.　Will, at length, Thy wrath be satisfied?　Jesus is commanded to lay Himself down on the cross.　He respects His Father's holy will in the order of His enemies; He obeys without resistance; He lies on this bed of sorrows without any thing else whereon to lean His head, but the thorns with which it is crowned; He presents His adorable hands; two gross nails driven through them, fasten them to the cross; He stretches out His feet, which are pierced and fixed to the wood with the same relentless cruelty.　Behold the great altar of the whole world, on which is offered to God the only Victim that can effectually appease Him. From His four wounds, issue forth four springs of sacred blood, which, like so many salutary streams, flow upon the earth, to cleanse it from its iniquities.　Adore that precious blood.　Offer that Victim to the heavenly Father.　Beg pardon and mercy through Him. Beg Jesus Christ to crucify you with Him, that you may say with St. Paul, "Cum Christo confixus sum cruci— With Christ I am nailed to the cross!" Beg Him to crucify your flesh, with all its lusts; your heart, with all its vicious propensities. Beg to be crucified to the world, and resolve to lead a crucified life from this time forward.

THIRD POINT.

Jesus raised, living and dying, on the Cross.

Consider what your Saviour suffered when they dragged the cross to the hole prepared to receive it, when they let it down, and when they fastened it by driving wedges with repeated strokes. It was then, according to the Prophet's prediction, that His bones were dislocated, so that they could be counted — "Dinumeraverunt omnia ossa mea." Place yourself now at the foot of the cross. Contemplate your crucified Saviour. View every part of His body, and see if there is one without suffering. Enter into His interior, and behold the extreme desolation of His blessed soul. Hear Him amorously complain to His Father, that He had forsaken Him. What do I say? His Father! Ah! it seems that He does not dare, any longer, call Him by this tender name. He calls Him, His God. "My God! My God! Why hast Thou forsaken Me? — Deus meus, Deus meus, quare me dereliquisti?" He lives three hours in these torturing pains, and pangs of death; hanging between Heaven and earth, as the Mediator between God and man; praying for our reconciliation, and offering Himself as an holocaust to repair His Father's glory. In fine, all is accomplished; and Jesus, with a loud cry, recommending His soul into His Father's hands, bowing down His sacred head in sign of submission, expires! — "Clamans voce magna expiravit."

Here it behooves us to imitate Him, and to unite together in our hearts all the sentiments which have animated them during the course of our meditations of our Saviour's sufferings: of admiration, compassion, love, sorrow, gratitude, fervor, and mortification.

ASPIRATIONS.

"Cum Christo confixus sum cruci! — With Christ I am nailed to the cross."

"Mihi mundus crucifixus est, et ego mundo — The world is crucified to me, and I to the world."

"Amor meus crucifixus est — My love is crucified."

"Christus passus est pro nobis, vobis relinquens exemplum ut sequamini vestigia ejus—Christ suffered for us, leaving you an example that you should follow His footsteps."

"Si compatimur, ut et conglorificemur—If we suffer with Him, that we may be glorified with Him."

Read "Following of Christ," book ii. o. 12.

FOURTH WEEK.

VIA UNITIVA.
THE WAY OF UNION BY LOVE.

DURING this Week we meditate on the glorious mysteries. We rise with Christ in His triumphant Resurrection; we ascend with Him into Heaven; and there associating, with the seraphim around His throne, we catch some sparks of that fire of love with which they are all aglow. In this heavenly school we learn, thoroughly and practically, that love is indeed the fulfillment and complement of the law.

Sursum Corda! Lift up your hearts! even to the heavenly Jerusalem, where dwelleth, in light inaccessible, and in glory ineffable, our blessed Jesus, ever living at the right hand of His Father, to make intercession for us! He went thither on our behalf, in our name, as our Leader, to prepare a place for us. He loved us

even unto the end; He will love us through all
eternity, with an eternal love. He wishes to
unite us to Himself for ever more, by the sweet
and golden bonds of love.

The practical fruit, then, of this Week's exercises, is to *unite* ourselves with Christ by love
in this world, that we may be *united* with Him
by love inseparably and eternally in Heaven.

Rise, then, my soul, from the lowliness and
darkness of thy present place of exile; look up
to Heaven, thy real and eternal home; shake
off the dust from thy feet, and wipe away the
tears of sorrow from thy eyes; the hour of thy
redemption and final triumph draweth near!
Yet a little while, and thou wilt be able to take
the wings of the dove, to fly away, and to be at
rest forever more in the bosom of God, who is
love — thy FIRST BEGINNING, and thy LAST END!
Courage, my soul! One brief day for sorrow, an
eternity for joy! The crown is well worth the
small labor and the trifling privations necessary
for its attainment. Shalt thou win and wear it,
or shalt thou through pusillanimity lose it forever?

O my Jesus, having strengthened my good resolutions by Thy holy Passion and Cross, do Thou vouchsafe now to complete the work which Thou hast begun, and to *transform* by Thy love into Thyself what Thou have deigned already to *confirm* by Thy grace, thus verifying the the motto of this Week—

CONFIRMATA TRANSFORMARE.

EIGHTH DAY.

FIRST MEDITATION.

ON THE RESURRECTION OF JESUS CHRIST.

Preparatory Prayer.

First prelude. When our Lord had breathed His last sigh, His body, taken down from the cross, was placed in the sepulchre: His soul descended into Limbus to deliver the souls of the just; then returned to the sepulchre the third day, and withdrew from it His body, which was then united to it never more to be separated. The risen Saviour appeared, first, to His blessed mother, then to the holy women, and at different times to the disciples and apostles.

Second prelude. Represent to yourself the sepulchre from which Jesus Christ arose, and some of the places that witnessed His apparitions—for example, the road to Emaus, etc.

Third prelude. Beg the grace to participate in the joy of Jesus Christ and of His blessed mother.

FIRST POINT.

The glory of Jesus in His resurrection.

Consider the glory of the Saviour in His resurrection, and how faithfully His Father rewards all the sacrifices of His suffering life.

1. In His passion Jesus Christ had made the sacrifice of His body. We have seen this sacred body scourged and on the cross, only offering to the eye one bleeding wound, and scarce allowing the features of the Son of man to be recognized: "From the sole of the foot unto the top of the head there is no soundness therein;" (Is. i. 6;) "There is no beauty in Him, nor comeliness; and we have seen Him, and there was no sightliness." (Is. liii. 2.) In the resurrection, the body of Jesus Christ takes a

new life — an immortal life. He is raised in a manner to the nature of spirits; like them He is endowed with agility and impassibility. In the place of that beauty destroyed by His executioners, He is clothed with a splendor surpassing that of the sun. This glory of the body of Jesus Christ is promised to our body also, but on the condition that, after the example of Jesus Christ, we offer up ourselves by penance: "Yet so if we suffer with Him, that we may be also glorified with Him." (Rom. viii. 17.) Let us courageously embrace Christian mortification, of which the following are the three principal degrees: (1) to suffer patiently all the trials that are independent of our will,—for example, sickness, infirmities, the inclemencies of the season, &c.; (2) not to allow our senses any criminal enjoyment; (3) to resist our senses, whether by imposing voluntary afflictions on them, or by refusing them allowable enjoyments.

2. In His passion Jesus Christ had made the sacrifice of His honor and glory. Before the tribunals and on Calvary we have seen Him, according to the oracle of the prophets, treated as the lowest of men, with the reproach of mankind: "The most abject of men," (Is. liii. 3; "The reproach of men." (Psalm xxi. 7.) Classed with the wicked; "And was reputed with the

wicked." (Is. liii. 12.) Loaded with ignominy; trodden under foot like a worm of the earth: "A worm and no man." (Psalm xxi. 7.) Now, in the resurrection, all is repaired: Jerusalem is filled with the news of His triumph; the judges who condemned Him are confounded; the soldiers, who insulted Him as a seducer and a madman, are the first witnesses of His glory; His disciples and Apostles who had abandoned Him, everywhere proclaim His resurrection; the angels and the holy souls He has delivered from Limbus bless Him as the conqueror of death and hell: "Thou wast slain, and hast redeemed us to God in thy blood, and hast made us to our God a kingdom and priests. The Lamb that was slain is worthy to receive power and divinity." (Apoc. v. 9–12.) Conceive a holy contempt for the opinion and esteem of men; place your honor in the hands of God, and know how to make the sacrifice of it to Him when He requires it, being assured that He will faithfully return it to you a hundredfold: "I also suffer; but I am not ashamed. For I know whom I have believed, and I am certain that He is able to keep that which I have committed unto Him against that day." (2 Tim. i. 12.)

3. In His passion Jesus Christ had made the sacrifice of His interior consolations. His soul

was steeped in bitterness: in the Garden of Olives we have heard Him cry out, "My soul is sorrowful even unto death," (Matt. xxvi. 38;) and on the cross, "My God, My God, why hast Thou forsaken me?" (Mark xv. 34.) Now the time of desolation is past never to return; His soul enters into possession of a happiness without end; it is inundated with the delights of Paradise, with all the joys of the divinity which is united to Him. Animate your hope by your faith. Recall to yourself that you are called to share this felicity of the Son of God one day in heaven. And when sacrifices alarm you or trials depress you, say to yourself with the Apostle, "For that which is at present momentary and light of our tribulation, worketh for us above measure an eternal weight of glory." (2 Cor. iv. 17.)

SECOND POINT.

The apparitions of Jesus Christ after His resurrection.

Consider to whom Jesus Christ appeared, how He appeared, and why He appeared.

1. *To whom Jesus Christ appeared.* He appeared, (1) according to the general opinion, to his blessed mother; not only on account of the incomparable dignity of Mary, but above all, because no one had participated so much in His

sorrows and in the opprobrium of His passion. So Jesus Christ teaches you that you will only participate in His consolations in proportion to your constancy in suffering, after His example, and for His love.

(2) He appeared next, not to the Apostles, but to Magdalen and the holy women. And why to these holy women? To reward their simplicity and fervor, and to teach you that it is to simple and fervent souls that He is pleased to communicate Himself: "His communication is with the simple." (Prov. iii. 32.)

(3) Lastly, He appears to the Apostles; but it is after Peter and John have been to the sepulchre and have merited the grace of seeing our Saviour by the zeal of their search. Learn from this, that to find Jesus Christ we must seek Him long by prayer and desire. Happy they who know how to draw Jesus Christ to them! Happy they who know how to retain Jesus Christ with them! "It is a great art to know how to converse with Jesus, and to know how to retain Jesus is a great prudence." (*Imit. of Christ*, book ii. ch. 8.)

2. *How Jesus appeared.* All the apparitions of the Saviour brought joy and consolation to their souls. He appeared to Mary; and who can express with what a torrent of spiritual delight

22

Hé inundated her heart? He appeared to Magdalen, saying to her, "Mary!" and this word alone, making him known, transports and ravishes the soul of Magdalen. He appeared to the Apostles, saying to them, "Peace be with you; and He said to them again, Peace be with you;" (John xx. 19, 21;) And the sight of Him and these words filled all their hearts with joy: "The disciples therefore were glad when they saw the Lord." (John xx. 20.)

Let us learn to recognize by these signs the presence of Jesus Christ, and the characteristics which distinguish the action of His spirit in our souls from the action of the evil spirit. The one announces himself by obscurity, trouble, depression and agitation; the other, on the contrary, announces Himself by light, peace, interior consolation. Above all, let us know how to profit by the visits of Jesus Christ; and let us not forget that to lose His sensible grace and the consolation of His presence, it suffices only to bestow too much of our thoughts on exterior things: "You may easily banish Jesus and lose His grace, if you give yourself too much to exterior things." (*Imit. of Christ*, book ii. ch. 8.)

3. *Why Jesus Christ appeared.* For three reasons, which the Gospel indicates to us;—to strengthen the still hesitating faith of the Apos-

tles; to prepare them for an approaching and long separation; to animate them to the sacrifices He is going to ask of them. The interior visits with which Jesus Christ favors souls are for the following purposes. If He honors us with lights and consolations, it is always to impress a greater liveliness on our faith,—to prepare us for interior desolation and trials,—to animate us for the sacrifices He will soon ask of us in the practice of virtue.

COLLOQUIES.

1st. With the holy Virgin. Congratulate her on her happiness, and join in her joy.

Regina Cœli.

2d. With our Lord Jesus Christ. Adore Him in the glory of His resurrection, and consecrate yourself anew to Him as to your Saviour and your King.

Prayer—Suscipe.

CONSIDERATION.

ON DEVOTION TO THE BLESSED VIRGIN MARY, MOTHER OF GOD.

FIRST EXERCISE.

Preparatory Prayer.

First prelude. Salute Mary, Mother of God, with the angel Gabriel.

Second prelude. Ask of Jesus Christ a high esteem and great veneration for His mother.

Consider —

1. What union the Divine maternity established between Jesus and Mary.

2. What virtues this august title presupposes in her.

3. What authority it confers on her.

FIRST POINT.

Mary is not only the privileged daughter of the Father, the beloved spouse of the Holy Ghost, she is also the *mother of the Son of God.*

1. In this quality, she is united to Jesus in the eternal decrees and in the promises of the Saviour, made in the beginning of all time. It is by her that the head of the serpent is to be crushed. (Gen. iii. 13.) She is united to her Divine Son in the oracles of the prophets. Isaias announces this branch of Jesse, and the blessed fruit she is to bear, (Isaias xi. 1;) the

Virgin Mother and the Emmanuel her Son,
(Isaias vii. 14;) Jeremias predicts this marvellous woman, mother of a perfect man, (Jer.
xxxi. 22;) David sings of this Queen seated on
the right hand of the heavenly King. (Psalm
xliv. 10.) The book of Wisdom describes the
wonders of the temple that Wisdom had chosen
for its dwelling. (Wisdom ix., etc.)

2. She is united to Jesus in the figures of the
ancient law. Eve, says St. Augustine, was, in
more than one point of resemblance or opposition, a figure of Mary. Eve was drawn from
Adam's side; Mary draws all her merits from
her Divine Son. Eve, seduced by an angel of
darkness, was the first cause of our ruin; Mary,
persuaded by an angel from Heaven, began the
work of our redemption. Her intercession and
power are figured by Esther obtaining grace for
her people, by Judith victorious over Holo-
phernes; her Immaculate Conception by the
burning bush, which the flames surrounded
without touching, by that wonderful fleece which
alone in a vast plain received the dew of
Heaven.

3. She is united to the Son of God, above all,
at the moment of the incarnation. Then her
Creator became her Child. (Ecclus. xxiv. 12.)
The blood of Mary became the blood of Jesus;
Jesus is flesh of her flesh; He lives with her
life, breathes with her breath; He is in her, to
her, of her entirely. Thus the angel says: "The
Lord is with Thee." (Luke i. 28.) Elizabeth
says, "Behold the mother of my Lord." (ib. 44.)

And the Church, in the third General Council, declares: "If any one refuse to call Mary Mother of God, let him be anathema." (*Act of the Council of Ephesus.*)

4. But, above all, the holy soul of Mary is united to the adorable soul of Jesus. She conceived Him in her heart before receiving. Him in her bosom, says St. Bernard. She unites herself to Him by the most lively faith, the most ardent charity, by the consent, the memory of which we revere in the "Angelus" three times a day, ánd which associates her with His whole destiny. So Mary is found with Jesus at Bethlehem, in Egypt, in Nazareth, in Jerusalem, and, above all, on Calvary, where the sword of sorrow pierced her soul when the lance opened the heart of her Divine Son.

5. Jesus ascends to Heaven, and Mary is soon placed on His right hand, that is, associated with His glory and His all-powerful action in the salvation of the world; united to the King of Heaven by an ineffable union. Here on earth the Son and the Mother are united in the praises of the Fathers, in the prayers of the Christian Liturgy, in the definitions of councils, in the solemnities of the Church. We see Christians honoring, always in union, the Incarnation of Jesus, the Conception of Mary; the birth of Jesus, the nativity of Mary; the presentation of Jesus, the presentation of Mary; the baptism of Jesus, the purification of Mary; the sufferings of Jesus, the dolours of Mary; the ascension of Jesus, the assumption of Mary; the

sacred heart of Jesus, the holy heart of Mary. The names of Jesus and Mary live always united in the hearts and the songs of the faithful; their temples and their altars are always near together, and nothing is more inseparable in their pious remembrances, their confidence, their invocation, their love, than JESUS AND MARY.

SECOND POINT.

And what creature was more like to Jesus than Mary?

The laws of nature ordain that the son should resemble the mother; the laws of grace ordained beforehand that the mother should possess all the characters suitable to the son. Here recall with profound respect —

1. *Her Immaculate Conception;* which renders her a stranger to sin and its consequences, and to all the occasions leading to sin. This privilege alone, which separates Mary from the mass of iniquity out of which we have all come, raises her above all the saints as much as the Heavens are above the earth.

2. *Her celestial virginity;* which the approach of an angel alarms; that would shrink from the Divine maternity, if the Mother of God could cease to be a virgin; which the Holy Ghost renders fruitful and a mother by an ineffable miracle.

3. *Her profound humility;* which, says a holy Father, made her merit the Divine maternity: "Behold," said she, "the handmaid of the

Lord. He hath regarded the humility of His handmaid. He hath exalted the humble. He hath filled the hungry with good things." (Luke i. 38, 48, 52, 53.)

4. *Her perfect charity;* which made her so prompt in visiting Elizabeth, so faithful in preserving in her heart the words of life, so attentive at the marriage of Cana, so devoted, so heroic during the labors and sorrows of her Son, so useful to the Apostles, so dear to the infant Church.

THIRD POINT.

What authority does not this Divine maternity give to Mary? Jesus Christ the Son of God, and Himself God, obeyed her thirty years; thirty years He executes her will, consults and forestalls her wishes. What a lesson does the docility of this true Son give to us sons by adoption; to us sons of Adam the docility of the Son of God! (St. Bernard.)

Jesus Christ on the cross gave her to us for our Mother. The Mother of God is, then, our Mother, exercising over us the maternal authority in all its meaning and extent.

Jesus Christ in Heaven, say the holy Fathers, still obeys the humble prayers of Mary. He has made her intercession all-powerful; He has established her the distributor of graces, the succor of Christians, the defense of the Church against infidelity and heresy. Giving us Jesus through Mary was to give us all through Mary.

From the conception of Jesus the way was thus traced: "We receive all from her who gave us Jesus." (St. Bernard.)

How great, then, is the authority of the Queen of Heaven, how extensive is the power of the Mother of God! In what peril are those who forget her or insult her! how safe are those she protects!

COLLOQUY.

Say to her, with the angel, "Hail, Mary, full of grace," etc.; or, with St. Cyril, the oracle of the Œcumenical council, "Glory be to you, holy Mother of God, masterpiece of the universe, brilliant star, glory of virginity, sceptre of faith, indestructible temple, inhabited by Him whom immensity can not contain. Virgin mother of Him who, blessed for ever, comes to us in the name of the Lord, by you the Trinity is glorified, the holy cross celebrated and adored throughout the universe, the Heavens are joyful, the angels tremble with joy, the devils are put to flight, man passes from slavery to Heaven. Through you idolatrous creatures have known incarnate truth, the faithful have received baptism, churches have been raised all over the world; by your assistance the Gentiles have been led to repentance. Finally, through you the only Son of God, source of all light, has shone on the eyes of the blind, who were sitting in the shadow of death. But, O Virgin Mother, who can speak your praises! Let us, however, celebrate them

23

according to our powers, and at the same time adore God thy Son, the chaste Spouse of the Church, to whom are due all honor and glory now and through all eternity. Amen." (St Cyril's Homily against Nestorius.)

SECOND MEDITATION.

ON THE BLESSED LIFE OF JESUS CHRIST IN HEAVEN.

Preparatory Prayer.

First prelude. Represent to yourself our Lord seated on His throne at the right hand of His Father; beside Him the Blessed Virgin; around the throne the angels and the elect.

Second prelude. Beg for an ardent desire of heaven, and the courage to suffer on earth with Jesus Christ, that you may one day reign with Him in eternity.

FIRST POINT.

Jesus Christ in heaven suffers no more.

Consider that our Lord in heaven is free from all the trials and pains which He experienced in His mortal life. His body, since His resurrection, is withdrawn from the empire of weakness and death.   His soul, inundated with the delights of the divinity united to Him, is henceforward a stranger to sadness and desolation.

In heaven, the Christian, like his Divine Head, will be forever freed from all bodily pains, and from all afflictions of the soul.

1. *In heaven there are no more infirmities.* The body, clothed with the glory of Jesus Christ, will be raised, like that of the Saviour, to a state of impassibility: "Who will reform the body of our lowness, made like to the body of His glory." (Philipp. iii. 21.)   In this abode of perfect beatitude the blessed no longer know what it is to suffer and die: "And death shall be no more." (Apoc. xxi. 4.)

2. *In heaven there is no more grief or sorrow.* "Nor mourning, nor crying, nor sorrow shall be any more." (Apoc. xxi. 4.)   Here below, what is life but one long, unceasing affliction?   In heaven all tears are dried: "God shall wipe away all tears from their eyes." (Apoc. vii. 17.) They remember past sorrows, but this memory is for the elect a part of their beatitude.   Each one of them, like the prophet, applauds his past trials.   Each one of them says, Happy tribulations, which are now repaid by an immense weight of glory; "We have rejoiced for the days

in which Thou hast humbled us; for the years in which we have seen evils." (Psalm lxxxi. 15.)

3. *In heaven there are no more separations.* Here below, to poison the sweets of friendship, this thought alone suffices: "How long will the society of these friends, of these relatives so tenderly loved, continue?" But once in the bosom of God, the elect meet to part no more. What joy for a Christian family to meet again, after the long and sad separation of the grave! What joy to be able to say with confidence, "We are again united, and it is for eternity!"

4. *In heaven there are no more temptations.* Here on earth is for the Christian a struggle of every day and every moment; and in this struggle a continual danger of losing the grace of God, his soul, and eternity. Hence the groans of the saints, who never cease crying out with the prophet, "Woe is me, that my sojourning is prolonged," (Psalm cxix. 5;) or with the Apostle, "Unhappy man that I am, who shall deliver me from the body of this death?" (Rom. vii. 24.) The lament of the exile is never heard in this country. There is no longer any thing to fear from the world, which has no more illusions; nor from hell, which is conquered; nor from our own hearts, which only live for Divine love. There every thing says, as did formerly holy

King David, "He hath delivered my soul from death, my eyes from tears, my feet from falling. I will please the Lord in the land of the living." (Psalm cxiv. 89.)

5. *In heaven, above all, there is no more sin.* Recall what you have meditated on the malice of sin. It is the supreme evil, the one only evil of time and eternity; the sole evil of the creature, the great evil done against God. Banished into hell, sin can not penetrate into the kingdom of charity. Oh, the happiness of that day, when, entering into heaven, the elect shall say, My God is mine, and I am His! "My beloved to me and I to Him." (Cant. ii. 16.) I am united to Him forever, and sin can never separate me from Him: "I held Him, and will not let Him go." (Cant. iii. 4.)

SECOND POINT.

Jesus Christ in heaven has no longer any thing to desire.

What our Lord asked of His Father is accomplished: "And now glorify Thou Me, O Father, with Thyself, with the glory which I had before the world was, with Thee." (John xvii. 5.) The holy humanity of our Saviour is glorified, and His glory is this blessed possession of God, in which His soul loses itself in the plenitude of all good.

To possess God, and in God to possess all good—such is also the bliss which awaits us in heaven; a sovereign and universal beatitude, which will be the full satisfaction of the entire man.

1. *Beatitude of the senses.* The body raised up at the last day and united to the soul, whose servant it was, will partake of its felicity. The ear will not weary of hearing the sacred songs of the elect; the eye will never tire in contemplating the light of Paradise, the splendor of the glorified saints, the sweet majesty of Mary on her throne, the lustre of the adorable humanity of Jesus Christ;—all the senses will be inebriated with these pure and spiritual pleasures, which appear to belong only to the celestial intelligences: "They shall be inebriated with the plenty of Thy house; and Thou shalt make them drink of the torrent of Thy pleasure." (Psalm xxxv. 9.)

2. *Beatitude of memory.* With what joy will the saints recall the graces they have received from God, the virtues they practised on earth! How will a martyr congratulate himself on his sufferings, an apostle on his labors, a confessor on his sacrifices! How each one of the elect will return thanks to God for His mercies! With what an effusion of gratitude and happiness

will they say to themselves, On such a day God inspired me with the desire to serve him alone; and it is this inspiration that has led me to heaven: on such a day God preserved me from this temptation, withdrew me from this occasion or habit of sin! What care His providence took for my salvation! and what had I done to merit that He should save me in preference to so many who are lost forever?

3. *Beatitude of the intellect.* Closely united to God, the intelligence of the elect sees all truth in Him as in a mirror. Suppose the rudest man in the world, the most ignorant of science, enters heaven; that moment his soul is inundated with lights so vivid that before them the lights of the greatest geniuses are but darkness: it sees God without veil and face to face; and in God sees all things,—the wonderful laws that govern the world; the mysteries of providence; the secrets of the redemption of men and of the predestination of the elect; the attributes of the Divine nature,—wisdom, power, goodness, immensity, eternity; the Three Persons of the Trinity, with their relations and ineffable operation. The soul sees God, and this sight, in a manner, transforms it into God Himself, according to the words of St. John: "We know that

when He shall appear, we shall be like to Him; because we shall see Him as He is." (1 John iii. 2.)

4. *Beatitude of the will.* This beatitude will be to love and possess God. To love God is the true object of our heart. But here below how weak is this love, how it is mingled with lowness and imperfections, how subject it is to change and inconstancy! In heaven, scarcely does God show Himself to the soul before He subjugates it and ravishes it forever;—sovereign love which rules all the affections; love so pure that the blessed forget themselves to be lost in God; love so ardent and so strong that it absorbs and exhausts all the power of loving; love so ecstatic that the soul goes out of itself and passes entirely into God to be consummated in unity with Him. It is the expression of our Lord; "The glory which Thou hast given Me, I have given to them, that they may be one, as We also are one." (John xvii. 22.)

"O God! when shall it be given me to see the glory of Thy kingdom? When will the day arrive that Thou shalt be all in all to me? When shall I be with Thee in the mansions which Thou has eternally prepared for Thy beloved?" (*Imit. of Christ,* book iii. c. 48.)

THIRD POINT.

Jesus Christ in heaven has no change to dread.

The reign of Jesus Christ in heaven is safe from all vicissitudes: it will have no end. He will reign eternally at the right hand of His Father, always triumphant, always sovereign, always the object of love to the saints and angels, as of the sweetest approbation of His Father: *Cujus regni non erit finis*, "Of whose kingdom there shall be no end."

The beatitude of the saints is immutable, like that of the Son of God. It is the inseparable condition of worldly goods to be accompanied by fear or distaste, sometimes by both at once: fear, because each moment they may escape; distaste, because we can not long enjoy them without recognizing and feeling their vanity. It is not so with the goods of eternity. These are unchangeable, and therefore have no end or diminution. Add ages to ages; multiply them equal to the sand of the ocean or the stars of heaven: exhaust all the numbers, if you can, beyond what the human intelligence can conceive, and for the elect there will be still the same eternity of happiness. They are immutable, and this immutability excludes weariness and disgust. The life of an elect soul is one succession, without end, of desires ever arising and ever satisfied, but desires without trouble, satiety, or lassitude. The elect will always see God, love God, possess God, and always will wish to see Him, love Him, and possess Him still more.

This beatitude is the end destined for all; God has given us time only in order to merit it, being and life only to possess it. Reflect seriously on this great truth, and ask yourself these three questions at the foot of the crucifix:

What have I done hitherto for heaven? What ought I to do for heaven? What shall I do henceforward for heaven?

Colloquies with the Blessed Virgin and our Lord glorified in heaven.

Anima Christi. Pater. Ave.

THIRD MEDITATION.

ON THE LOVE OF GOD.

First remark. True love consists in fruits and effects, not in words: "My little children," says the beloved disciple, "let us not love in word, nor in tongue; but indeed and in truth." (1 John iii. 18.)

Second remark. The effect of true love is the reciprocal communication of all good things between the persons who love each other; whence it follows, that charity can not exist without sacrifice. Do not, then, content yourself with tender and affectionate sentiments; "For," says St. Gregory, "the proof of love is in the works: where love exists, it works great things; but when it ceases to act, it ceases to exist."

CONTEMPLATION.

Preparatory Prayer.

First prelude. Place yourself in spirit in the presence of God, and figure to yourself that you are before His throne in the midst of saints and angels who intercede for you with the Lord.

Second prelude. Ask of God the grace to comprehend the greatness of His benefits, and to consecrate yourself without reserve to His love and service.

FIRST POINT.

Recall to yourself the benefits of God. These benefits are of three principal orders; *benefits of creation, benefits of redemption, particular benefits.* In the first order are comprised all the natural gifts; — the soul with its powers, the body with its senses, life with the good things which accompany it. In the second are comprised all the supernatural graces, the sufferings and death of Jesus Christ, the Sacraments, etc. In the third are all the graces that we receive every day and every hour from Divine Providence.

Consider attentively these three orders of the Divine benefits, and in each one meditate on these three circumstances, in which St. Ignatius shows us the characters of true charity. In each you will find:

1. A love which acts and manifests itself by works. What more active than the charity of God in the creation, preservation, and redemption of man?

2. A love that gives, that lavishes its goods. Has God any thing of which He has not given part to man? Has He not given Himself on the cross for an example, and in the Eucharist, His body, His blood, His divinity, His life, and all His being?

3. A love never satisfied with what it has given, and that would always give more. Is not this the love of God towards us? Is it not true that His greatest gifts have not been able to exhaust the prodigality of His heart? Is it not true that there is in Him a desire to do us

good which will never be satisfied until He has given Himself to us entirely and for ever in Heaven?

After having meditated on these characters of Divine charity, return to yourself and ask yourself what gratitude and justice require in return for such marvellous generosity. You have nothing of yourself: you hold all from God; what else, then, can you do but offer Him all that you have and all that you are? Say to Him, then, with all the affection of your heart:

Suscipe, Domine, etc.: "Take, O Lord, and receive my entire liberty, my memory, my understanding, and my whole will. All that I am, all that I have, Thou hast given me, and I give it back again to Thee, to be disposed of according to Thy good pleasure. Give me only Thy love and Thy grace; with these I am rich enough, and ask no more."

SECOND POINT.

Consider that God, your Benefactor, is present in all creatures and in yourself. If you look at every step of the visible creation, in all you will meet God. He is in the elements, He gives them existence; in plants, He gives them life;

in animals, He gives them sensation. He is in
you; and, collecting all these degrees of being
scattered through the rest of His creation, He
unites them in you, and adds to them intelligence.
And how is this great God in you? In the most
noble, the most excellent manner. He is in you
as in His temple, as in a sanctuary where He
sees His own image, where He finds an intelli
gence capable of knowing and loving Him.
Thus your Benefactor is always with you; He is
more intimately united to you than your soul is
to your body. You ought, then—and this is the
second degree of love—you ought as much as
possible not to lose sight of Him. You ought
to think and act in His presence, to keep yourself
before Him like a child before a tenderly-loved
father, studying the slightest sign of His will
and wish. Finish this second point by a renewed
offering of yourself, and one, if possible, still
more affectionate and unreserved.

THIRD POINT.

Consider not only that God your Benefactor
is present, but also that He acts continually in
all His creatures. And for whom is this continual action, this work of God in nature? For
you. Thus, He lights you by the light of day; He

nourishes you with the productions of the earth ;
in a word, He serves you by each one of the
creatures that you use; so that it is true to say
that at every moment the bounty, the wisdom,
and the power of God are at your service, and
are exercised in the world for your wants or
pleasures. This conduct of God towards man
should be the model of your conduct towards
God. You see that the presence of God in His
creatures is never idle; it acts incessantly, it
preserves, it governs. Beware, then, of stopping
at a sterile contemplation of God present in
yourself. Add action to contemplation; to the
sight of the' Divine presence add the faithful
accomplishment of the Divine will. Meditate
well on the two characters of the action of God
in the world, so as to reproduce them as much
as possible in your own deeds. What more
active than God, and at the same time what
more calm and tranquil? He is incessantly
occupied with the care of His creatures; and
yet He is never distracted from the interior contemplation of His essence and of His attributes.
Learn in the exercise of the presence of God,
to unite movement and repose, work and recollection. Think always of God, but in such a
manner that you do not cease to act; act, but
in such a manner that you do not cease to think

of God. And to arrive at this high degree of
perfection, endeavor to seek only one end even
in the diversity of your occupations; that is, the
good pleasure and holy will of God. End by
offering yourself as in the preceding points.

FOURTH POINT.

Recall what you meditated on the first point;
that is, that there is in God an ardent desire,
and as it were a need to communicate all His
perfections to you, as much as the infinite can
be communicated to the finite. Consider that
you find the weak and rude image of these perfections in created things. All that there is
good and beautiful in creatures, what is it but
an emanation of the Divinity? The power, wisdom, goodness of men, from whence do they
come if not from God, as the rays come from
the sun, and the stream from the fountain?

From this consideration arises a double consequence, which is the fourth and last degree
of the love of God: detachment from creatures,
and detachment from ourselves.

1. *Detachment from creatures;* because they
have only very limited perfections, and those
lent to them; while God possesses all perfection
and in an infinite degree.

2. *Detachment from ourselves;* because all our being and all our happiness depend, not on us, but on God, as the light of the ray depends on the sun, the water of the stream on the fountain. According to the words of our Lord, to find ourselves is to lose ourselves, because in us and of ourselves there is only nothingness: "He that loveth his life shall lose it," (John xii. 25;) and, on the contrary, to hate ourselves, leave ourselves, lose ourselves, is to find ourselves, because then we find ourselves in God, who alone is our life, our happiness and our being: "He that hateth his life shall keep it unto life eternal." (Ibid.)

From this double detachment springs true liberty of spirit, which consists in no longer being bound either to creatures or to ourselves, and in reposing perfectly and solely on the love of God. In this state the soul is absolutely indifferent to all that is not God. For in it there is only one thought—to please God in all its actions; only one desire—soon to quit this earth, in order fully to possess God in heaven.

Finish as in the preceding points.

Sum up, in order to profit better by them, the four degrees of the love of God, as they are proposed to us by St. Ignatius.

24

1. A God from whom I hold all; I ought, then, to render Him all. Hence entire oblation of myself.

2. A God who is present in every creature and in myself; I ought, then, to live in God by a constant and happy remembrance of His presence.

3. A God who acts in every creature, and for my service, but without losing any thing of His infinite repose; I ought, then, to act in God and for his service, without ever losing sight of His presence.

4. A God who wishes to communicate all His perfections to me, and who beforehand shows me the image of them in a faint degree in His creatures; I ought, then, to leave both creatures and myself, in order to attach myself only to God, in whom I find, as in their source, and in an infinite degree, all perfections.

Colloquy according to the accustomed method.

Suscipe or *Pater.*   *Ave.*

APPENDIX.

BISHOP DAVID'S MANUAL

OF THE

RELIGIOUS LIFE.

TO MY BELOVED DAUGHTERS OF NAZARETH.

ALTHOUGH your rules, dictated by the heavenly wisdom of your holy Founder, My dear Daughters, are sufficient, if faithfully observed, to lead you to a great perfection; yet to promote that perfection, which is the object of my most earnest desires, I have, this long time, felt myself moved to write for you some advices on your religious duties, and to form of them a sort of Manual, which you might have often in your hands, to animate you to an exact observance of them. A want of leisure, at first, and then many other obstacles have hitherto hindered me from accomplishing that design; which I hope to be able to do now, with the help of Heaven. This Manual will consist of four parts; the first shall treat of the general notions and maxims of a religious life; the second of the spirit and virtues peculiar to your institute; the third of the exercises and practices of the institute; the fourth of the duties annexed to the various offices.

GENERAL NOTIONS AND MAXIMS OF A RELIGIOUS LIFE.

ARTICLE FIRST.

Eight marks to know whether a religious community is well regulated, and retains its primitive spirit.

1. If all things in the community be faithfully held in common, so that no one will pretend to say : *This* or *that* is mine ; for then the community exhibits an image of the first and most perfect community that ever was, and of which it is said, "And the multitude of the believers had but one heart and one soul. Neither did any one say, that of the things which he possessed, any thing was his own, but all things were common unto them ; Neither was there any one needy among them." (Acts iv. 32, 34.)

2. If charity and concord flourish in it, by means of the mutual respect and honor, which all the religious bear one to another.

3. If ambition is banished from it, with all desires of honor and preferment ; so that every one shuns offices, in which there is some appearance of honor, yet without ceasing to qualify herself for any, in case the will of God should call her to it.

4. If solitude and silence are cherished and observed by all, with a perfect obedience to Superiors, without any exception or hesitation.

5. If there is but little frequentation and visits of parents, relations, or other persons of the world : and if, when necessity compels them to receive such visits, the Sisters make it a practice to speak with them of spiritual things, besides those which are necessary.

6. If the Sisters entertain a great desire of advancing in virtue and perfection, and to obtain it, employ all their care, labor, and industry.

7. If the rules are faithfully observed, and if penances and mortifications are duly imposed, and exactly accomplished by those who have transgressed them.

8. If all the Sisters zealously apply to the practice of mental prayer, particular and general examinations of conscience, the frequentation of the Sacraments, the reading of good books, and such other exercises as are prescribed by the rule, for the acquisition of virtue and perfection ; which is the end, for which they have entered into a religious life. To this add —

ARTICLE SECOND.

The four interior supports of a religious community.

First. Mental prayer ; Second. The spirit of faith ; Third. Interior recollection ; Fourth. Fraternal charity ; and the four exterior supports, namely :

First. The accusation of their faults, made with exactness and humility ; Second. Mutual admonitions given with charity, but without human respect, and received with gratitude and docility ; Third. The rendering an account of their consciences, made with openness and docility ; Fourth. The manner of spending the recreations.

ARTICLE THIRD.

The nine fruits of a religious life, pointed out by St. Bernard.

In religion a soul first, leads her life more purely ; second, falls into sin more rarely ; third, rises from it more quickly ; fourth, walks more cautiously ; fifth, is watered with grace more frequently; sixth, reposes more securely; seventh, dies more confidently; eighth, is purified more speedily; ninth, is rewarded more abundantly.

ARTICLE FOURTH.

The nature and excellency of a religious life.

Religion, or a religious life, is no other than a certain state tending to Christian perfection, by means of the three vows of Poverty, Chastity, and Obedience, which are made in religion, for the love of God, and through a desire of pleasing and serving Him. It is a state instituted by Jesus Christ Himself, first, in His apostles and disciples, and ever since continued and observed in His Church, by a great number of men and women, who have embraced and followed this holy manner of life. It is a state of perfection, in which all those virtues meet together, of which every religious person ought to make a profession. It is, says St. Basil, an institute high and sublime. It is a perpetual sacrifice of one's self, which the religious offers continually to God, by means of the three vows aforesaid, whereby he sacrifices to God all the goods he possesses, with his body and soul. It is a perfect way of living by the perfect imitation of the life of Jesus Christ, who has exhorted us to this excellent manner of life, both by His words and by His example. It is, says St. Ephrem, a heavenly and angelical life. It is, says St. Bernard, an imitation of the life of the apostles, and a profession of apostolical perfection, a high and elevated state of sanctity, where we find the excellence of that spiritual life, which renders religious persons alike to angels, and different from the rest of mortals, by reforming in man the image of God, and making him alike to Jesus Christ. It is a state of penance, say the holy Doctors ; a state, which contains, not only the perfection of charity, but also the perfection of penance. St. Thomas observes, that there is no satisfaction that can be compared to the penance of those, who have consecrated themselves to God in a religious state. The flower of religion, is sanctity ; the proper office of which is to offer to God our heart and soul, pure, entire, and free from all defilement of sin ; and to consecrate that soul to His service, with all its powers, by means of prayer and devotion, which are the two daughters of the sanctity of life.

What is a Monastery ?   A Monastery is a heaven upon earth.   Therefore, concludes St. John Climacus, in the fourth degree of his Spiritual Ladder, as we believe that the angels in heaven serve God with the purest and most ardent love, so we must serve our Brothers and Sisters in the Monastery. A Monastery is the fortress and citadel of God, fortified and furnished with every thing necessary for defense.   It is the field and farm of the Son of God, from which He continually draws great and abundant revenues to His own honor and glory ; says St. Bernard.   A Monastery is the inclosed garden of the Spouse, His Paradise of delight, His nuptial bed, pure and undefiled.   It is the school of virtue, the tabernacle of the Covenant, the closet of the Spouse, the fort of His soldiers, the house of sanctity, the bulwark of chastity, the academy of piety, the abode of devotion, and the dwelling of perfection.   A Monastery is Jacob's ladder on which the angels of heaven are ascending and descending.   It is the house of God, and the gate of heaven, says St. Anthony. There is to be found the fairest and soundest part of the Church of God, and of the flock of Jesus Christ.   For, as St. Gregory Nazianzen remarks, those ought to be counted wiser and more prudent than the rest of the people, who have retired from the crowd and the bustle of the world, and have consecrated their lives to God. A Monastery is a Mount Thabor, on which Jesus Christ transfigures Himself; a fertile and fat mountain; a mountain in which God is well pleased to dwell. There we find Peter, that is, Obedience; James, that is, Evangelical Poverty; and John the blessed disciple, that is, Chastity, which all the inhabitants of that holy mountain vow to God, and faithfully observe. These three things are so agreeable to God, that He permits, in this miserable life, the true religious to enjoy here below a portion of that heavenly glory and felicity, which He has prepared for His elect in Heaven; so that religious persons, faithful to their institute, are moved to say, with St. Peter, "Lord, it is good for us to be here."

Religious persons are the domestics of God; they are the chosen members of the family of Jesus Christ, says St. Bernard. "I know not," continues the holy Doctor, "what more worthy title I can give religious persons. Shall I call them heavenly men, or earthly angels, who dwell on earth, but whose conversation is in heaven? It is the occupation of angels to be always in the exercise of praising God and doing His will: and it is also the constant occupation of the religious woman. She applies herself, by fervent prayers, to appease the anger of God, and to obtain graces for her neighbor. The holy will of God is the sole rule of all her actions. She continually employs her mind, sometimes in reading good books, at other times in the exercise of good works. Separated from all unnecessary communication with persons of another sex, one religious person inspires life into another and keeps guard over her."

"How excellent is that life," exclaims St. Ambrose, "in which there is nothing to be feared, and much to imitate." (Ep. xxv.) He may have a sweet assurance of being admitted into the heavenly Jerusalem, who has been called into the assembly and congregation of the just. For it is a great sign of the Divine predilection and predestination, to be called to the enjoyment of that religious company and confraternity. "It is a great honor, a great glory to serve Thee, O Lord, and to despise all things for Thee. For they who willingly subject themselves to Thy most holy service, shall have a great grace ; they shall find the most sweet consolation of the Holy Ghost, who, for the love of Thee, have cast away all carnal delights." "They shall gain great freedom of mind, who, for Thy name's sake, enter upon the narrow way, and neglect all worldly care." "O pleasant and delightful service of God, which makes men equal to angels, pleasing to God, terrible to devils, and commendable to all the faithful ! O service worthy to be embraced and always desired, which leads to the Supreme Good, and procures a joy that will never end !" (Following of Christ, book iii. c. 10.)

"Embrace, my dear Sisters," says St. Bernard, "embrace this life. Carefully preserve this precious pearl of religion. Embrace that sanctity of life, which makes you alike to the saints of Paradise, and the familiar friends of God."

ARTICLE FIFTH.

Some particular sentences of the holy Fathers and Doctors of the Church in favor and recommendation of the three vows of religion.

OF RELIGIOUS POVERTY.

1. "To sell all and distribute it to the poor ; and ·being thus disengaged from all things, to take one's flight towards Heaven, where Jesus Christ is, is an act of apostolic elevation and perfection, and the effect of a heroic virtue." (St. Jerome, Ep. viii.)

2. "Wilt thou be perfect and ascend to the first degree

of dignity; do what the apostles have done: forsake all things and follow Jesus: sell all things and give them to the poor, and follow thy Saviour, carrying the cross, naked and alone." (St. Jerome ad. Hebr., Ep. cl.)

3. "The beginning of perfection and of a spiritual life, is a renouncing of all earthly things; and the end of it is charity." (St. John Climacus—last degree of his Ladder.)

4. "Poverty was not seen in heaven, but it was found every where on earth, yet the world did not know its value. The Son of God came down from heaven upon earth, in order to render it precious and acceptable to men, by the choice and esteem He entertained for it, in taking it upon Himself, and cordially embracing it for our sake." (St. Bernard.)

5. St. Francis of Assisium used to say: "that religious poverty was the way of salvation, the support of humility, and the root of perfection; that this virtue produced many and divers excellent fruits, although hidden, and known to but few persons; and that nothing rendered man more commendable and agreeable in the eyes of God than this evangelical virtue." (St. Bonaventure, in his life of St. Francis.)

6. God says to the religious the same as He said to the tribe of Levi, consecrated to His worship: "In this land you shall possess nothing, neither shall you have a portion among them; I am thy portion and inheritance in the midst of the children of Israel." (Numb. xviii. 20.)

7. "Blessed are the poor in spirit, for theirs is the kingdom of heaven." (Matt. x. 3.)

OF CHASTITY.

1. "Jesus Christ, who was the first to teach humility, was also the first to teach chastity." (St. Augustine.)

2. "It is a deed of great faith and of great virtue, to become the most pure temple of God, to offer one's self as a holocaust, and to be, as the apostle says, holy both in body and mind." (St. Jerome.)

3. " The life of those who are chaste and continent is the life of angels," say the holy Fathers Chrysostom, Basil and Ambrose.

4. What happiness is it not, to be the servant-maid of Jesus Christ, not a mortal husband but the immortal Spouse of religious souls; not to obey the flesh, but to obey the spirit ! "For he who adheres to the Lord, is one spirit." (1 Cor. vi. 17.)

5. "The life of virgins and religious souls, is the life of angels.   It is a most beautiful and odoriferous flower, and a most precious stone among the riches and treasures of the Church." (St. Jerome, Ep. xvii.)

6. " Virgins and religious persons are the blossoms of the germ of the Church, the honor and ornament of a spiritual life.   They are subjects worthy of praise and honor, a perfect and immortal work, an image and representation of the Divine Being, corresponding with the sanctity of our Lord ; in short, it is the most illustrious part and portion of the sheepfold of Jesus Christ." (St. Cyprian.)

7. " Virginity, (this is understood of that which is vowed or forever preserved in our hearts for the love of God,) is the sister of angels, the victory over lusts, and the possession of all goods," says St. Cyprian.

8. " Perpetual virginity and chastity is a most agreeable sacrifice to God, and the most fit to obtain His favors," says St. Ambrose, and also Origen.   "It is truly a very great and a most beautiful virtue, which, to say all in one word, makes the person, who is pure in soul and body, to be alike to God Himself," says St. Basil.

9. "As much as an angel is above man, so much is virginity, consecrated to God, more honorable than marriage; for virginal chastity is an angelical life." (St. John Damasc.)

"Purity bringeth near to God. No price is worthy of a continent soul." "Oh how beautiful is the chaste generation with glory! For the memory thereof is immortal; because it is known both with God and with men!"

Oh Chastity, mother of love and charity, angelical way of living! (Eccl. xxvi.) Oh Chastity, ever pure in thy heart, ever bright to the sight, and glorious to the speech! Oh Chastity, haven of grace and salvation! Oh Chastity, that fillest thy professor with joy, and givest wings to the soul to fly to Heaven! Oh Chastity, thou bringest gladness to the heart, and drivest all sadness far away! Oh Chastity, thou subduest passions and freest the soul from trouble! Oh Chastity, spiritual chariot that bearest upwards the soul that possesses thee! Oh Chastity, that as a budding rose, openest thyself and flourishest amidst the body and the soul, and fillest the whole interior house with thy delightful odor!

OBEDIENCE.

1. "Obedience," said Samuel to Saul, "is better than sacrifices;" for this reason, says St. Gregory, "that by sacrifices the flesh of other animals is immolated, but, by obedience, we immolate our own will, which is an oblation of inestimable value before God."

2. "Obedience is an admirable virtue, that causes man to forget himself, and to tend continually towards his Redeemer." (St. Thomas.)   .

3. "The way of obedience is the King's highway, which leads, in all safety, those who practise it, to the top of the ladder of perfection, on which God appears leaning."

4. "Man can not give to God any thing greater, than to submit his own will to the will of another, for the love of God." (St. Thomas.)

5. "Obedience is a virtue, which, in a rational creature, is as the mother and guardian of all virtues." (St. Augustine.)

6. "An obedient man shall speak of victory." "We indeed," says St. Gregory, "combat Satan by every sort of virtue, but we vanquish him by obedience. Those come out victorious who obey."

7. "Obedience is the only virtue which implants in the soul the other virtues, so that as long as obedience shall flourish, the other virtues shall never wither away." (St. Gregory.)

8. It is a deed much more meritorious, to submit our will forever to the will of another, than to chastise our body by long fasts, and to afflict our soul by a continual penance.

ARTICLE SIXTH.

A summary of the rules of ancient Monks.

We learn, by the venerable monuments of the ancient discipline of Monks, many very important points for the conduct of the religious, whether superiors or inferiors ; the observance of which is capable of preserving monasteries in all the lustre of their primitive institution, and to make of the religious so many models of regularity, sanctity and edification in the Church of Jesus Christ.

1. We see in the first place, with what zeal and attention the principal leaders of the monastic state of former times formed assemblies for the maintenance of regular observance, and the encouragement of the religious in the duties and virtues of their state ; and what was, at the same time, their

charity, their meekness, their patience, their prudence, and their firmness in the government.

2. We see the strict obligation incumbent on superiors, never to seek their own interest; never to appropriate to themselves any thing belonging to the Monastery; never to absent themselves without necessity, that they may watch continually over all the souls committed by Providence to their care; to have an equal charity for all; never to judge their brethren through passion or caprice, but according to the rules of the most exact equity; to instruct them in sound doctrine; to nourish them spiritually with the bread of the word of God; to hear and console them in their troubles; to correct them in their faults; to stretch out to them a charitable hand in their heavier faults; to employ, sometimes rigor, and sometimes weakness, to recall them, when they go astray; to remove from them the occasions of scandal; to provide, without predilection or preference, for all their temporal needs, both in health and sickness; to give to them all good examples; to be always at their head in all the regular observances; finally, to govern them, as being persuaded that they are to give an account of them, soul for soul, to the Sovereign Judge.

3. We see what ought to be the conduct of inferiors, towards their superiors, towards their brethren, and in the observance of their regular duties for the salvation of their own souls. They ought to fear their superiors as their masters, love them as their fathers in Jesus Christ. They ought to receive their instructions with a spirit of piety, their admonitions with respect, their corrections with meekness and in silence, their penance with docility and humility. They ought to obey them through virtue and religion, with diligence and exactness, never doing any thing without their orders, never disposing of any thing without their permission;

conforming themselves to their will in all things, and living with them in a filial confidence, and in an entire dependence. They ought, with regard to their brothers or sisters, to consider them in Jesus Christ, as supplying the place of the brothers, sisters, and other relatives, whom they have left in the world; to cherish them with tenderness, to consider them as other themselves, and to observe towards them, by their meekness, their patience, their affability, their humility, all the rules of that charity which our Lord has recommended to us in the Gospel.

Finally, with regard to themselves, they ought to be mortified in their senses, to love labor and occupation preferably to repose and the conveniences of life; to apply themselves to cultivate their souls by the practice of virtue and the exercise of piety; to render themselves assiduous to all the duties of the Monastery, especially to those of prayer; to obey quickly the signal which calls them to those various duties; to acquit themselves of them, not through constraint, or with negligence, but for the good of their souls and with a holy fervor. They must go abroad but very seldom, and never without necessity; love their cells or work rooms, as the paradise of the earth; and there employ themselves either in prayer, or reading, or labor, as they are directed; shun the commerce of the world and all unprofitable communications with secular persons, and above all, with those of another sex, even with those who make a more particular profession of piety, such as priests and other clergymen or religious; show themselves exteriorly, only to edify, and procure Jesus Christ to be glorified by their words and their modesty. They ought, in a word, to live as angels in the house of God; since, by their holy vocation, God has drawn them from the world, that they might consecrate themselves entirely to Him; looking on their Monastery as an abode of sanctity, and on their habit as a garment of sanctity ; on all that surrounds them in the house of God, and on all their exercises, and the practices of of their state, as so many means of sanctity. Behold the end of the holy rules prescribed by those fathers of the religious life.

Behold, then, what they taught their disciples, and procured with so much care to be faithfully observed. And behold the true spirit, which ought to animate the good superiors in religious houses, and the good religious under their guidance.

ARTICLE SEVENTH.

Description of a Monastery of true Religious.

The order of Tabenna might be considered as a prodigy, which God had wrought for the salvation of souls, and as a model, to be proposed to all those who wish to assemble souls together, to lead them to the most eminent perfection. St. Pachomius himself did not consider it in another light ; not through a vain complacency of self-love, but by a sentiment of the mercy of God on a work which he had undertaken only by His orders. There was to be seen at Tabenna, an almost innumerable multitude of fervent religious, whose whole study was to disengage themselves from the weight and embarassment of worldly concerns, to carry with more facility the amiable yoke of Jesus Christ ; of religious persons solely devoted to the care of their own souls, and wholly intent on acquiring the sanctity of their state ; of religious persons, for whom the world was now nothing, and who seemed to live almost no longer upon earth, but already began, in some measure, to enjoy the bliss of heaven ; because seeking, as they did, God with uprightness of heart, and serving him with a sincere affection, God in return filled them with the sweetness of His divine consolations, and caused them to enjoy an interior peace a thousand times more consoling, than all that can be enjoyed here below in the vain pleasures of the world. Those holy religious lived intimately united to one another by the tie of a most pure and holy charity. They mutually encouraged one another, to make daily progress in the life of the spirit. They fed their souls, with a holy avidity, with the food of the word of God. They conversed together only on the means of triumphing over their passions and the devil, and of arriving at a most eminent sanctity; and although many of them were no other than peasants gathered from the neighboring villages, and consequently with illiterate and uncultivated minds, they were full of the wisdom of God, by their assiduous study of the maxims of the Gospel, and the communication of the light of Heaven, which they received in great abundance. Hence it will not appear astonishing, that several among them were elevated to the episcopacy, and that the Monastery of Tabenna soon acquired a great celebrity throughout the world; that men should flock to it, not only from every part of Egypt and Armenia, but also from the West, and the utmost boundary of the known world; the former to assure themselves, by their own eyes, of the wonders which they had heard related, and the latter to place themselves under the discipline of the great Pachomius.

ARTICLE EIGHTH.

Exhortation of St. Pachomius to his Religious, after the vision in which God revealed to him the future decay of his Order.

"Oh! my brethren, so long as we shall have a breath of life, let us fight courageously for the salvation of our souls;

lest, when it will be too late, we should repent for having neglected that important affair. Let us exercise ourselves cheerfully in the pursuit of God, and let us shun even the least appearance of sin. Ah ! my brethren, if we could pay due attention to the promises made by Almighty God to faithful religious souls, and to the frightful punishments which are prepared for negligent and remiss religious, we would exert all our strength to attain sanctity, according to the rules prescribed by Jesus Christ. Wo to him, who having renounced the world to consecrate himself to God, does not live conformably to the promises he has made to Him! How much I fear lest our parents and kindred, whom we have forsaken and left in the world, and who hope that our prayers and good works will be profitable to them before God, having made the sacrifice of being deprived of us, that we might consecrate ourselvee to Him ; How much I fear, I say, lest in the day of judgment, they may be covered with great shame and confusion, when they will see that, by our own fault, and against their expectations, we shall be ranked among the reprobate ! Therefore, my brethren, let us labor with all the ardor we are capable of; let us, above all, make use of the frequent remembrance of death, which is so efficacious to disengage our affections from the earth, to smother in our hearts the love of the world, and to elevate our minds to God. Let us think on it every night, when we go to take our rest. Let us then reason with ourselves ; let us address every member of our body, let us make our soul thus speak to them : 'O my feet, that have now the facility of walking, be ye ever ready to do it in order to accomplish the will of God, before death comes to render you stiff and motionless. O my hands, the time shall come, when you too must become stiff, cold, and incapable of motion ; but before this will happen, make a good use of your time, while you have the power; whatsoever you are able to do, do it earnestly. Extend yourselves to every good work, and raise yourselves to God in prayer. O my body! before we part, and thou be dissolved in dust, let us labor together to render to God the service which we owe Him. Act now with courage; often prostrate thyself before God; furnish me with abundant tears; submit thyself to the yoke of the Lord; help me to walk with Him, and to embrace with a holy joy all that belongs to His service. Think not on taking rest nor remaining idle in this world, lest thou shouldst precipitate me with thee into eternal flames. If thou now hearken to me, thou shalt share with me the heavenly inheritance; but if thou resist, wo to me for being so closely united to thee, as we are. Thy perdition will necessarily draw mine after it: we shall both be eternally tormented.'

"If you thus encourage yourselves every day, my brethren, you will see that God will abide in you, as in His own chosen temple; and being with Him, you will have no occasion to fear the artifices of the devil, but you shall be enlightened with the light of the Holy Ghost, who will conduct you better than a thousand masters, and will impart to you a spiritual knowledge which no human words could convey to your minds."

To this exhortation of St. Pachomius, I will join that of Orsisius, one of his successors; that you may know by the lessons of these great masters, the true spirit and fruits of a religious life. After having shown to superiors their obligations, he addresses his words to every religious in particular, whom he earnestly exhorts, with several texts of the Holy Scriptures, very happily applied, to labor in working out their own sanctification :—

"Be ye," says he, "as faithful servants, who are expecting their Master, with your loins girded, and burning lamps in your hands. Let not the length of the labor dishearten you, considering that you shall be one day introduced into the heavenly banquet. Serve the Lord with joy. Be submissive to your superiors. Avoid murmuring and vain reasonings. Apply to all your duties with simplicity, that being adorned with virtues and the fear of God, you may render yourselves worthy of the adoption with which God has honored you. Remember that you are the temple of God, and that He could exterminate you, if you were so unhappy as to violate this temple by sin. 'Grieve not the holy spirit of God.' (Eph. iv. 30.) Live in a great purity, that it may be said of you, that you are 'a garden enclosed, a fountain sealed up.' (Cant. iv.) Renounce all the vain desires of the earth; and let all your care be, to accomplish the holy will of God. I conjure you also to maintain yourselves continually in the resolution, which you have taken in embracing a religious state. Consider the lessons of your fathers, as a mysterious ladder by which to ascend to heaven. Desire no longer what you have once trampled under your feet. Content yourselves with what is barely necessary in the affairs of this life, and seek not what is superfluous. Good religious, who submit with humility and mortification to the yoke of religious poverty, of that happy poverty, which enriches them, by stripping them of all temporal possessions; good religious, I say, shall have, when they will happily lay aside that vile spoil of their body, the happiness of being associated with the patriarchs, the prophets, and the apostles; and they shall repose, as Lazarus, in the bosom of Abraham. But those who dare appropriate to themselves, in Monasteries, what ought to be employed for the common use of their brethren, shall be told when they go out of this world, as the rich man mentioned in the Gospel, that they have possessed goods in this life, while their brethren lived in labor, fasting, and mortification; and that it is but just that these latter should now, in preference to them, enjoy the goods and delights of eternity; since, to possess them, they have cheerfully renounced the conveniences of this life. But, as to those, who would not conform themselves to the Gospel, they deserve nothing but the torments and frightful misery of hell."

Orsisius shows thereby, how much he had at heart the practice of religious poverty. He insists upon this, more than upon any other point. He recommends that nothing useless should be retained, but only what is permitted by the rule. He says, "that if any one appropriates to himself any furniture, and keeps it to himself or gives it to another to keep for him, both are guilty, and ought no longer to be regarded as being in the number of the brethren; but rather as hirelings, strangers, scandalous subjects, and destroyers of the monastic discipline."

Although he recommends much charity and union, yet he will not have any of those human and natural friendships, which are contrary to the charity which should bind all alike together, and constitute singularities. When a superior reproves a brother for a fault, he specially forbids that another, under pretense of friendship, should presume to defend him, and to maintain his cause against the superior: "Because," says he, "but for your interference, he would have risen again and returned to his duty, and you prostrate him anew; he would have corrected his error, and you cause him to go still further out of the right way. Wo to you, who thus intoxicate your brother, by presenting to him a liquor that troubles his mind! Wo to you, who turn the blind from his right path! You inspire, with a proud independence, him who was ready to submit; you fill with bitterness the heart of him who was about to taste the sweets of charity;

you seduce him into rebellion, when he was disposed to surrender to discipline ; and you irritate his mind against the superior, who had no other view than to instruct him according to the spirit of God."

Finally, Orsisius ends his treatise by the following words, which are so very instructive, and which also show that he was approaching the end of his course, when he addressed them to his religious community :

"I will speak to you again, my dearest children, since the Lord would have me to take the charge of your conduct. I have not ceased to admonish each of you in particular, and to exhort you with tears, that you should render yourselves agreeable to God. I can not reproach myself with having concealed from you any thing which I thought would be profitable for the salvation of your souls. And now I commend you to God, and pray that His grace may fortify you, and conduct you to the possession of the heavenly inheritance. Be watchful, labor earnestly, never lose sight of the end which you proposed to yourselves, in embracing a religious life, and faithfully comply with the engagements which you have contracted. As to me, I feel that I am going, and that the time of my dissolution is approaching. I have fought, at least in part, a good fight. I have kept the faith. It now remains for me to receive the crown of justice, which God, as a just Judge, has laid up for me, and will render me at the last day ; and not to me only, but to all those who have loved justice, and have kept the precepts of their fathers. I conclude with these words, that contain all that I could say to you : Fear the Lord ; observe His commandments ; for He will examine in His judgments all the works of man both good and evil."

ARTICLE NINTH.

The happy state of a religious soul that has subdued her passions.

St. John of Egypt, exhorting the religious to banish vices from their souls, pointed out vanity as one of the most dangerous, and attended with the most pernicious consequences; and he observes that this subtle vice, attacks equally both those who begin, and those who are already much advanced in virtue. From vanity, the Saint passes to other vices, and exhorts the religious to combat them courageously. The means he suggests for succeeding in this is, to watch carefully in keeping a guard over their minds and their hearts, to prevent any vain desire, any disorderly will from taking deep roots in them. "For, besides, this would produce a crowd of distractions, which take possession of the soul in time of prayer, captivate the mind, cause the imagination to wander about on a thousand unprofitable and pernicious objects; soon many depraved affections open by sin the door of the soul to the devil, who comes and establishes his dwelling there, as in a house that already belongs to him."

He afterwards describes, in a few words, the deplorable state of a religious soul in whom the devil has established his empire by sin. "He never can," says he, "enjoy any peace or repose. The soul is always in trouble and disquietude. Sometimes she suffers herself to be carried away by a senseless external joy; at other times she will sink into a deep sadness, because she had introduced into her interior à miserable guest, by yielding to her disorderly passions." Then, to render the deformity of the soul of a religious, who by his vices and passions has become the dwelling of the devil, more sensibly felt, the Saint opposes to it the happy state of him who has opened the door of his heart to the Holy Ghost, by subduing his passions; which he describes in the following manner: "On the contrary, he who has truly and sincerely renounced the world, that is, who has retrenched sin from his heart, and left no doors open, whereby it may find an entrance into it again; he who restrains his anger, subdues his disorderly motions, shuns lying, detests envy; who not only avoids detraction, but does not even give himself the liberty of judging his neighbor; who looks upon the prosperity and affliction of his brethren as his own; and conducts himself on every occasion accordingly; such a one, I say, opens the door of his heart to the Holy Ghost; who having once entered into it, nothing is found therein but contentment, joy, charity, patience, meekness, kindness, and all the other fruits which are produced by this Holy Spirit of consolation."

After having shown them what the religious ought to avoid, St. John points out what he ought to strive to acquire. The Saint insists principally on purity of heart. He requires that he should aim at it by all combats against his passions, by every effort to purify his soul from all irregular affections, and by every spiritual exercise which he practices in his state. He assures him, that this purity of heart will dispose him wonderfully for contemplation, and for receiving the most signal graces. What he says on the subject deserves to be related in full, because it includes, in a few words and in a very simple manner, what the masters of a spiritual life have said, in greater detail and more extensively, of eminent prayer, and of the sacred commerce of the soul with God, and with the Blessed Spirit.

"If, therefore," says he, "we present ourselves before God, with a conscience pure and free from those defects and passions of which I have already spoken, we shall be able to see God, as much as He can be seen in this life, and to raise up to Him, in our prayers, the eye of our understanding, to contemplate, not with corporeal eyes, nor with sensible looks, but with the eyes of the mind and by an intellectual knowledge, Him who is invisible.   For let no one persuade himself, that he can contemplate the Divine Essence, such as it is in itself; nor attempt to form for that purpose, in his mind, some image that has any relation to a corporeal figure.   Let us not imagine any form in God, nor any limit, whereby He can be circumscribed; but let Him be conceived as a pure spirit, who can make us feel His presence, and penetrate the affections of our souls; but who can neither be comprehended, limited, nor represented by words.   For which reason, we ought never to approach Him, but with a profound respect and a very great fear; nor consider Him with our interior looks, but in such a manner, that our souls may know that He is infinitely elevated above all the splendor, all the light, all the brightness, all the majesty, which they are capable of comprehending; even though they were all pure, and perfectly exempt from all the stains and blemishes of a corrupt will."

After speaking thus of contemplation, the Saint comes to those extraordinary graces, which God sometimes grants a pure soul; such as the holy familiarity with which He honors her, the mysteries and the secrets He reveals to her, and the apparitions to her of blessed spirits.   "He who knows God after this sort, shall afterwards acquire the knowledge of other things, and even of the greater mysteries : for the purer his soul will be, the more will God reveal to him of His divine secrets; because He will then consider him as His friend, and as one of those to whom our Saviour says in the Gospel, 'I will not now call you servants, but I have called you friends.' (John xv. 15.)   And thus He will grant to him, as to a friend who is most dear to His heart,

26

the effect of his prayers. The angels and all the blessed spirits who are in Heaven will cherish him, as being the friend of their God and Master; they will fulfill his desires; and it may be said truly of him, that 'neither death, nor life, nor angels, nor principalities, nor powers, nor any other creature, shall be able to separate him from the love of God which is in Christ our Lord.'"

ARTICLE TENTH.

The happiness of a vocation to a religious life.

1. You can never conceive a sufficient esteem and love for your vocation. It is a favor that you should esteem a thousand times more than all the sceptres and crowns of the universe, and that you ought to love more than the dearest things you have in the world. Ah! Can you ever sufficiently esteem a state, which preserves you from a multitude of sins, which you would be incessantly committing in the world, had you remained exposed to its dangers; a state which keeps you continually occupied in exercises of piety, which causes you to merit every moment immortal crowns of glory; a state, which gives you God Himself for your portion and inheritance; which procures for you the advantages and honor of dwelling in His own house, where He makes you taste of ineffable delights; a state, in fine, that will conduct you infallibly to Heaven, if you faithfully comply with the duties thereof. It is an inestimable grace, the full value of which you shall never know till you are in eternity. What have you done for God to induce Him to grant you such a favor, and to give you the preference over so many others who perhaps deserved it more than you, and would have made a better use of it than you do? Let,

then, this grace be most dear and precious to you. Give
thanks to God for it every day, and fail not to renew also
every day the vows which bind you to it. This renovation
is the confirmation of the alliance, which you contracted
with God on the day of your profession; and as often as you
make it, it draws upon you new graces from His divine
liberality.

2. Endeavor to comprehend well the excellence of your
state, that you may conceive for it a still greater esteem and
love. There is nothing greater in the Christian religion. It
seems that nothing equals the excellence and perfection of
martyrdom; because charity, in which perfection consists,
can not be carried to a higher degree, than to suffer for
Jesus Christ. But the religious state is not only a martyrdom, but it includes a multitude of martyrdoms. For the
consecration of ourselves to the service of God, especially by
religious vows, is a martyrdom, in the judgment of the pious
person; because it makes us die to the world, and immo-
lates us to God. Obedience is a martyrdom, according to
St. Theodore; because it makes us die to our own will.
Chastity is a martyrdom, in the opinion of St. Ambrose;
because it makes us die to the pleasures of the body. Poverty is a martyrdom, if we believe St. Bernard, because it
engages us to suffer many inconveniences, and makes us die
to the love of riches. Mortification of vices is a martyrdom,
as St. Gregory, Pope, assures us; because it crucifies the
flesh with its vices and concupiscences. Penance is a martyrdom, in the sentiment of St. John Chrysostom, because it
afflicts all the members of the body, which had become an
instrument of sin. Purity of the heart is a martyrdom, in
the opinion of St. Jerome, because it makes us die to sin.
The love of God is a martyrdom, in the judgment of St.
Bridget, because it consumes us with its fire, and makes us

die of grief to see God so little loved, so ill served, and so much offended. The love of our neighbor is a martyrdom, according to St. Gregory Nazianzen, because it makes us share in his sufferings, and suffer with patience his defects, his persecutions, and his injustices. All christian and religious virtues are, finally, so many martyrdoms, in the estimation of St. Cyprian, who calls them the glorious martyrdoms of virtue; because they make us die to the opposite vices, and because we must offer to ourselves a great violence in order to practise them.

The religious state includes in itself all those sorts of martyrdom, because it engages us to practise all those virtues. We may say that a true religious soul resembles those heroes of the Christian religion, who suffered a great many martyrdoms by the various tortures which the cruelty of tyrants inflicted upon them; but with these three differences, which are very glorious to her: first, That her martyrdom is voluntary and of her own free choice; whereas that of other martyrs was often forced upon them: she offers herself freely unto death; whereas the martyrs were dragged thereto; second, That the other martyrs were the martyrs of faith; but she is the martyr of perfection. They suffered that they might not lose their souls; she suffers to make herself more perfect and more agreeable to God. They were the martyrs of the war made upon the Church; she is the martyr of the peace which the Church enjoys. Third, The torments of other martyrs soon had an end; but hers last as long as the ordinary course of human life. Now all these divers kinds of martyrdom shall be for her an immortal crown of glory in heaven. Think now how happy you are, to have been called to a state, in which you may merit so many rich crowns! How precious your vocation ought to be in your eyes, since it procures to you so many rare advantages!

Apply yourself, then, with so much fervor to the practice of all the virtues which it requires of you, that you may render yourself worthy of all those great rewards. A pious author says : "The spiritual nuptials of a religious soul, between her and Christ, begin in the noviciate, are ratified and confirmed in the profession, and are perfected and consummated in the heavenly glory, where the soul is inseparably united to Christ." St. Bernard having been ordained Abbot of Clairvaux, is said to have thus addressed the novices who came to his Monastery : "If you hasten to the acquisition of the goods that are within, leave there out of doors those bodies, which you have brought from the world. Let your spirit alone enter ; the flesh availeth nothing." The founders of religious institutes had no other view, than to assemble together only such as were willing to give themselves to God with all their hearts, and who sought, through the sweetness of grace, the virtue of the sacraments, and the light of truth, to establish themselves in the precious life of sanctity ; a life of true devotion, which has no sweeter pleasure than to converse with God, to meditate on the things that God has done for us ; a life of charity, that moves souls to help one another as brothers and sisters ; a life of mortification, that does not permit us to suffer any evil in ourselves ; a life of humility, which delights in submitting itself to every body, and in anticipating others with good offices ; a life of penance, which subdues the flesh and represses the instincts of nature by holy austerities. It is for this end that religious communities have been instituted. But if the contrary take place, if religious persons seek only the repose of nature and the satisfaction of the senses, honor, esteem, reputation, and praise, they plainly resist the designs of God, and should have remained in the world.

THE END.